Betrayal

Including Prequel Stories

Imposter

Holidays

Laura Stapleton

Table of Contents

INTRODUCTION .... **V**

IMPOSTER **3**
   ACKNOWLEDGEMENTS 5
   DEDICATION 5

HOLIDAYS **55**
   ACKNOWLEDGEMENTS 57
   DEDICATION 57

BETRAYAL **139**
   ACKNOWLEDGEMENTS 141
   DEDICATION 141
   CHAPTER 1 143
   CHAPTER 2 187
   CHAPTER 3 223
   CHAPTER 4 255
   CHAPTER 5 283
   CHAPTER 6 293
   CHAPTER 7 311
   CHAPTER 8 323
   CHAPTER 9 333
   CHAPTER 10 347
   CHAPTER 11 365
   CHAPTER 12 387

ABOUT THE AUTHOR **401**

Introduction

Welcome to the first book in my Nova Scotia Murder Mysteries series. Usually, I like having a short story to kick off a series. It's so much fun writing what happened before chapter one's "brick through the window" beginning.

This series is different. Imposter and Holidays breaks the mold by being a duo of short stories. Together, they provide a thrilling and romantic beginning to Betrayal.

From watching SCTV in the late 1970's to the Netflix bounty of Canadian shows and movies, I've been in love with the amazing country just north of the United States. This is my love letter to the entire country and its people. I hope you enjoy.

Laura Stapleton

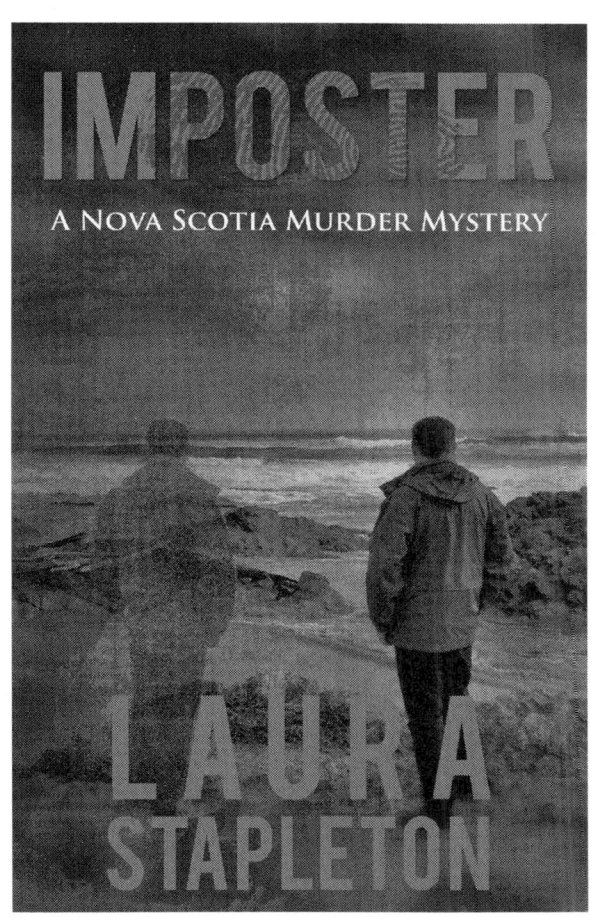

Laura Stapleton

Imposter

A fake doctor played the medical hero with Dr. Aaron Nicholson's credentials. No one died, but what about the next patient the identity thief treats? Afraid of the next time this guy impersonates him, Aaron must find out who his imposter is before someone dies.

Laura Stapleton

Text Copyright © 2015 Laura L Stapleton

All Rights Reserved.

No portion of this book may be reproduced, stored in a retrieval system, or transmitted in any form or by any means, mechanical, electronic, photocopying, recording, or otherwise, without written permission from the author or publisher.

Names, characters, and some incidences are imaginary and complete fiction.

Acknowledgements

Huge thanks to everyone in this anthology. Each person has made this experience fun, and a definite do again for me. Extra special thanks to Miranda Nadine, thriller author extraordinaire.

Dedication

For Dirk.

Laura Stapleton

Imposter

A knock on his office door got his attention. It opened before he could say anything and a couple of suited men strolled in. Aaron stood. "Excuse me? Can I help you?"

"Dr. Aaron Nicholson?" At his nod, the taller gentleman continued, "I'm Detective Paolo, and this is Detective Stewart with the Vancouver Police. We'd like you to come with us. Answer a few questions."

Aaron scanned the two men's badges. He'd felt fear before, but this time? Panic clung to his insides like static electricity dancing on plastic wrap. "Am I being arrested?"

Paolo shrugged. "Not formally, no. At this point, it's more of a request. You've been accused of admitting and treating patients without authorization at various hospitals around the province."

"That's ridiculous. What if I refuse?"

The detectives exchanged a look before Stewart, the shorter one said, "Then it's an arrest."

With that assertion, he realized he would be taken in either with or without a fight. Aaron knew the accusation was false. The hospitals he did have privileges with gave him plenty of work. He stepped from around his desk. "Do you need to handcuff me?"

Detective Paolo gestured toward the door. "No, not as long as you come along willingly."

"All right. I need to make some arrangements for my work during the rest of the afternoon." He reached back and picked up the desk phone's receiver.

"No need. We've talked to Dr. Jones already." Stewart stepped outside motioning for Aaron to follow.

Aaron let the receiver fall back into place. Shit. "Does anyone else know why you're here?"

"No." Paolo went to stand behind Aaron. "We thought it best to keep it quiet."

"It is, thank you." He left the office. The taller detective lagged behind as they led him to their unmarked cruiser. Dread and fury mixed in his stomach like drain cleaner and a hair clog. Neither man said a word as Aaron got in the car. He texted his brother, Brad, on their ride to the station house. Hitting send, he stared ahead. The men in the front seats seemed decent enough. Aaron shifted in his seat. He hated the pitying expressions on their faces. This was a mistake. It had to be.

Imposter

At the station house, he walked up the steps in front of the detectives. His phone hung silently in his lab pocket, and he resisted the urge to check yet again for new messages. Calling attention to the device could get it confiscated. "What do I do first? Fingerprints? Mugshot? Rake a tin cup back and forth across the cell's bars?" He opened the district offices door for all of them.

Detective Paolo snickered. "Funny guy."

Stewart replied, "Nothing so dramatic. First, a lineup. We have a couple of witnesses in to identify you."

Aaron paused to let a uniformed constable pass in front of him. "Or not. Because I wasn't there."

"All right, or not. Either way, they're here, you're here, so let's get started."

A coat rack hung to the right of the door. Most of them were light, thanks to the warm fall temperatures. He realized he still wore his lab coat. "Should I take this off?"

"No, leave it on. It'll help the witness." Detective Stewart opened a door with a frosted window.

He stepped into a tiny room with four other men, all dressed like him. "Jeeze, did they get a memo?"

"We want this to be accurate. Good luck."

Aaron looked back at the irritating Detective Stewart. What was this? An audition? He examined each man there. Intuition told him three of them were police officers, and the fourth was someone randomly picked. An out of work actor who need the practice, maybe? He didn't know but hoped they fooled the witness.

A speaker crackled followed by a flat voice. "Line up and get ready to walk in."

The younger detective opened the door, and the events played out in his mind like a twisted, surreal television show. All of them faced forward. "Turn to the left," continued the metallic voice. "Face front." Sweat bubbled on his upper lip. A minute had stretched into two before the orders were repeated. Left, then front. He studied the others, staring into the two-way mirror. They seemed bored. The extra radiated guilt. Aaron studied himself and couldn't guess how he'd appear to anyone else. The door opened, and fresh air rushed into the stuffy room. The voice instructed, "You may leave."

When Aaron stepped out, the older detective began, "You have the right to retain counsel without delay...."

He moved aside so the others could go around him. Thanks to television dramas, he knew the litany of his rights. He tuned them out, his mind racing, searching for a possible friend or even acquaintance with legal knowledge. He didn't want to rely on Google for this. "Didn't you say I'd not be arrested?"

Stewart led him down the hall. "After witnesses pointing to you, what do you think, doc?"

The condescending tone angered him. "I'm not a degenerate."

"No, never thought you were, but with five people nearly killed, we didn't want to take the chance on you skipping town."

"May I call someone?"

"Go ahead. Make it quick."

At the top of his speed dial, Brad's phone rang several times before going to voicemail. Aaron choked back an expletive. The beep sounded. "Hey, give me a call. No, wait. You can't. I'm at the main police station and need you to come get me. I'll owe you big time. Please." He swallowed hard while ending the call. Detective Stewart sat on a desktop nearby, so he asked, "If I have to leave a voicemail, does that count, or do I get to try again?"

He stood up. "Don't worry about it, eh? Give it thirty minutes and I'll let you try again."

Aaron wanted to argue that now was a better time, but didn't want to push his luck. The station buzzed with activity. Not many criminals, he noted. The observation seemed promising unless all the offenders were already locked up and waiting for him. Detective Stewart opened a door with the sign "Booking Area" in front. The "Area" was more a small room with mug shot equipment on one side and a fingerprint device on the other.

"I'll need an id." He waited until Aaron handed him his driver's license. "You've been fingerprinted before, right?"

"Yes." The detective fussed around with the computer next to the print scanner. "For my medical license."

"Thumbs first."

Aaron's thumbprints showed on the scanner. The young man nodded in silent approval. "Good. Now right fingertips." He did as instructed. "Left." He figured they were finished and stepped back. "Fingers one at a time."

"Really? Isn't that overkill?"

"Nope." He moved Aaron's right forefinger side to side before going to the middle finger. "Let me guess, you were ink printed the last time?" At his nod Detective Stewart continued, "Yeah, it's different. No mess."

Both stayed silent as each print scanned and showed on the computer. Aaron inhaled, not realizing he had been holding his breath. "Mug shots?" he asked.

The detective flipped on the brighter lights. "Stand in front of the height chart."

Aaron did as requested and faced front. He waited as Stewart entered his information.

He took the photo. "To the right, please." The digital camera made the sound of a click as more a warning an actual shutter grabbing the shot. "Okay. We're done here." Stewart clicked off the lights and pressed a key on the computer. "I'll take you to lock up." He stopped. "Wait, you'll want to make another phone call."

Glad he didn't have to ask, he offered, "I can just use my cell."

"Fine. I'll take your personal effects afterward." He motioned. "This way."

Shit. Aaron stopped at the counter with the detective and speed dialed Dr. Jones' number. She picked up on the second ring, and he almost cheered when hearing her voice. "Tina, I need help."

"I know. How fast do I need to be up there?"

"Now is good."

"On my way."

He turned to the waiting man. "She'll be here soon."

Stewart went around the counter, pulling out a large envelope. "Empty your pockets, take off your belt and any jewelry. Do your shoes tie?" He looked down as Aaron lifted his pant legs. "No? Keep them on. Put everything in the bag." He nudged a younger female officer at the computer. "Murphy? Could you take down Dr. Nicholson's belongings while I show him our hospitality?" At her nod, he grinned at Aaron. "You can wait in a luxurious holding cell while I get the paperwork ready for you to leave."

"Is that all it will take? Paperwork?"

Imposter

"No, your friend will need to sign for you. That you won't commit a crime in between now and your court appearance."

He took a deep breath and stepped into the cell. "Pretty easy since I didn't do it in the first place."

"Sure you didn't." Stewart closed and locked the door. "Prison is full of innocent men."

Aaron wanted to reach through the bars and choke the guy. "I'm not joking. It wasn't me."

"Hey, tell it to the judge." He chuckled. "Love saying that, every time." He went to the outer door. "Hang tight until your friend gets here."

He leaned against the wall, a bit amazed at how empty the jail was. Television made cells seem like a hub of activity, not this barren wasteland. He didn't expect everything around him to appear as antiseptic as his workplace. Time appeared to run backward in its sluggishness until the heavy outer door swung open.

The younger officer, Murphy came in. Smiling, she unlocked the cell. "Dr. Nicholson, your friend is here. This way."

He followed her out, seeing Tina in the holding area. She looked him up and down. "Gee, Aaron, not bad for a jailbird."

"Thank you?" He turned to the official as she closed the heavy door behind him. "Can I sign paperwork and leave, now?"

"Yes, follow me."

His boss raised her eyebrows at Aaron before falling in step with him. "I have some documents for you to review, too. Is your car here?"

"It's still at work." He scanned the court appearance agreement and asked the officer, "Do I get a copy?"

"Here." She pulled apart the carbonless papers. "Ours, the court's, and yours." He took the pink copy she held out. Murphy added, "I'll get your personal effects."

Tina handed him a stapled stack of papers. "Sign these, if you choose to."

He read the absence with leave form, saying he'd relinquish his rights and responsibilities with the university hospital during the investigation. Hairs on the back of his neck rose for the first time. The arrest was one thing. He could get a lawyer. Losing his medical license meant losing himself. "This doesn't have an end date. What happens if I don't sign?"

"You're terminated. Either way, I'll need your current badge."

Imposter

A cold lump of dread settled in his stomach. "They have it with my wallet and cell phone."

She leaned over and tapped the blank line next to date on the form. "Take a deep breath. The probation is open ended until your court case is settled."

"Fine." Aaron signed every highlighted x. He gave it back to her just as the rookie returned with an evidence envelope. "Thank you. Am I free to leave?"

"Yes, sir. Thank you for your cooperation."

"Sure. It's the least I could do." The woman narrowed her eyes as if he were sarcastic. "I mean it. This wasn't like television. You all are a lot nicer."

"Come on." Tina took his arm. "Kiss up on your own time. Unless you want the board to kick you out on your ass, I'll drive you back to the office."

He began to protest until being fired sunk in. "What's there?"

"Evidence"

"What kind?" He slid into Tina's passenger seat. "Other than the witnesses I've encountered back there."

She glanced over her shoulder and pulled out from the curb. "Video, badge records. The detectives asked if you'd worked certain dates and at certain hospitals. I scribbled them down, and the locations. Then, while waiting for your phone call, I checked with a few friends."

"You knew I'd call?"

"Ok, hoped you would. So, after checking with legal and my friends, it seems you were living a double life."

"How? I don't have time for the one I'm in right now."

"This other Dr. Nicholson, yes, he's Aaron, too, is a hero."

"Then why arrest him? Rather, me?"

"Because he came in, the patient coded, and he worked to save their life. Several times, several hospitals, several patients."

"Shit."

"Yep. Their proof is convincing."

They both fell silent. He had no idea what she was thinking, but his mind raced with possible suspects and lame solutions. The guy had saved people's lives. Until complications set in, and what if they did? Murder, or homicide? Aaron stared out the car window as Tina pulled into her parking spot. He didn't want to go to prison for someone else's crime.

"Let's go over what I have and see if there's a solution." He followed to her office where she unlocked her door. "Come in. Close it behind you, please." Once he'd done as she asked and settled into the chair, she pushed a paper across the desk toward him. "I need to formally ask. Have you been admitting or seeing patients at these hospitals?"

He studied the printout. Five locations and Aaron knew something about each of them. He'd been in one, but only for a childhood accident. He looked up from the list. "I've referred patients to doctors practicing at some of them, but haven't been there myself."

Dr. Jones tapped a pencil on the desk. She opened her desk drawer and pulled her phone from her purse. "I'll tell you everything, now that I know your answer. First, can I record our session together? It'll be for any future legal ramifications."

Aaron stared as she swiped across the screen of her phone and opened the recorder app. He shook off the unease. "Sure. I have nothing to hide."

"I know." She gave him a smile and pressed record. "This is Dr. Tina Jones at Vancouver Regional. I'm with Dr. Aaron Nicholson. We're discussing his admission privileges at area hospitals." Dr. Jones straightened in her chair. "Now then, doctor. Do you currently have admission privileges at Lion's Cove, BC General, St. Anthony's of Abbotsford, Royal Campbell, or Richmond Medical Center?"

"No."

"Have you been to visit patients at any of these hospitals in the past six months?"

"Not that I'm aware of," was his knee-jerk response. He searched his memory for a more definitive answer. "No."

She bit her lip. Tina frowned at first her computer, then at him. "You're certain you've not been to any of them, not even for a visit?"

Panic raced through him like an electric current. Had he not? From Dr. Jones' eyes staring him down, it seemed she wanted him to say yes. He couldn't lie. "I'm sure I haven't been to any of them in the prior six months."

"I have absolute proof you've not only been there but admitted patients and signed documents while there. Witnesses say each time you've said it's an emergency."

Aaron shook his head. "No, they're wrong. I would remember hospitals, patients, and the emotional stress."

"I would think so, too. Especially since every person you admitted almost died." She read from her computer screen. "The patients coded before you brought them back."

She had said the same thing in the car. "Yes, I was not there at any of those incidents. I'd remember anything that serious." He stared out of the office window at the snow-capped mountain range. "How are they sure it's me and not some other doctor with the same name?"

"CCTV and your photo id. Plus, he used your name on everything he signed." She gave him photocopies of sign-in sheets.

The signatures were his, every one of them. Aaron's lunch threatened to make a repeat performance, and the ham sandwich wasn't that tasty the first time. "He also has my handwriting?"

"That's improbable, don't you think? For someone who isn't you to have your penmanship, your name, your appearance, your expertise?" She gave him a hard stare. "I don't see how this isn't you."

"I agree." He examined the top of the pages for dates and times. After a quick check of his phone's calendar, Aaron knew work couldn't be his alibi. All the incidents happened during his off hours. "Do you have a video of me, rather, him?"

"Not all of them. One hospital's camera wasn't working when you were there." She shrugged at his sharp glance. "Sorry. Another's lens was dirty. They're cleaning those images as much as possible."

"They are?" He started jiggling his left leg for a moment, nervous. Not every crime warranted video enhancement, but it looked like this one fit the description. "Sounds like I'm in serious trouble. What happens if I can't prove this isn't me?"

"For a start, loss of privileges in the hospitals you do have. Wrongful death lawsuits if any of the patients die later. Losing the trust of the community, and ethics charges from the Canadian Medical Association at least. Maybe jail time. Fraud?" She leaned back in her chair, rubbing her temples. "I don't know enough about that to tell you anything substantial. I suggest getting a lawyer."

"I agree. We're done here until I hire an attorney."

"That concludes our discussion." Dr. Jones tapped off her phone recorder. "Look, right now, you're something of a low-key hero who's colouring outside of the lines. You rushed in and saved five lives. In some of the witness statements, the nurses mentioned seeing you cry."

"Ridiculous." He scanned the witnesses' reports for other inaccuracies. "I wouldn't cry in public, and certainly not in front of staff."

"I know. That's why I suspect you weren't there for any of it." She took back the papers and slid them into a folder. "It's why I'm giving you all of my evidence." She reached over to the printer and pulled fresh pages as they emerged. "Here, you'll want these, too."

He scanned the documents, each one more incriminating than the last. "Damn."

"Exactly. It's not likely you have a twin, is it?" She shrugged. "Unless your mother should have told you something."

Aaron needed an alibi, however small. "No. A brother, but he's not a twin."

"Everyone looking into this wants to be doubly sure you're the man on the video. They'll want concrete evidence before any punitive action is taken." She rubbed her eyes, smearing her mascara a little. "So go, read everything over. Double check where you were and try to find alibis." Dr. Jones pulled a tissue and wiped under her eyes. "Since you know everything I do, I'll forward whatever new I learn until told not to."

"I appreciate that." Her derisive look unnerved him. "No, I mean it sincerely. I'm just thinking ahead to when the well of info dries up, and I'm back to being clueless."

"Let's hope you can find evidence proving you weren't there." She gave him a wan smile and started working on her computer.

Feeling dismissed, Aaron left in a fog, clutching the file folder with the damning proof. He walked down the hall and thumbed through the pages. More like the damning insinuation. He'd not been near any of these hospitals and especially not on his own time. At the little table he used as a desk, Aaron glanced at the time before reading every page given him. He double checked each location and day despite already knowing the answer. Stunned and a little weary, he pushed the papers away in unconscious denial.

It couldn't have been him in each hospital. His phone's caller id flashed. Brad? He noticed his fingers shook as he swiped on the device. "Hello?"

"Hey buddy, I got your text. Everything all right?"

"Hey." He decided against asking where the hell was he, instead saying, "Yeah, crisis averted."

"So, you free tonight? How about dinner?"

Aaron's brain struggled to ignore his problem and stalled for time. "Yeah, I think so. Let me see." Did he really want to spend the evening feeling vaguely guilty for putting off seeing Brad until now? "I'd planned on hanging out, catching up on laundry."

"Do that later. Come on, eat with me. Unless you're too good to hang with us little people."

Brad's favourite guilt trip worked on him. "You know better than that." He stared at the file, wanting to be anyone but himself right now. Dinner out might be a good distraction. "Sure, why not? I have a problem to run past you."

"What?" He laughed. "You saying I can help you?"

"Yeah, I am. You're always out in the field, and I could use some answers to some shady activities."

"Sounds fun. All right, Pourhouse at seven?"

"Make it six. That'll give us a chance to talk before the music starts."

"Good thinking. See you then."

Aaron slid the phone into his lab coat pocket. All this had taken too much of his afternoon. If he wanted to be out of here in time for dinner, he'd have to hustle. After an inner debate over putting the folder on his desk, he decided against leaving it in the office at all. He headed out to the parking lot, intent on locking the evidence in his car.

In the Pourhouse, the air buzzed with the end of workweek joy. The imposter problem kept Aaron's own mood glum as he stepped aside to let another group in. He found his brother before the hostess could say anything to him.

"Hey! There's the man." Brad stood, nearly knocking his chair over in his haste. "How ya doin'?"

Aaron returned his hug, then bent to retrieve his brother's tweed jacket. "As fine as always." They both settled into their seats, and he continued, "Is that a local brew?"

"Yeah, not bad, either." He drained the glass and motioned to the waitress. "Highly recommended."

"Sounds good." Aaron closed his menu. "I might just stick with the beer tonight."

"Big lunch?"

"No, more like big worries."

"So? They can't be that much." Brad reopened the menu. "Try to eat something."

Aaron tried to smile. "I'm not hungry, really. Work problems."

"That's a shame. I'm not a doctor, but can listen." He lifted up the arm of his jacket and let it fall. "If you'd brought your lab coat, I'd have worn it so you'd let me help."

The waitress arrived with their drinks, and he welcomed the distraction as his brother ordered a steak. When Brad finished, Aaron said, "I learned something disturbing this afternoon."

A grimace passed over Brad's face as a group passed behind him with several members bumping his chair. "That drives me crazy." His voice grew louder. "You'd think some people could be less clumsy."

Wanting to stop a problem before it started, Aaron stood. "Come on, trade me places. Then I can tell you all my dirty laundry." Once settled in the opposite chair, he stared at Brad. How much could he admit to outside the medical and legal system? Probably not a lot, but he needed to confide in someone. "There's been something odd going on around town.

Someone has been using my credentials to admit patients."

"Damn!" He stared at Aaron. "How are they using your creds?"

"He has a badge—"

"Wait." Glass in midair, Brad asked, "How do you know it's a he? Could be a she."

He nodded to the waitress for another beer. "Witness reports."

"Ah. So? Was there a description of this guy?"

"Yeah, and he looks like me."

Brad chuckled before glancing up at his brother with a guilty look. "Sorry. Just seems weird. Happens in movies or on TV, not real life."

The waitress interrupted. "Here you are, sir." She set the plate down in front of Aaron and looked at Brad. "Are you sure you're fine? I could bring an appetizer for you."

Reaching forward, Brad took his plate and retorted, "I'm good as soon as I get my meal."

"Oh! Sorry, I didn't realize."

"Don't worry, we switched while you weren't looking," reassured Aaron. "It's okay, and I'd like water when you get a chance."

Imposter

Brad began cutting his steak. As soon as the girl left, he said, "See what I mean about the doctor-mister thing? It's a pain in the ass."

"Yeah, I can see why." He fidgeted, not wanting to deal with the mundane. Aaron wanted to get back to both his car and the reports Dr. Jones had given him. He ignored an urge to leave. Instead, he stayed there to get Brad's point of view. "What would someone have to gain with this, outside of fiction? They're not stealing drugs. Just saving lives."

"Not yet. Maybe stealing is what's next."

"True." He scanned the restaurant's customers. The pharmaceutical angle was worth exploring. Perhaps in all the excitement, no one had noticed the intruder taking anything. He glanced at Brad's plate. None of Aaron's appetite had returned. "Right now, it's just an ethics issue. Add in drugs or patients dying from botched care and it's a criminal one." He shook his head, hating the lack of solutions. "I should have Dr. Jones call the authorities on this. They have detective skills and forensics to find out who's impersonating me."

"Police?" He pushed away his plate and motioned for another beer. "Naw, I don't think it's that bad. Probably just someone pranking you."

Aaron stared at him. "Pretty shitty prank. I could lose my medical license over this."

"Maybe I can get you on at LifeTech. I hear we're hiring. Or is that beneath you?" He nodded thanks as the waitress set down a new drink.

Jibes from Brad pissed him off more than usual. He glanced at his watch. Still too early to make an excuse to leave and his brother wasn't being helpful with the kidding around. Aaron leaned forward, waiting for him to stop chewing. "How's things with you? Okay?"

He wiped his mouth. "Other than never seeing you, I'm good. It's been a while."

"You're right, I could do better." He opened his hands. "Like Thanksgiving. We're planning one, aren't we?"

"I hope so. It's in a couple of weeks."

"There you go." The packed restaurant and bar almost drowned out his thoughts. The live band tuning up to play helped seal the deal for him. He motioned to their waitress and mimic signing a receipt. She nodded, and he went back to watching his brother.

Imposter

She came over, giving each of them a check. "Again, gentlemen, sorry about the mix up earlier."

"Eh, no prob." Brad smiled. "We get this all the time. Before you ask, we're not twins, either."

She returned his grin and nodded, scooping up their credit cards. Aaron watched her for a moment with a memory rattling around in his mind. As if his brain took a photograph, everything clicked into place. "Do you know when we last hung out together?"

"I don't know. A few months ago, I guess." He shrugged, placing his fork to the side. "Why do you ask?"

"That's about the time I last saw my old work badge. Have you seen it around?"

"I have no idea what your ID even looks like."

"If you had found and maybe dropped my badge on the way to returning it to me, I'd understand. This identity thief might have the card. He's probably running around, having fun, but his joke is a serious deal to me."

"That would be rough, guy." He shook his head and signed the receipt brought to him. "I've not seen it. Haven't lost it, either."

Aaron didn't want to let this go. "You've been to several of the hospitals I'm supposed to have been in." He leaned back in his chair. "Who knows? Someone might have seen you there, saw your last name, and thought you were me."

"You think I'm doing a prank on you? I don't have time for something like that." Brad stood and pushed in his chair. "I have a life."

He stood as well. "Hey, what's with the sudden defense? I'm not saying anything like that, it's cool."

Brad drained the last swallow of his beer. "Sure as hell feels that way." He crossed his arms and stared at his empty plate.

"Calm down a minute and let me tell you what I suspect. You were carrying my badge with good intentions, but dropped it somewhere." He shrugged. "I'm sure if you lost the thing, it was an accident."

"Stop saying that. I don't have your badge." He started for the door. "Look, I gotta go. I'll see you at Thanksgiving."

"Wait up." Aaron followed him. "Look, I'm sorry, but my reputation and career are on the line."

"How is that my problem?"

Imposter

"It's not, but I'd just feel better if you'd go over the incident list. Do me a solid and see if you were there at the same time this con artist was. I know it's a pain, but I'd appreciate any help. Please?"

He paused and sighed. "Sorry about being a jerk. All right. Email it to me and I'll get back to you." Brad held out his hand. "Really. Your problem bothers me, man. Wish I could help."

Aaron did the shake hands and pulled him into a half hug before going back to his car. At home, he reviewed everything in the file given him. He wasn't sure how much to write Brad about the pseudo-hero. Everything and risk him knowing too much? Just enough to end up being not enough? He didn't know. Every action had consequences. Finally, he typed up the schedule for fraudulent hospital admissions and hit send on the email. Aaron hoped his younger brother knew something useful.

*****

He stood on Brad's welcome mat. Aaron had received his brother's texts about Thanksgiving all week. But not a one about his missing badge. Before delaying any longer, he knocked on the door. A muffled *come in* sounded through the wood so he stepped inside. "Hello?"

"In here." Brad glanced up from setting the turkey down on the small table. "You didn't bring anything? Good, 'cause this is on me."

Thanksgiving decorations sprawled across the walls. A stuffed animal turkey sat on the coffee table. Even the sofa had fall foliage patterned throw pillows. If not for the last two weeks, he might have appreciated the effort. "Mom would be proud."

"And dad would be annoyed." He grinned. "Don't even try. You and I both know it."

"He'd still eat everything and get seconds."

"Like you?"

Aaron laughed. "Yeah, probably. I wasn't hungry until the smell hit me. Now I'm starving."

"Oh? Something bothering you?"

He glanced up at his brother. The smirk Brad wore pissed him off. "You know it is, shithead."

"Love you, too." The younger man placed knives next to both of their plates. "I'd say tell me about it, but if it's upsetting, I can't eat all this myself."

Imposter

"I might be able to overcome." Aaron sat and began dishing up his plate. He enjoyed how Brad had fixed all their mom's dishes. "All of it's to do with the fraud charges brought against me."

"Have you been to court?"

He shook his head before swallowing a bite of turkey. "No, my lawyer says that's next month."

"I'm sure it'll turn out."

"Yeah." He ate, not wanting to say anything more unless it was about his id. They both ate until at last Aaron couldn't stay quiet. "You know what would help? Finding my old badge."

"I've searched the place. It's not here."

He took a deep breath, resisting to yell how Brad could have sent a text. Just one saying searched but didn't find would have saved Aaron some sleepless nights. Hell, a couple of sleepless weeks. "Too bad you couldn't have texted me back. It would have helped clear my name in all this."

"How's that going? Don't tell me the cops left Tim's long enough to do their jobs."

Brad's sarcasm grated on his nerves. He set down his fork. "Yes, they are, but no, they've not found him yet."

"Shame. It's keeping you from work, isn't it?"

Aaron really didn't like the smirk on his brother's face. He resisted the urge to fling the last bite of his mashed potatoes at him. "Have you not received a single one of my messages?"

The other man shrugged. "I have, but things have been crazy busy. I read and listened to the first few words but didn't know anything."

"So not answering seemed like a good idea." A sharp ache hit his stomach. A stress pain, now? Aaron waited for the gas bubble feeling to pass before adding, "Maybe next time you tell me right then so I'm not bothering you."

"All right, maybe I will so you'll be less of a little bitch."

Brad's curtness matched the radiating pain from Aaron's center. He examined what little food remained on his plate. "Did you put jalapenos in anything?"

"No, why?"

He took a deep breath, trying to ignore the burning in his gut. "My stomach is trying to kill me."

"Man, calm down." Brad stood and took Aaron's glass. "Here, let me get you some more water."

Imposter

He glanced over at the television, irritated by the electronic whine emitting from it. Trust Brad to still have an old school TV instead of a flat screen. "Hey, do you mind if we switch off the noise. It's starting to bother me."

"Sure." He set down the water and grabbed the remote. "There. Better?"

Aaron turned his head. "No, I still hear it."

"Hear what?"

"This ringing. Sounds like static, AM radio static."

"That's weird."

"I know." He tried to shake the noise. "Look, all the work stuff must be getting to me. Between my stomach and my ears, I'll just go home and sleep for a while."

"I have something you could take for the pain." Brad went to a cabinet and started rummaging around.

"Thanks, but I'm good."

He held out some generic pain relief. "Here, at least take these with you. Just in case."

"All right. Couldn't hurt." He took the bottle of pills from Brad.

His brother stood in front of him and peered into his eyes. "Hell, you don't look good at all. How about we go for a drive? Get you some fresh air?"

"I'd rather crawl to bed."

"Humor me, will ya?" Brad handed Aaron his coat. "We'll go to Whytehouse Park, stand around, then I'll drive you home. Sound good?"

"Not really, but a few minutes of salt air might help."

"That's what I'm talking about."

Aaron watched with bleary eyes as the landscape passed by. "Thanks for driving. I'm still not a hundred percent."

"Whatever it takes to get you feeling better."

"I guess." They topped the hill just before Whytehouse Park. The movement gave him motion sickness. "Do you come up here often? I never seem to have the time."

"Eh, bout once a week."

He nodded and decided to make more time for the outdoors. "So you know the pathway pretty well? That'll be handy when I need to pass out."

Brad laughed. "I know all the best places for that."

Aaron grinned instead of replying. All the witty retorts had deserted him at dinner earlier this afternoon. "We're taking a short way around, right?"

"Yeah, if you want." He glanced over and put the car into park. "Maybe we should do this some other time. You're looking bad."

"Thanks for the vote of confidence." Unsnapping the seat belt, Aaron added, "Come on. Let's get my outdoors therapy over with."

"All right." Brad locked the car and followed for a while before taking the lead. "We really need to talk."

"Sounds good." He hated starting off on an argument. Still, he wanted to know why. "We can begin by talking about why you didn't text me when I asked you to."

"Can't let it go, huh? I told you, I have a life." He glanced back at Aaron. "Not my problem if you don't."

He struggled to catch up, the uphill climb winding him. "Up yours."

"Back at ya." Brad stood a little way ahead on the pathway. "I suppose you're still trying to figure it out, huh? Who pretended to be you, the big hero, saving lives?"

The sneered description rankled him. Sure, some doctors might consider themselves superhuman. Aaron didn't. "I'm not a hero."

"Mom always thought so. Dad too." He shrugged and moved on. "Doesn't matter now. They're gone, and you're as good as dead to me."

"What the hell does that mean? It matters a hell of a lot." Aaron hurried to catch up to him. "We're family. We have to stick together."

"Sure. I'll remember that the next time I have to harass you into spending time with me." He interrupted himself with a laugh. "Never mind. I'm not doing that again." When Aaron caught up to him, his brother poked him in the chest and said, "Ever again."

"Knock it off, you shit." He pushed away Brad's hand. "Look, I'm sorry you feel like you're begging me. You're not. I'm just really focused on work."

"Oh? Your important work as a doctor? I suppose my peddling drugs in the hospitals wouldn't be good enough for you."

Everything clicked into place. The missing id, the fraud who looked like Aaron, and his sudden illness. He stared, slack-jawed, as his brother walked away. "*You* did all this." He struggled to catch up. "You took my id, impersonated me, and I'm betting you poisoned me, too."

Brad stopped and sneered over his shoulder. "If you're too stupid to know when you've had too much acetylsalicylic acid, that's not my problem."

"Stupid?" Aaron grabbed Brad by the arm and spun him around. "Trusting you to be the last person on the planet to do this is stupid? They arrested me. You have no idea what that's like."

The younger man jerked free. "Fuck off! I didn't want you arrested. I wanted you discredited and your ass out the door."

He could barely hear him and followed Brad to a scenic overlook. "My what? What did I ever do to you?"

Brad stared out at the ocean, scowling. "You have no idea what it's like to be the doctor's brother. I go around, and people think I'm you all the time. They treat me with respect until they find out I'm *Mr.* Nicholson, not *Dr.* Nicholson. It's humiliating." He shook his head. "I'm done with accepting it."

Aaron stared at him. Brad had been the athletic one, always on the team, voted Biggest Flirt. Women swarmed him like fruit flies. The guy could be anything he wanted and still be successful. "So poison is the best solution? Why didn't you just quit your job and do something else?"

"Me quit? Fuck that! You quit."

A laugh escaped Aaron before he could stop it. "Don't be ridiculous. I can't stop being a doctor, it's who I am. You can do sales anywhere with anything. You're good at it."

"Sure." Brad exhaled hard as if letting out the fury. "Sure. I can quit pharm, go into siding sales. Or maybe used cars. How about that? Doctor Nicholson's brother, used car salesman. I'm sure it's how you'd introduce me to all your swanky friends."

"If that's what you enjoy and are good at it, why not?" Aaron had to hurry to keep up as his brother walked on. "There's no shame in honest work."

Brad's words were harsh and cold. His voice grew louder with each word. "You don't understand now and you never will!" A calm came over him. He stared across the bay at Vancouver and took a couple of steps closer to the outlook's edge. "I might as well face it and end everything."

Shit. He sounded suicidal, and Aaron moved toward him, prepared to keep him from jumping over the cliff. "A little morbid, don't you think?"

Imposter

"Yeah, but I like the thought."

Silence. Brad seemed mesmerized by the opposite shore. Aaron shifted from one foot to the other. Eager to get his brother away from the path's steep edge, he tried, "C'mon buddy. You're scaring me. Isn't it me you want dead?"

"I can't decide if you're a chicken or a whiner. Maybe both." He indicated the trail to the left and ahead of them with a nod. "You first?"

Aaron hesitated for a moment before continuing on as the path wound around a glacial boulder. He paused, waiting until hearing his brother behind him. Ahead, the forest opened up as the trail climbed along a cliff. With Brad's chatter about death, Aaron wanted to keep the guy from flinging himself down the rocky wall below them. "How about we backtrack? I'm not feeling too steady."

Brad said from behind, "Funny how you asked if I wanted you dead."

His brother's composed voice sent a shiver through him. He turned to see Brad stopped and staring out at the bay again. Damn it. He'd had no idea about his brother's building depression. Going over to him, Aaron said, "It wasn't a joke." He tried to lighten the mood by asking, "Why give me the aspirin if you want to end it all? Isn't that a step in the wrong direction? Why don't we go to your car and really talk about this?"

A sea breeze lifted his hair, and he breathed in deep. "This is my favourite part of the hike."

Not liking how close the edge was, Aaron turned back toward the hill and took a few steps. "Mine too. Great view. Come on. How about we head back and talk about how I'll—"

A blinding pain and sharp crack dazed him. "What the hell?" He yelped hit him again, almost knocking him unconscious. Falling to his knees, he cried, "Brad, stop!"

"My educated guess is your death will be caused by a fall."

"Son of a bitch!" Aaron struck out, not connecting with his opponent. "This is a bludgeon—" He staggered to his feet, intent on getting away, but stumbled back to the ground.

Brad kicked him in the ribs, knocking Aaron to his side. He rolled away before hopping to his feet as the younger man laughed. "No, it's blunt force trauma that'll kill you." With that, he shoved his older brother over the cliff.

Aaron grabbed at the air before landing on his arm. He bounced down several feet to the water's edge. He laid there for a moment, the air knocked out of him. After prying open his gritty eyes, he saw Brad looking down at him.

The younger man eased to the edge, his eyes searching. "I need to be sure," he muttered. After taking a slow step, the stone wobbled under his foot. Brad slid down a little before catching his balance. He pulled his leg back and hollered, "If you're still alive? You know the tides. Goodbye and sorry about your accident. Glad mom and dad weren't here to see this. They'd be heartbroken." He paused, looking at him. "Gotta go, someone's coming." Brad threw down the rock he had smacked Aaron with and disappeared.

He braced for another hit, but the stone bounced over him. Fighting to stay conscious, he struggled to keep his eyes open. People talked while walking the path above him. He cried, "Help!" a couple of times. His voice sounded breathy, and water splashing against the rocks drowned him out. Sunlight blinded him each time the clouds parted. His chest ached, keeping him from getting a deep breath. His ribs hurt enough to be broken. Aaron coughed into his hand and looked, not seeing any bloody specks. He had a little time.

The tide lapped against his other hand. Brad was right. He'd be underwater if he passed out cold. Feeling the wet and his moving toes were good signs. Hell, even lifting his head to see his feet meant he'd survive this. Aaron first rolled to his side, then belly, before pushing up to his hands and knees. Everything hurt and the salty spray stung his face. He stood, wobbling as he checked his pocket.

Despite the cracked screen, his cell phone worked. He scrolled through his contacts to Doctor Jones but paused. What would he tell her? He sank down on a flat rock, knowing what she would say. Blood dripped onto his cell from his nose. He wiped the device and dialed 911.

"Nine one one, what's the address of your emergency."

"Whytehouse Park."

"What's the number I can call you back on?"

A dark fog clouded his brain as he tried to remember. "Whatever caller id says."

"604-555-8978?"

"Yes." He coughed, covering his mouth with the back of his hand. Looking down, phlegmy blood covered his knuckles. Not good.

"Who am I speaking with?"

Imposter

"Doctor Aaron Nicholson."

"What is your exact problem?"

"Hemoptysis with some pain."

"I'm not sure what that means, oh wait, coughing up blood. Do you have pain with that?"

He didn't have time for this. "Please, just send an ambulance. The EMTs will know what to do."

"Where are you in the park? Is anyone nearby?"

"On the walking trail, near the end. I don't have enough breath to call for help."

"At the end?"

"Yes. Off the trail, at the water's edge." Brad's aspirin overdose was wearing off, fast. He wanted to be carted to hospital, given as much morphine as possible, and sleep until the pain ended. His brother had been right about one thing. Aaron was glad his parents weren't here.

"An ambulance has been dispatched. If you're stable and comfortable, they'll be there in a few minutes."

"Thank you." He ended the call and stared up at the rocky slope. Brad had left him for dead. Aaron's left knee began aching. He lifted up to his elbows, wincing as various injuries protested. He'd landed on his left leg hard enough to tear up his jeans He reached forward to pull away the ragged fabric but couldn't reach that far without his ribs digging into him.

Exhausted, he leaned back against a smooth boulder and speed dialed Tina. She picked up on the third ring, and he said, "We need to talk. I know who my imposter is."

"Who?"

Pebbles rained down and pelted his feet before bouncing down into the water. "What the hell?" He turned and looked up, pain stabbing his chest.

"I knew it!" Brad hollered. "Should have stayed and made sure." He kicked at the rocks lining the path.

He froze, letting the gravel bounce around him until a chunk of the cliff fell. Aaron ignored his body's protest and rolled sideways. He used his good leg to hobble behind a boulder and hid there, protected from the assault. He glanced down to find his cell phone lying in the water.

Aaron shivered and began to yell for help. "Hey! Someone!" Each word pierced him, so he stood to ease the pressure on his ribcage. He heard Brad laugh and watched as his brother stumbled toward him.

Imposter

"Nice try. Thanks for letting me know where you are." Brad slid down closer.

His brother's grunts and curses grew louder as he climbed down the slope. The noises almost drown out the siren in the distance. Aaron wasn't someone who prayed, but now? He didn't mind learning whatever it took to get out of here in anything but a body bag.

Brad had been silent for a little too long. Aaron took the chance to get to his feet. He scooted over to the edge of the boulder and peeked up where he suspected Brad to be.

A face peered over the rocks above. "Hey, buddy. What are you doing down there? Which one of you is Doctor Nicholson?"

"Damn it all to hell!" roared his brother. "I swear to God this is the last time I'm called doctor."

Aaron couldn't breathe or holler to the EMTs. Instead, he dug into his last bit of strength. He scrambled and put the overhang between them. Focused on staying safe, he barely heard shouting from the witnesses and dodged the rocks thrown at him.

"I'll kill you with my bare hands!" Intent on his prey, Brad stumbled a few more feet to him. He stopped to throw a few orange sized rocks before continuing his stalk.

A slab of stone rising up trapped him. He wrapped an arm around his injured ribs. His pain angered him. He wanted to kick his brother's ass, but the pulsing burn in his lung stopped him.

"Shit!" hollered Brad.

Aaron also looked up the slope. Several police officers climbed down to them, the paramedics watching. He sunk to the ground, avoiding another rock and sliding lower against the rock wall.

The younger man pointed at him and said, "This isn't over, mark my words."

"Yes, it is. We're done," Aaron whispered with what little air he had.

The police swarmed Brad, tackling him to the ground. One of them handcuffed him as the other began, "You are under arrest for assault. Do you understand? You have the right to retain and instruct counsel—"

A roar in Aaron's ears drowned out the rest. He closed his eyes, knowing his blood pressure dipped too low. He heard Brad protesting the tight restraints as the police hauled him uphill. Asshole. The guy deserved the injuries.

Imposter

"Hey, doc. We're going to get you up and out of here. Stay with me, okay?"

He glanced at the EMT and nodded. "Just a little tired," he breathed as the paramedic held the stretcher steady for him. Aaron eased onto the carrier, and the EMT strapped him in.

"You're going to be all right, buddy."

"Thanks," Aaron managed, knowing that the guy was right. He'd be okay with medical care. Every bump on the way to the top and ambulance stabbed him in the chest.

"Hang in there."

He nodded. A final jolt as they pushed him into the vehicle, slapping a mask over his face. He breathed in as much as his ribs allowed. The oxygen helped clear his brain. Brad had washed out of medical school, playing social butterfly instead of student. Aaron closed his eyes when they hit a pothole. He'd never thought less of his brother for dropping out. The guy had aced every pharmaceutical class.

"Get ready, doc. We're pulling up to the doors, now."

He nodded, and opening his mouth to ask which hospital, he realized it didn't matter. His one family member had tried to kill him. Aaron lost consciousness knowing he was safe but alone.

Holidays

Laura Stapleton

Holidays

Freshly divorced, Mandy Hays breaks with family tradition and books a tropical vacation for Christmas. When a handsome guy moves in the apartment across from hers, she's curious. What is her new neighbor's secret?

Laura Stapleton

Text Copyright © 2015 Laura L Stapleton

All Rights Reserved.

Covers by Cheeky Covers.

No portion of this book may be reproduced, stored in a retrieval system, or transmitted in any form or by any means, mechanical, electronic, photocopying, recording, or otherwise, without written permission from the author or publisher.

Names, characters, and some incidences are imaginary and complete fiction.

Holidays

Acknowledgements

An immense thank you to everyone who read Imposter, the first short story in this series. Especially now since you're reading the second installment. I hope this and the novels continue to entertain you.

Dedication

To Wayne, Crystal, and Doug.

Laura Stapleton

Holidays

Thanksgiving

Mandy Hays pressed her parent's doorbell. The Nova Scotia air sparkled, and she shivered, the tiny crystals of frozen drizzle flying around her. A movement and whoosh as the wooden door opened.

"Why are you standing here like a stranger?" asked Karen Hays. "Get in and get warm, young lady."

"Goodness, Mom. It's not that cold, yet." Doing as ordered, she stepped inside, suffocated by the warmth. The thick, delicious smell of turkey, ham, and desserts filled the air. The television in the next room blared updates from a game. Judging by her father and brother's hollers, they were watching hockey, and their team just scored.

Karen walked down the hall to the kitchen. "It will be a lot colder by the time you leave tonight, mark my words."

She grinned while hanging her jacket and scarf. Who said that anymore? Mandy followed her mother. She had news for everyone and wanted to ease into telling them. Her heart pounded hard enough to feel it in her veins as she entered the hotbox of a room. "It's finally done,"

The other woman paused in grabbing an electric mixer from the cabinet. She said, "Oh, dear," before going to her daughter.

"No, it's fine." Her throat hurt before a sob escaped. "I'm all right."

"Come here," admonished Karen before enveloping Mandy in a hug.

The tender touch triggered a tidal wave of sobs from her. "I hate him, Mom. I'm glad we're divorced. Why does this hurt so much?"

"What's going on?" asked Mandy's father, Shawn.

Mrs. Hays spoke above her daughter's head. "Nothing dear, just the loss of Geo."

"Good riddance, I say." He held his arms open, wiggling his fingers.

Mandy chuckled and went to her father. She snuggled into her dad's flannel shirt. "I'm better off without him, I know."

He kissed the top of her head before resting his cheek there. "Yes, you are. He's not worth a single tear of yours."

She tried to stop sobbing. "He's a jerky jerkface, and I hate him."

He snickered, giving her an extra squeeze before letting her go. "Why do I

Holidays

think you've cleaned up your language for me?"

"I might have," admitted Mandy. "Only a little."

Mrs. Hays hugged her daughter again. "Come on, no more crying. He's the past, and you have a better future ahead."

She took the paper towel from Shawn and wiped her tears. "I'd like to think so."

"Of course you do, sweetheart." Karen held her out at arm's length. "Now come help me with the turkey."

Mandy shook her head at the food. Every square inch of counter space held a side dish or dessert. She'd been so focused on her troubles to the point of coasting through the first two weeks of October. "I should have brought a dessert."

"You did. You brought yourself." Karen handed her the large serving plate. "Hold this while I carve."

"Hey! There's the baby!" Marty hurried over to her and grabbed her in a bear hug. "Want me to go kick Geo's ass? Cause I will. No one messes with my sister."

She gave him a watery laugh. "That's the problem. He wasn't messing with me. Just everyone else."

"Aw! Pumpkin." He hugged her. "He's not worth it. The divorce is final?"

She nodded against his shoulder. "Good! I never liked him."

She held out the plate for her mom and gave Marty a wry look. "Hoser, he's your best friend."

"Was. Now let's eat." He took a small slice of meat from her. "You are hungry, right?"

"Starved!" She breathed in, enjoying the roasted sage from the dressing in the oven. Her family fussed, her mom smacking the hands of both turkey thieves. She grinned at her father and brother's antics. This place was heaven today and what Mandy needed.

Karen gave the men one last shaming look before smiling at her daughter. "How is everything at the shop? Are your booths rented out, yet?"

"All but one. I don't get to have any fun thanks to the paperwork." She tried to keep the food from her brother, but he managed to steal a couple of pieces.

"I could have told you that," interjected Marty. "Everyone else gets to work on cars while I'm cooped up in the office." He shrugged before popping a bite of turkey into his mouth. "It's not claustrophobic in winter, but summer? I can't get out to test drive a repair or two."

Holidays

"That sounds awful!" Karen took the full platter from her.

Shawn filled glasses with ice. "Sounds like my life without the test drives, son."

"Marty, mash the potatoes. Mandy, get the other sides, and Shawn? Wine glasses, too, please." The older woman looked behind her. "Who wants the wishbone?"

Her brother shouted over the hand mixer, "I do."

A little later, with less noise and everyone seated at the dinner table, Mandy cleared her throat. She wondered how to give the family her news. They'd protest, and she didn't blame them. She'd spent every Christmas with them since her birth and Marty since his. Mandy took a deep drink of wine. "I need to tell you my holiday plans." She waited until she had everyone's attention. "You might not be happy, but I've planned to spend Christmas in Florida."

"Where?" asked Shawn.

Karen put down her fork. "No, you can't."

"Are we going, too?" Marty punched his dad on the arm. "Family vacation!"

"I'm going alone." She stared at her plate, toying with a piece of ham. "I'd thought about spending time in the sun where it's warm and away from everything."

Her mother crossed her arms. "Hmph. I see. You're running off from us."

"That's not it." Her prepared speech left her for a moment, wondering how to convince her family how her decision had nothing to do with them? Mandy decided to say flat out, "I don't want to think about Geo and his new little family during the holidays."

Shawn patted her hand. "Well, it sounds as if you've made up your mind."

Mandy smiled at him. "I'm sorry, but I have." She looked at her mom. "If I stay, I'll mope around and bring down everyone else."

"Don't worry, sweetheart." Karen grinned at her. "Just do what's best for you."

Tears filled her eyes when she saw them nod in agreement. "Thank you for understanding, everyone. I love you, too."

Holidays

Halloween

The doorbell rang. Mandy jumped up and grabbed the big bowl of candy. Her first group of kids at her new place! She opened the door and saw a princess, a frog, and a caped crusader who hollered, "Trick or treat!"

"How about a treat?" she asked. At their yells, she gave each of them a handful of mini chocolate candy bars. They said thank you before turning to the apartment across from hers. She didn't have time to close the door before new children came up the steps, their faces hopeful. Mandy smiled back at them, not pretending to hide inside.

When the opposite door opened, she caught sight of her new neighbour. She'd caught glimpses of him yesterday, from a distance. This close? Their gazes met. His medium gray eyes grabbed her attention first. The colour reminded her of an overcast day. His dark hair went every which way as if he'd woken up minutes ago. The man's face looked the rugged side of handsome until he smiled at her. Mandy couldn't help but return his grin. Her heart did a flip, like when she'd been caught peeking at the answers during a test. She stood for a moment before feeling a tug at her tutu.

"Ma'am? Can we have our treats?"

The boy's mother behind him tugged on the child's superhero cape. "Jeffrey! Say trick or treat, first!"

Mandy grinned at the horrified mom. "It's ok...."

"Trick or treat!" the boy yelled.

"Trick!" shrieked Mandy before laughing. She noticed her new neighbor trying not to chuckle. The little guy seemed confused. "Sorry. Your costume scared me." She gave him a handful of candy. "I mean treat."

Other kids crowded around both doorways. After awhile, they formed queues up and down the stairs. She shook her head and wondered if all these children lived in her apartment complex. When a break in the tide of fictional characters and monsters slowed, the man closed his own door and walked over. "Hi, I'm Aaron."

They shook hands as she said, "Hi, I'm Mandy." She set down her bowl of chocolates and looked at him. Taller than her by a good half foot and he had a rather deep voice. He smelled like soap, spices, and mint. He seemed the perfect neighbor so far.

"I live next door now."

Holidays

"I see," she kidded and loved how he blushed. Mandy hadn't meant to embarrass him. "Moved just in time to give away all your candy. Such a shame."

He laughed. "Yeah, but I've kept a bag back for me."

She gave him a thumbs up while reaching over to her own bowl and taking a handful of candy for later. "Great idea! Welcome to the neighborhood. If you need anything, they have a website from the 90s. Very helpful." Mandy decided she enjoyed hearing him chuckle. "I'm kidding. I've lived in the province all my life and don't mind answering questions."

He nodded as more kids climbed the stairs. "I'll keep that in mind. So, catch you later, then?"

"Sure." She backed into her apartment, bumping against the threshold in her clumsiness. The kids hit Aaron's place first and gave her time to get the candy. They soon left, the coast clear, and she closed the door. She liked hearing him talk to the children. His voice caused tingles in the nerves to her ears, tickling them in a sexy and wanting more way. She'd snuck peeks into his apartment every chance possible. No boxes and the furniture came with the furnished apartments. Mandy had stuff Geo let her take, so she'd been able to have her own belongings. This Aaron guy didn't appear to own much.

Fewer kids rang the doorbell. She had some candy left over. Mandy got up and looked outside to check the coast was clear. Aaron's door opened a little, and he looked outside, too. She said, "I think it's over for the night. Everyone else is old enough for a party."

Aaron raised a hand. "Or too old to be at one."

She chuckled and raised her hand. "Or too tired."

"That's true." He switched off his outside light. "Did you save back anything for yourself? I ended up using my reserves."

She had to kid around with him. "Poor guy! What are you doing for dinner?"

"Dinner? Haven't thought about it."

She took a handful of the leftover treats and held them out to him. "Here's your dinner."

"Ah." Aaron accepted them with a wry smile. "Chocolate. A major food group."

"Oh! That reminds me. Give me a second." She left her door open and went to her kitchen to grab a bottle of wine. Mandy opened her fridge, looking for her best bottle.

"Is it ok if I come in?"

Holidays

She glanced over to see him standing outside. "Sure! Close the door behind you. Both doors, for both our sakes and tell me if you like wine."

"Love it and thanks." He walked into the house. "Your place is nice. All this furniture must be yours."

"It is. I had everything and didn't need the furnished option." She handed him the bottle. "Here, the second food group and a welcome to the neighborhood."

He laughed, taking the wine. "Are you the official greeter, or just a decent person?"

"Might be since I'm the only person I've met at the complex besides you and the office people." She felt a blush begin when he glanced up at her through his lashes.

Aaron arched an eyebrow. "Really? Your place has that cozy vibe. As if everything was picked for this exact apartment."

"I think that's called messy. I've been here a month tomorrow."

He grinned, going back to reading the bottle's label. "It's fine, not cluttered. I may have to return the favor and welcome you to the neighborhood."

"Sounds good. You'll have to offer the third food group, coffee." She picked her coat up from the back of the sofa.

"I can do that."

She hung her winter gear and turned to him. "You're a wise man."

"Hope so." He held up the wine. "Thanks for this. It's nice."

"You're welcome. Let me show you out." She followed him, noticing he walked as if his legs hurt. His movements reminded her of the day after a tough run. "Will you be okay?"

"I'll be fine." He opened his apartment, turning back to her. "Goodnight, Mandy. See you around."

She closed her door at the same time he did. Aaron had a fit body, looked like he worked out. Mandy would be lying to herself if she might be only interested in him helping her bring up groceries or carry heavy things. She grinned and sank into her sofa. The heavy lifting was Marty's job. This new guy? Total eye candy and a possible new friend.

If his outside matched his insides, he'd be a great boyfriend, too. She shook her head, but not great for her. Mandy crossed her arms and stared at the blank television. Her ex-husband of three weeks getting engaged didn't lead her to be in the same rush. She'd need more recovery time before jumping back into the dating pool.

Holidays

"Hey, you all right?"

Mandy startled a moment, glancing up from the document. Her vision swam until the tears fell. She glanced around to see if anyone else but her and Aaron were next to the mailboxes. "Hey. I'm fine. Just sad news." The official documents sealed her fate as a divorcee.

"Those cable bills can hurt. My satellite one left me despondent."

She snorted more than laughed and wiped her cheeks. "These are divorce papers, and I'd prefer utility bills. Neither are the best, but always a treat, eh?"

He checked his own mailbox. "Divorce, huh? Sorry to hear that."

Mandy figured she had put him on the spot with her admission. She should have laughed it off or blamed the popular something in her eye for the tears. She patted his arm. "Don't be, it's ok. I need to remember this is good news and one final cry before starting the celebration." She folded the paper back into the envelope, slipping everything into her purse. "Geo's been calling me every day to ask if I'd received the documents, yet. I shouldn't have waited this long to check mail."

"Rip off the band aid sooner rather than later?" He tapped the prior occupant's catalogs against his palm.

"Exactly." Mandy smiled at him, wanting to think his fidgets were irritation over Geo's callousness. Probably not, but she liked pretending. "Well, enough of this. I need to get going. Thanks for the sympathy."

"No problem, take care." He headed toward the parking lot.

She watched for a moment, before realizing if he turned around, he'd catch her staring. Mandy shook her head. She had better things to do. His walking had improved. Not much, though, and she made a note to ask how often he went for a run or lifted weights.

An hour later and with a clean house, she opened the door to find him locking up. With his back turned to her, he didn't see how his full laundry bag echoed the basket resting against her hip. She didn't want to startle him. "Hello."

He glanced over at her and grinned. "Great minds, huh?"

She gestured toward his clothes bag. "Best minds ever."

"The laundromat downstairs?" At her nod, he continued, "Wait a second." He eased the bag over his shoulder with a wince before letting it drop back to the floor. He gripped the cloth top with one hand, near the

Holidays

top of the sack, and led the way. "Let me go first. That way if you slip, it's on me."

"What a gentleman! I'll try not to trip and crush you."

He laughed. "Don't worry. Your laundry basket would hurt more than you would."

She noticed he took each step carefully. "Are you okay? You seem to be somewhat stiff." After the innuendo had escaped Mandy, she was glad he didn't face her. If the guy were the same as Marty, he'd pounce on the chance to kid around about the double entendre.

"Yeah." He stood out from the bottom step, waiting for her to reach him. "I took a hell of a fall on Thanksgiving and am not a hundred percent."

Since he'd mentioned it, she noticed a healing cut under his chin. "That was a few weeks ago. You're still limping, so the accident must have been painful." She led the way to the laundromat. "Your face looks good."

"Thanks, but you should see the rest of me." He chuckled, holding the door open for her. "Not as pretty."

She blushed while passing by him; glad he didn't know everything she'd thought about him. Mandy stopped at an empty machine and set her basket in front. "What kind of fall was it?"

Aaron gave her a glance before searching the area. "I didn't bring soap. And I don't see them selling any."

She didn't like his distraction. It kept her from learning more about his accident. "You can have some of mine."

"Thanks." He thought for a moment. "How about I start my wash, courtesy of your soap, and you watch our clothes while I hit Horton's for coffee?"

"Sounds wonderful. I want a single single."

"You bet. Be back in awhile."

"Before the rinse cycle?"

"Long before, I promise."

She watched him. He'd been breathing a little harder than she'd expected a healthy guy to do. She'd also noticed his limp seemed more pronounced than before. Mandy wanted to ask him everything about the fall he'd mentioned. The usual questions, when, where, what, how, and why. Her ex-husband's snarky words about butting in where she didn't belong played in her mind.

Mandy retrieved her cell phone, opened her e-book app, and stared at the screen without reading. Aaron stayed in her thoughts like his cologne lingered in the air. She smiled at the metaphor. Or did the fresh

Holidays

scent come from his dryer sheets? She'd have to ask how he'd been hurt, what he did for a living, and anything else when he returned. Which might be much later, so she refocused on the latest book.

He came in, carrying two coffees on a tray and a bag. "Hey. I thought you might want lunch, too."

Mandy stood and took her coffee. "Food and drink both? Thank you." She led the way back to the seats, enjoying how the hot cup warmed her hands.

He rummaged around in the Timmie's bag before handing her a wrapped sandwich. "Hope you don't mind chicken. It's their latest."

"I've heard but haven't had the chance. Why don't you sit and tell me what happened to you." She settled in for lunch and a chat, her stomach growling at the aroma.

Aaron paused in unwrapping his food. "Didn't sound like a question."

She laughed, seeing how his frown didn't reach his eyes. "Didn't mean it as one. Unless it's a super secret government spy thing."

"Should I be worried? What do you do, again?" He took a bite.

"I hang out, visit my family, go to work, and come home. Work on my plans for world domination through force and intimidation. The usual." She liked his laugh. His amusement reassured her he'd not been offended by her questions. "In my spare time, I run a styling salon."

He grinned. "That sounds good. I'll need someone to cut my hair carefully while my stitches heal."

"Let me look, then I can give you a time estimate. Though we would be careful with you. That whole butcher thing is due to the shop down the street." She put her coffee on the table as he tilted the top of his head toward her. "I don't see... Oh wow, Aaron! Were you in a car wreck, too?"

"No, just one accident. I fell down a cliff while hiking in a park." He leaned away from her. "It aches sometimes, but looks worse than it is."

Her stomach dropped for him, sure the experience had to hurt. "Were you alone? Did your cell still work?"

"I was alone, and yes, for a little while. I could call for help." He stood, crumpling his sandwich wrapper and putting it in the nearby trash. "No dramatic rescue, just an embarrassing and painful trip."

"Literally, it sounds." She did the same with her paper as he had, both of them opening the quiet washing machines. She wondered how long they'd been done and

Holidays

joined Aaron in transferring everything to a dryer. Mandy glanced at his clothes, trying to not be nosy while being curious. When spying medical scrubs in the mix, she took a chance and said, "Being a doctor had to help. You could guess how bad your injuries were."

He smiled at her. "It did help. How did you guess I wasn't a nurse?"

"I'm observant when I want to be." She put the money in the coin holders and started her machine. "You poor guy. It's rotten no matter how it happened. Here's a dryer sheet. You'll need one for static."

"Thanks." He threw it in the machine, started it, and went back to his seat beside hers. "Now I'm intrigued. Tell me more."

"Your car says you're practical and from British Columbia. Your heavy weather gear means you're used to colder temperatures than this. And your shoes?" She peered at his feet. "They're a puzzle. They're high-end running shoes which say you're very active, but I've not seen you out first thing in the morning." He laughed, and she grinned. "Unless you're out before dawn, of course."

"Is that it?"

"No, there's more, but it's speculative. You're single because there's no wedding band or car seat. Plus, I've never spotted you with anyone. From the lack of ear piercings or tattoos on the lower arms, I'd guess you're either a subversive rebel or a guy who plays by the rules."

"Really?"

When he had an odd expression on his face, Mandy knew she'd hit the mark. She wanted to learn more, but the stubborn clench of his jaw said he wouldn't be willing to add details. Maybe an indirect approach would work. "Yeah, I'd also guess over thirty-five, even if you look twenty-nine to thirty."

"I'm thirty-five, just turned." He stood, crunching the fast food bag. "That was fun. An interesting example of your powers of observation."

"Thank you. I sometimes need to observe more than a client tells me."

"Is that why hairdressers have the reputation of being nosy?"

"No, not at all." His insinuation irritated her. "I don't usually want intimate details, information that helps me give the best style for a person."

She pulled out her phone, reopening her e-book application. When a handsome new guy starts saying the same things as the ex-husband? Time to tune out and ignore. Mandy felt fine letting Aaron find someone else. A gal who wasn't curious, would be stick thin, and be able to lead married men astray with a single wink.

Mandy glanced over when his actions caught her attention. He had his own phone out. His movements mimicked hers when she deleted spam from her inbox. She turned back to her own little screen.

"Probably nosy wasn't the right word for you. Sorry. Alert and curious are more accurate." He glanced over at her as she looked at him. "As long as you're not snooping through someone's underwear drawer, you just see what's there."

"Exactly!" she said, glad he saw the real side of her personality. Before thinking, she blurted, "I wish Geo—. Never mind. I'm glad you see the benefits."

He stood to get clothes from the dryer. "Trust me, I'm the last person to complain about what you learn from a customer. When a patient is unconscious, it's on me to save a life. I have to do what I can." He folded each article and placed it in the laundry bag. "Even if it means rifling through their underwear." He put the boxer brief on top of everything else and grabbed his coffee.

"Oh, gross." His laugh told her he'd been kidding. "I'm glad you're not serious!"

She went to her dryer as it eased to a stop and began folding.

He picked up his laundry bag. "I'd try other things first. Blood pressure, temperature, pupil dilation, testing reflexes."

"Wait, let me pay you for lunch before you leave." She dug around in her pocket. "I hope quarters are ok."

Aaron backed up to and opened the door. "Don't worry. I have errands to run, so you'll pay next time?"

"Sure." Before Mandy could say anything more, he was out, the door closed behind him. Presumptuous of him to assume they'd do this again. She smiled. Maybe he wasn't so bad after all.

Holidays

Christmas

Through the next week, she only saw Aaron in passing and when one of them needed to be somewhere else. Several days more of this and she'd resort to taping an envelope to his door with her part of laundry day lunch. Mandy stepped outside with her trusty snow shovel. Last night's storm gave them a new blanket around four inches deep. She and Aaron were the only ones who used this set of stairs. A part of her didn't want to slip on them, but a larger part didn't want him hurt, either. She began clearing, the snow heavy and wet.

"Hey, great idea."

She turned and saw Aaron holding his own snow shovel. She held a hand out to shield the sun and the gleam from the scooper's chrome. "That looks new."

"It is. I finally have a chance to use it." He came down slow and easy, pausing when he reached the step above where she stood. "How about I start at the bottom and we'll meet in the middle?"

Mandy shrugged, not wanting his help, but not dumb enough to turn him away. "Sure. Why not?" He grinned and continued to the ground. She shook her head. He wasn't wearing a hat. The man needed a cut since his hair was way shaggy. A little crack in her heart's ice began when she remembered his stitches and how painful they'd looked. She started clearing steps, pushing snow to the side and off. "So, did you get the dissolving stitches or the ones you had to pull out?"

Aaron didn't pause with the shoveling. "Some were, others weren't. It depended on the injury."

She hadn't thought of where else he'd been cut or broken. "You had more than the scalp?"

"Yep. Knee, chest, arm. Most were surgical after the fact, others when it happened."

"Damn, Aaron." She paused, dying to ask more without being intrusive. "Have you not healed enough for a haircut or are you going for a wooly mammoth look?"

He laughed, stopping to look at her from his lower step. "You're right. I've probably healed by now. Can you recommend anyone who can tame this mess?"

"I might have a stylist brave enough." Her cell buzzed in her pocket. She ignored it, certain the message was a payment acknowledgment from her phone company. Mandy smiled at Aaron, not wanting a text to stop their chat. "So, the day after tomorrow is the big day. Are you ready?"

"For?"

"Christmas! Don't tell me you forgot?" She threw the last clump of snow over the railing.

"No, I know it's Christmas Eve today."

"Sure, I'll believe that." Mandy turned toward her own apartment, looking back and saw him following. She slowed to let him catch up.

Aaron leaned forward, tapping her middle back with his shovel's handgrip. "At least I have a wreath on the door. Who's festive now?"

"You are." She grinned back at him before taking the last step to the landing. "I'm proud of your festive spirit."

He gestured at her front door. "So where's yours?"

"In a box with my other decorations." At his wry smirk, Mandy laughed. "I'm leaving this afternoon, spending my holidays in the tropics."

"I'll be here, freezing to death."

"There's a cure for that." She handed him a gift card for Timmie's.

He took the present, looking it over with a smile. "Thanks, you didn't need to do this."

"Yes, I did, and don't be too impressed. It's only ten dollars, but I can renew it for your birthday, Appreciate a Doctor Day, World's Best Snow Shoveler. The usual reasons." Her phone buzzed again in her coat pocket, reminding her of a text. "I'll see you next year?"

He grinned and held up the card. "Hope so. I like the way you think."

Mandy slipped inside, leaving her shovel on the inside mat. She had several other tasks to do before this evening. She hung the damp parka on the closet doorknob before prying off her boots. The tickets, her passport, ID, swimsuit were already sitting out on the coffee table. She grinned, ready to be blinded by white sand and not snow.

A couple of hours later, her packed bags sat by the front door. All she needed was a light jacket to bring instead of her usual coat. Mandy paused. She'd need something warm when returning, plus her phone was still in the pocket.

She locked up, pulling one suitcase and carrying another. The stairs shone under the streetlights with a freezing mist covering them. She put a tentative foot down to test if the step was slick. Nope, only wet, so she hurried to her car.

Mandy suspected something was wrong while in long term parking. She secured her car, remembering to get her cell phone before leaving her heavy coat in the front seat. A harder, colder rain fell, freezing to everything it hit. She picked her way to a bus stop and pulled her hoodie over her head. Might as well check the text and make sure her account was accurately charged. She tapped the screen and opened the message. *All flights canceled due to storm of the century.*

She stared at the sky before instantly regretting that decision when a cold splat hit her between the eyes. Insurance took care of the cancellation, so she wasn't out much money. She looked at her car. Ice began to cling to the trunk and roof. Great. She'd have to hurry home before conditions became worse. She drove behind a salt truck most of the way and found the bright side of staying home. Her family would be happy she'd spend Christmas with them.

As she inched back to her place, she remembered her brother. He'd probably be bitter and angry over missing out on the rum she'd promised to bring him. The complex's asphalt gleamed with ice. She eased in, slow and careful, into a distant space. She the keyless entry for her trunk helped and pulled out her suitcases. She walked upstairs, the baggage banging into her legs. A couple of steps more and her foot slipped. A current of fear buzzed her during the stumble forward.

A masculine voice saying, "Hey, what are you doing here?" got her attention. Aaron stood at the top, pausing for a second before coming down and taking her luggage. "I didn't mean that. Let me help. The flat surfaces are starting to get slick."

She liked how he seemed happy at first, then embarrassed. "Only as long as you're careful, too. I've heard doctors make horrible patients." She gave him her backpack and kept the heavier rolling case for herself.

"It's true, we do. I take it you're not going anywhere?" He paused beside her welcome mat.

She nodded and unlocked her door. "Remember that text I ignored?" He nodded, so she added, "Yep. They canceled it. Come on in and I'll make our coffee."

He shook his head. "I'd love to stay, but I'm due at work in thirty minutes."

Mandy ran her hand along the coated railing. "In another fifteen, it might take you an hour to get there."

Holidays

"Right." He went to his door and locked it. "I'll get going. Can we compare holiday woes on Boxing Day?"

She wanted to agree but knew her mom. "I'll probably be busy with family."

"And I'll be busy with drunk drivers and new gift accidents. Like, the bullet is supposed to come out where? Or, that knife didn't look sharp at first."

She laughed. "Fish hooks go in easier than they come out?"

"That, too. Later?" He brought her in for a half-hug. "Merry Christmas."

"You bet and Merry Christmas to you, too." Mandy closed the door and took off her coat. Poor guy with nothing but work on Christmas. They'd known each other, what, a month? She had learned not much more about him now than when they'd first met. A dozen questions floated around in her mind, but first, she started the coffee and settled in to text her family her change in plans.

Flight canceled. I'm here for the holiday.

What? No rum?
Oh, good! Your father was worried.
Can we have two Christmases?
I vote yes, mom.
Sure. I'll add a ham.
More presents?

She laughed over Marty looking at the bright side. *Yes, Mar, 'cause I love last minute shopping.*
Good.
Being facetious.
Whatever.
Kids, noon dinner. Mandy, bring the pies. Marty, bring the casserole.
Sure, mom.
'k.
Hugs to you all.
You too!
Glad you're here, sis.
I suppose. ;)

She looked up from her phone. Hazelnut coffee aroma filled her home, and the sweet smell reminded her of dinner. Her refrigerator was empty on purpose. She opened the freezer portion, staring inside for a quick meal.

A Salisbury steak heated in the microwave, and Mandy leaned against the counter. She needed to text her assistant manager to close the salon for the rest of the day. As soon as she hit send, Mandy's dinner beeped ready. She began eating, wondering how Aaron was getting home if it got much worse. A text came in from Fiona saying she was on top of things, now locking the doors. In between bites, Mandy replied a thanks and Merry Christmas. She

Holidays

had bonuses set to hit their accounts tomorrow and couldn't wait. The year's profits allowed her to be generous.

Mandy spent the rest of the afternoon watching holiday specials, trying to stay awake. She yawned, certain she had better things to do. Like presents. The Hays had an early gift exchange, sure. But to not open anything on the Day? She went for the coffeemaker, filling it again. As the vital liquid brewed, she grabbed the remote and turned to the forecast, hoping the temperature planned on melting the ice later today. She glanced at the television, the news still on with no forecast in sight. She needed to check texts anyway. After reading messages, she clicked the weather app. Shopping for gifts in the warming afternoon, back home before dark and refreezing. Perfect.

Mandy managed to carry every bag with two hands. She smiled, seeing Aaron get out of his car. She blurted, "There you are," before realizing how clingy she'd sound. "Hey, beautiful weather we're having. And since you're off work, you can help me wrap presents."

He fell into step beside her before lagging back to let her ascend the stairs first. "Yeah, I've got to go. This is my lunch hour." He laughed when she frowned at him. "Really."

"Wow, long hours." She unlocked her apartment door and set the bags inside. "Is this normal and you're home for the day?"

"Not quite. I'm covering for someone else tomorrow. So tonight, when I'm iced in, I'll need a few things." He motioned behind himself before unlocking his own place. "Another change of clothes and a phone charger are at the top of the list."

"They don't have chargers at the hospital that fits or one of those bars that recharge when you put electronics on it?"

"You caught me. I'm here for other stuff, too. Instant tea, fresh socks, and a bag for the dead body." He held his door open. "Come in and keep warm for a second or two."

She stepped in, closing the door behind her to keep in the heat. "Thanks, hey, it's nice in here. No, I just figured there'd be a row of various cell chargers in the doctors' lounge, ready and waiting. Hold on. Did you say dead body?"

"I'm kidding." Aaron held up a grocery bag with a jar of instant tea showing through the thin plastic. "No cadaver in the

Holidays

place." He put the phone accessory in the sack and motioned for her to follow.

"Right. Good to know." She stopped short of following him into his bedroom. "Where are we going?"

"Here." He opened a dresser drawer. "But you can hover outside the room if you're chicken."

She rather liked his wicked grin. "I'm not. I don't want to intrude on your privacy."

Aaron laughed outright, shoving clothes into the bag. "Sure you don't."

The remark hit her in the heart. She mentally shrugged it off. Geo said the same thing when she'd wondered where he'd slept that night and several others when he'd not been home. She'd said nothing to Aaron about her past. And who was he to her, anyway? He wasn't that close of a friend. She turned and left the doorway, saying, "I actually don't want to intrude. So, see ya."

"Hey, I was kidding around." He came up behind her, tapping her shoulder. She didn't face him, so he continued, "Come on, I invited you over because I enjoy our conversation."

She shrugged. "No worries. I'm just respecting your space."

"Thank you, I appreciate that." He bumped into her while walking by. "But never tell anyone of the horrors you saw in my bedroom. The unmade bed, dirty clothes, old school TV. I'm trying to build a reputation." Aaron knelt a little to look her in the eyes. "Please?"

Mandy chuckled. "Secret's safe with me."

"Good." He straightened and went to open the door. "As much as I'd love to stay and chat, they need me at the hospital." Aaron followed her out, putting the key in the lock. "Hey, wait." He finished securing his place and looked at her. "You know I meant it, right? I'd rather spend the rest of the day with you. I mean, not to be intrusive or anything, I'm sure you have plans."

Was he blushing? She grinned, glad she had such a chance to kid around with him. "I do have plans. Christmas with the parents and kid brother." Similar to a sharp cold front ahead of a storm, Aaron's expression changed. What the hell, she wondered. "I mean, Marty's not an actual kid, we're a year apart."

"That's cool." He tapped his keys. "So, later?"

"Sure." She watched him for a moment until the chill got to her and she shivered. Mandy hurried into her own home, amazed at the change in her neighbor. The

Holidays

bags to the entry's side reminded her she had gift-wrapping to do before leaving.

She wrestled with the red and green paper, managing to get more tape on the presents than herself. All the while, Aaron's reaction lingered in her mind. Family couldn't be an off-limit topic. Otherwise, what would she talk about? Work? "Ha!" She looked up from writing out the gift tags. "I need a hobby."

A fire roared in the wood stove, adding to the cozy atmosphere in the Hays living room. Every Christmas light glowed, giving the night a festive air. The tree bowed under a century's worth of ornaments. Mandy sipped at her hot chocolate and wiggled her toes. Her mom had made her, and Marty new socks for a Christmas Eve present. They fit perfectly, too.

"So? Tell me about him," said Mrs. Hays.

"There's not much to tell. He lives across the way, is standard issue tall, dark, and handsome."

"A foreign guy?" asked Shawn.

She laughed. "Almost, British Columbia."

Her dad went back to his newspaper. "Humph."

"Now, don't be silly." Karen ushered Mandy into the kitchen. "Come on and help me with the sides, please?" She took out the cranberry relish and butter out of the fridge. "Is this Aaron your rebound guy you think?"

She took the items from her mother while saying, "Mom! It's a little soon for that."

Karen led the way to the dining room table first, then back into the kitchen. "Probably. After Geo, I wouldn't blame you if you dated the next great catch you saw."

Mandy took and filled four glasses with ice. "Just to show him?"

"Yes, he deserves to be taken down a peg or two. Or hundred." Karen had four stemmed glasses and a bottle of wine.

"I'd like that, but not at Aaron's expense." She set down the glasses at the same time as her mother.

"Hm." Karen went back into the kitchen and began pulling back the foil on their turkey.

The non-comment amused Mandy. "No, don't try to match make. He's a friend who lives next door, that's all."

"Didn't you do laundry together? And see his bedroom?" teased Karen, carving the meat.

Marty strolled in, grabbing a bite of turkey. "She what? Saw whose bedroom?"

Holidays

His mom slapped his hand and said, "Marty, either help out or get out."

"Ma! Who're we talking about?"

"You don't know him." Mandy gave him a piece of ham.

He took the slice, grinning. "Thanks. Who is he?"

Karen seized the platter from her daughter's hands with a frown. "Mandy's new neighbor. He's a doctor. I'll have to check on him. Shawn? Dinner's ready."

"Finally!" he said from the living room.

Marty followed his mother after grabbing a couple of side dishes. "That's all? He's the neighborhood doctor? Why is Mandy hung up on him?"

"Shut it, I'm not." She hollered at him while grabbing the tea pitcher.

As Mandy walked in the dining room, her brother teased, "Mom says you are."

The older woman shook her head. "I did not. She's a friend to someone new in town."

Marty snarfed his tea and flicked the back of her neck. "Yeah, you're going with that, Man?"

She shot him a mean glare. "No. He's new, lives in the apartment across from me, that's it."

Her mom sat last. "They had coffee and did laundry together." She patted Mandy's hand. "Tell Geo to go suck it."

"Mom!" she choked out.

"Mandy!" Karen retorted. "He needs to hear you're not the last berry on the bush."

Mr. Hays pointed his fork at Marty. "No, you tell Geo our little girl isn't the only berry in town. He lost out when he started beating around other bushes."

"Ha! Call me or video it when you do, would ya?" stammered her brother.

Mandy flopped a spoonful of mashed potatoes a little harder than she'd intended. "I'm telling him nothing."

Marty guffawed, "Yeah, I'll tell him for ya."

"No, not a word." She shook her head.

Her father glanced up from getting turkey slices. "She's right. George doesn't need to know anything." He winked at Mandy. "He made his choice, and he's lucky you keep him on at the garage."

Marty took the plate from Shawn. "As soon as a decent transmission guy appears, Geo is out of there."

Shawn poured himself a generous glass of wine and passed the bottle to Mandy first. "You mean to tell me that no one on

Holidays

this side of the province can do what he does?"

Her brother stared at his plate. "I need to look harder for a new mechanic."

Mandy sympathized with him. Geo had been his friend longer than he'd been her husband. She knew their divorce put Marty in a tight spot. "Don't worry, Mart. Just keep looking for a new guy and don't expect us to be friends."

"Sure. I'll take out a bigger ad."

"You took out one at all?" Karen patted her son's arm. "See, Shawn? Marty's trying to be a good brother."

"Humph."

"Ok, so. I'll put another ad out for a new trans man." Marty sat straighter, reaching for the dinner rolls. "Tell us about this neighbor. He's not a serial killer, eh?"

"His mug shot didn't say he was." At her father's grimace, she grinned. "You know he isn't. New in town, and like I told Mom, we did laundry at the same time. He's a doctor at the hospital, from BC, doesn't want to talk about his family."

"Red flag right there, sis. Keep your distance."

She laughed. "Tough to do when a few feet separates our front doors."

"You know what I mean."

Karen leaned in. "He's right, sweetie. How a man treats his mother shows how he treats women in general, right, dear?" Their dad nodded at Karen's question, and she continued, "I'll ask around at work. I'm sure the other nurses have heard about the newest doctor in town."

Mandy smiled at her father. "What do you think, Dad? You've been far too quiet."

"I'm chewing." He waited until they finished chuckling. "Not every family is postcard perfect, sweetheart. Whatever kind of man he is, there's no rush until you're comfortable."

"Thanks, Dad." Tears threatened to fill her eyes, and she glanced at her plate. He'd always been her staunchest supporter.

"Send him to me between now and May. I'll do his taxes and see if he's hiding anything from you." Shawn nodded toward his office. "Before you leave, go to my room and get one of my cards for him. Tell him to call me for an appointment."

Marty shifted sideways in his chair, digging out his billfold. "Yeah, take my card, too. He needs oil changes, right? Send him in and I'll make sure he's decent."

"Sure, Mart." She put his card in her pocket, certain Aaron would enjoy the motor oil fingerprints printed on them. Mandy took a bite of her cranberry orange compote. Judging by the ordinary one he drove, she didn't think the guy loved cars.

"'Course, if you saw his bedroom... I mean, you may already be crazy about him."

She glanced up to see her brother staring at her as if looking for a clue. Mandy had to admire Marty's way of weaseling information from her. "Yes, I saw his bedroom. He invited me in, so I followed. Wanna hear what happened next?"

"Nope!" Marty cried.

"Sweetie, I don't think so."

Shawn held up a hand. "None of our business."

She laughed at all of them leaning away from the table, sure their imaginations ran wild. "Aaron retrieved a change of clothes, and we both went right back out. In fact, I didn't even walk into the room properly."

"How about improperly?" her brother snickered.

"Not even that."

"Behave, young man." Karen smacked her son with a dessert spoon. "So, Mandy, what did his bedroom look like? Is he someone who needs a maid service?" She dished up a second helping of candied yams. "Because I'd advise against dating someone you'll need to clean after. You're too busy to be someone's housekeeper."

She took a deep drink of her water. This whole having them dating after a couple of chats didn't surprise her. The entire Hays clan had a fetish for planning ahead. Shawn set up next year's finances in November. Karen circled doctor and dentist appointment deadlines on the calendar by New Years. She grinned at her brother's wink. He penciled in the times she'd need maintenance on her car as soon as she left his shop. And her? The Florida trip was the first spontaneous thing she'd done in a long time and look how that turned out.

"I'm glad you're smiling." Karen stood and gave her daughter a brief hug as she passed by to the kitchen.

"Me too. I'm glad to be here."

"Ha! I'd be happy to be on warm sand and hot ladies on the beach." Marty gave Stewart a high five when his dad held up a hand.

Karen came in with a blueberry cheesecake. "I saw that!"

Mandy shook her head at the two men of the family, snickering like boys. She helped clean the dinner dishes while her mom cut the cake. Alone in the kitchen, she put plates in the dishwasher. Alone in the quiet reinforced how terrible she felt for Aaron.

He'd had a small wreath on his door. No decorated tree inside, not a pine or cinnamon scented air freshener to brighten the place. He should have had something festive. When her mom walked in with leftovers, Mandy asked, "Hey, I'm wondering. Do we have any surprise Christmas gifts? Something I can take for Aaron and replace with something else later?"

"Aw, sweetie, of course we do and don't worry about replacing anything. I'll do that tomorrow at the sales." She set down the half full dishes and empty turkey plate. "Did you have something special in mind?"

"Gosh, I just now thought of giving him something. Maybe a gift pack?"

"I have the thing. It's a peppermint coffee set, and the cup handles look like candy canes." She went to the pantry and fished it out for Mandy. "Do you think he likes flavors?"

She took the box from her mom and replied, "If I wrap it and put on extra bows, he won't care about the contents. It's supposed to be the thought that counts, right?"

Her mom hugged her. "Right."

Pushed out of the door by her parents so she'd be home before dark, Mandy climbed the steps to her apartment. She brought a couple of bags of presents, unwrapped except one for Aaron. She paced once inside and warm. After a bit of inner debate, while standing in her own place, she finally said, "How silly." She scooped up his gift and went to his door.

After a couple of knocks and a long wait, Aaron peeked out. "Um, hi. What's going on? You have a good time today?" He ran a hand through his crazy hair. "Don't stand out there, it's cold. Come in."

"I'm sorry. You were asleep." She hesitated, holding the present out. "I should go."

"You should come in, it's freezing."

"All right." She did as he said, stepping aside to let him close the door behind her. "Here's a small gift. It's Christmas, and I thought you should have one."

He took the festive box from her as if the package held spun glass. "I didn't think to get you anything. It's been crazy at work." He turned the gift over in his hands, first shaking it, then reading the tag and smiling. "My name's on it, so this isn't a leftover no one else wanted?"

Holidays

"No, of course not." She grinned as he treated the present like a kid with something from Santa. "Okay, I'll come clean. My mom keeps extra gifts in the pantry, just in case. Marty, Dad, and I know that if we need one, she'll have it."

"Planning ahead. I like it." He set the box on the kitchen table. "Did you want something to drink? I'm still not awake." He punched a button on his coffeemaker. "How about a seat? You can take off your coat if you prefer."

"Sure. I'll sit, and you can have your Christmas." Mandy draped her jacket over a chair and bit her lip, toying with a bit of chapped skin. He seemed less interested in what she'd brought when hearing about the spare gifts. "So, going on with my story, when one of us can't figure out what to get someone for their birthday, Christmas, or whatever, we shop Mom's store."

"When should I open it?"

She loved how the happy had returned to his eyes. "Now is good. Go ahead."

"It's ok with you if I'm the only one with a present?" He looked around him. "I didn't think about something for me this year. Getting here and being employed were my presents."

"I've had two Christmases. I'm good for a while."

He grinned, tearing open the wrapping. His expression changed from amazement back to happy. "This is perfect. I love peppermint and needed coffee cups. I only have one and couldn't share." His coffee maker did a last gurgle as if agreeing. "Now I can ask if you'd like some, too."

"Yes, I would, thank you. Want me to rinse those out for you?"

"No, sit and be a guest. This won't take long."

She glanced around his apartment, wanting to be covert. Nothing hung on his walls. She could have given him a clock for the kitchen at least. But then, the microwave had a digital timer.

Aaron soon returned with both cups, full. "I know you like single single, but all I have is single."

"Sugar or milk?"

"Milk."

She took a sip and put down the cup. "I'm fine with this, then." If he kept his place as cool as hers, she would have used the coffee to warm her hands. In a little while, she smiled at him. "We're quiet, aren't we?"

"It's not a party, no. Considering work, though, I like the quiet." He grinned.

Holidays

"Not that we can't talk, of course. You must be around noise all day, too. Hair dryers, water sprayers, upbeat music for the customers."

Mandy sighed, glad Aaron understood. "Gosh, yes. It is good to be in the car on my way home and hearing nothing."

His eyebrows rose. "Not even the radio?"

"Nope."

He shrugged. "Me too. I'm behind on what's popular and what's going on in advertising."

"My work isn't always chaos. Walk-ins slow down at predictable times. Does that happen to you, too?"

"They do. We have a steady stream during the day. Not emergencies as much as urgent care or the person's usual GP is booked solid. I suppose walk-ins are something we both have in common."

"True, and we make people feel better before unleashing them back into the world."

Aaron chuckled. "That's always the goal, even if it doesn't happen every time. How did you decide on running a salon versus being a stylist? Did you need hair experience or business school?"

"I started out with dolls as a kid. When they were bald, I moved on to my brother." She had to wait until he quit laughing. This whole amusing Aaron thing was becoming addictive. "Nothing else happened in my career for a long while after he was bald. Mom locked up the scissors, but that was it."

"So he was completely bald?"

"No, mostly until Dad took him to the barber."

He stopped laughing long enough to ask, "Tell me this wasn't around the time for school pictures."

"No, thank God or Mom would have banned sharp objects for life."

"Until you moved out."

"Maybe not even then. I went to cosmetology school and loved it. Being in an actual salon wasn't as much fun. I loved the customers, but not being bossed around."

"Let me guess, you're the oldest?"

"Yep." She wanted to ask if he was an older brother as well but didn't want to stop their conversation. "I learned from Marty's incident as a child and then my former boss about what to do and what not to do to bring out the best in people."

Aaron grinned at her and went to the kitchen. "Wow. I might need to take lessons from you in that."

Holidays

She pulled out the garage's card she'd stuffed into her pocket at dinner. "Speaking of my brother, he wanted me to give you this." When he came back to refill their cups, she added, "It's good for one free oil change."

"Handy, since my car needs one. Haven't had one since BC." He replaced the coffee pot and looked at Marty's card. "I like the fingerprints."

"So do I, ingenious. I try to get in there for maintenance every five thousand kilometers."

"Me too, and now I have a decent mechanic." He put the card in his billfold. "I've been meaning to go in before now, but have had enough to do with work."

She nodded. "That and healing, I'll bet. You still need to come in for a trim."

He gave her a sly look. "Do you have a card for one free cut?"

"No, but I might offer you a discount. Or a trade." She grinned. "You get a cut, I get a flu shot."

"Deal." He held out his hand to shake.

She laughed, shaking on the deal. "So, did you always know you wanted to be a doctor?" The question slipped out before Mandy remembered to keep it impersonal.

She held up a hand. "Only if you want to talk about it."

He grinned and slowly spun the coffee cup around, staring into the liquid as if it held answers. "I considered veterinary school for most of my life. Found out humans being able to talk helped to diagnose a lot. My brother followed me into medical school but didn't take it seriously. His grades forced him to quit."

"Some parents might be relieved, financially." As soon as she'd spoken, Mandy wanted to grab back the words out of the air and unsay them.

"He, um, dropped out after our parents were killed in a car wreck."

His statement confirmed her worst fears. She'd stepped in it, and it was a mess. Mandy wanted to fix this. "Oh, Aaron, I'm sorry." She reached over and squeezed his hand. "How awful."

"Thank you. It happened nine and a half years ago. I'm used to it, as much as I can be."

"Gosh." She fell silent, echoing his actions by staring into her own cup. Words failed her when expressing sympathy, so she stayed quiet.

"I tend to not mention my family for just this reason." He shrugged. "My brother included."

Holidays

She wanted to put her elbows on the table and soak in every word. Aaron had intrigued her with how close he kept facts about himself. Nothing aroused her curiosity more than a person who didn't talk about their past. "It appears he's a touchy subject for you. You don't have to say anything if you'd prefer."

He replied, "No, it's ok, I'm thinking of how to answer."

The sad expression he wore bothered Mandy. Her need to know more wasn't as important as being kind to him. "Don't. It's ok. It was a boundary I soon figured out not to cross."

Aaron chuckled. "I'm that transparent? I'll have to work on that."

Her heart did a flip at his sudden smile. She grinned back at him, wanting to amuse him more. "Don't. I like winning at poker, and hey, you're a doctor. Lots of money to lose."

He laughed. "Right. I'll tell my creditors." Aaron waved his hand as if to ward off her worries. "I'm kidding. I'm close to being debt free."

Mandy stared into her empty coffee cup, knowing she'd been too expressive. "My dad will be glad to hear that. He has a thing about debt to income ratios."

"Wise man. Do you want a refresh?" At her nod, he eased to his feet as if sore from a workout. "I'm the same way about diet and exercise. Eat natural, move around, stay healthy."

"Thank you. How do Timbits fit into that ideal world?"

He laughed, pausing on his way into the kitchen. "As well as I fit in my pants after eating them."

When he yawned, she couldn't help herself and yawned, too. "If coffee isn't helping, I need to hit the bed. Tomorrow is booked solid."

Aaron returned with the coffee pot. "I'm betting tonight will be busy. Drunk driving, new ATV's, and mayhem in general."

"You work tonight?" She stood, taking her empty cup. "I'm sorry for keeping you from getting ready. Let me rinse this while you refill yours with what's left before I go."

"No, you don't get to do my dishes." Aaron gently took the cup from Mandy and pulled her into a hug. "Thank you for the present and the company." He let her go and stepped back. "I appreciate both."

"You're welcome. It was my pleasure." She eased to the door. "Be careful driving around tonight. To work, I mean."

Holidays

He pointed to the chair. "Don't forget your coat."

"No, ha!" Mandy grabbed her parka. "That'd be crazy." She stood there for a moment, wondering how to score another hug from him.

"First thing tomorrow morning, it would."

She felt her cheeks flame like the elements in an electric heater. "So, bye!"

"Bye," said Aaron as he eased his door closed.

She would have leaped out of his house and into hers, except for the locked door. Mandy rushed inside and leaned against the solid wood. Oh man! Aaron had felt perfect and smelled better. She closed her eyes and shivered at the memory. Panic jumped around in her stomach from how right she'd been in his arms and how much that mirrored her feelings with Geo. "Deep breath in, it was just a hug," she whispered. "Deep breath out." The calm, rational side of her kept Mandy rooted in place. Her wild side? Scared her with the desire to knock on his door until he let her in to ravage him.

She put a cold hand to her hot forehead. Did people use that word anymore? Didn't matter. Ravage was exactly what she wanted to do to him.

Laura Stapleton

New Years

Hey, sweetie! Learned abt yr dr.

Mandy grinned at the message. Her mom's grammar slid into a pit when she texted for more than a few minutes. Her prior conversation must have been a doozy. She almost sent back, "is not my dr," but decided against it.

Do tell.

Aaron Nicholson from Vancouver, er doctor, single, no kids anywhere Nurses adore him, even bad ones.

Bad?

Too old or too young, married too.

She laughed at that, imagining the expression on her mother's face. Her phone rang. "Hey Mom, too much to text?"

"Gosh, yes. The scuttlebutt is he killed several people, so I knew that couldn't be right."

Fear sparked along her nerves. If he were a psycho, her mom would find out for sure. "What did Google say?"

"I wouldn't snoop."

"And?"

"I'll forward the article to you. If that's him in the photo, I like him already.

Holidays

He has the kindest eyes and the cutest little smile."

Oh, dear God, she talked about him like he was a puppy. "He's housebroken, too."

"I should hope so." She glanced up to spot Neal loitering at her door with the cash drawer. "I need to get back to work, Mom, later?"

"Sure. I'll text if I find out he's seeing anyone."

"Thanks. You do that." Mandy ignored her odd dislike of him dating and grinned at her employee. "Yes, Neil? What's going on?"

The reed-slender man grinned while running a hand through his hair. "A party at Joe's house. Wanna go with us?"

She paused in standing. "Eh, which Joe?"

"Not gee oh, sweetie. Joe. He's the new guy Barb is dating. Don't say no, you need some fun."

"I can't say no for real?"

He set the drawer on her desk. "Come on. Close up and be our driver."

"That doesn't sound fun."

"It does to me."

She grinned at his pleading eyes. Mandy hadn't been out with her group since the Christmas party in the shop. She put the cash in her drawer and locked it. "All right. Is everyone done up front?"

"Yep, cleaned and ready for tomorrow. No excuses, ma'am."

"I'm not dressed for it." She waved a hand down her casual clothes.

"No one is. That's the fun of it."

She followed him out, pausing to lock her office door. Their cheers at Neil getting her out of the little room amused her. She checked the front before following everyone to the back. Arm the security system, lock yet another door, and they were off in her car.

It took Mandy only an hour before she began enjoying herself. She both liked and disliked how many men at the party were taken or uninteresting. The last thing she wanted was a relationship right now and yet some guy to hang out with sounded fun, too. She took a sip of the diet cola, ignoring that little "What about Aaron?" nag from her conscious.

"Is that a smile?"

She grinned at Fiona. "I'm having a tiny bit of fun."

Barb hugged her. "Good! You need it. How are you on drinks?" She sniffed Mandy's drink. "I don't smell anything good in here."

Holidays

"I'm double D tonight."

"I'm sorry. Next time for sure."

"For sure." She went back to watching the crowd. "Aw, Neil." He'd hopped onto the coffee table and began dancing. How good he was surprised her, and Mandy started clapping along. A couple of more people hopped up to join him. The group closed in around them, everyone cheering. She frowned, not sure how sturdy the table was.

A thumping bass beat drowned out everything but the screams as their platform gave way. Two of the dancers landed on people while Neil hit debris. She pushed her way through to him, hollering, "Cut the music." Kneeling by her friend, Mandy asked, "Do you hurt anywhere?"

"Just my butt." He tried to stand with her help. "Owww!"

"Still the butt?" she asked.

"No, my leg."

She motioned to a bystander. "Hold him up while I see how much he's hurt." After lifting his jeans hem, she shuddered. His ankle was already swelling. "You're not cut, but have a nasty sprain."

"It hurts like hell."

"I'm sure." She shook her head. "This will need urgent care."

Neil moaned. "It feels like it. I'm blitzed, and my foot hurts all the way up my leg."

"Okay, guys. We're missing the last half of the party. Let's load him up. Fiona, Barb, and Edie? You have rides home?" She saw each of them holler or nod yes before following the two burly guys and Neil out to her car.

She blocked out Neil's whimpers during their drive to the hospital. His noise made her tense with the need to help ease his pain. Mandy made a mental note to ask her mom how she coped at work with people in agony. She sighed in relief when spotting the ER sign. "Neil! We're here. They'll give you great meds, and maybe a cast."

He moaned, "I need a wheelchair," as Mandy eased the car to a stop inside the rotunda.

"Of course, you do." She put the car in park and shut it off. She almost added a reminder to stay put but figured he'd not be going anywhere. The ER waiting room was somewhat empty. She walked to the reception desk. "Hello, I have a friend who has hurt his ankle."

The woman began typing. "Is he conscious?"

"Yes, awake, but no, he can't walk."

Holidays

"I'll call for a wheelchair." She picked up a phone and started dialing. "Make sure he has his health card and id."

"Ok." Mandy went back to her car and saw Neil standing on his good leg.

"Even my other foot hurts."

"Hey, come on, sit back down." She opened the passenger side door and helped ease him into the seat as a male nurse arrived with the wheelchair. "Or not."

"I hear you need help."

The guy's voice sounded deep and strong. Both grinned at him and Neil spoke first, "Yeah, I fell off a coffee table."

Mandy laughed. While she and the nurse helped him into the chair, she teased, "More like you fell through a coffee table. Neil, the front desk needs your cards. You got them?" When he nodded, she patted his shoulder. "I'll park the car and be right there."

"Thanks, sweetheart. You're the best boss ever."

She smiled at the nurse. "He's still a little happy from the party, obviously."

"Eh, seems sober to me." To Neil, he said, "Come on party guy, let's get you fixed up."

Soon, Mandy was rushing back through the automatic doors. She scanned the waiting room but saw a couple of people in from the cold. The woman still sat at the information desk so Mandy went over to her. "Hello, my friend was in here."

"Yes, the nurse took him for x-rays." She stood, entering a code. "You can go on back and wait with him."

"Thank you." Once through the doors, she realized she didn't know which room they'd put Neil. Mandy didn't want to knock. She eased by, peeking into every open curtain. She saw a glimpse of him lying on the bed, his eyes closed, and gave a light cough to get his attention. "Hey, Neil."

"Oh, thank God. I didn't know how I'd get home."

She walked in, staring at his bare foot. "Come on, did you think I'd throw you out and leave?"

"It hurts too much to think."

"I'll bet." She went to the end of the bed. "Neil, have you looked at this? Your ankle is turning purple." She resisted the urge to poke at the huge lump forming. "It looks like someone put a half of a lemon under your skin."

"It hurt like hell when he took off my shoe and sock."

She patted his shoulder. "I didn't hear you scream."

"I was manly because that nurse is hot."

Holidays

"Ah. Good call." She grinned at him and went back to the head of the bed. "So the lady at the desk said x-rays."

"Yeah, The nurse did, too. He said the doctor would be in first to make sure I need them."

"Speak of the devil and here I am."

Aaron's voice gave her a little tingle in the heart, and she turned to see him walk in. "Oh, hello, Aaro--, um, Dr. Nicholson."

"Mandy, good to see you. So, we have…" He stared at Neil's ankle. "Yeah, we have a serious sprain. You a basketball player? I see a lot of them with this injury. This and mangled fingers."

Neil struggled to sit, and Mandy helped him. He winked at her before saying, "Not this time. I'm not that sporty. We were at a New Year's party, and things got wild."

"Ah. Sounds like it." He tapped first the toes, then ran a fingertip down Neil's sole. At his patient's laugh and then gasp from the pain, Aaron grinned. "No nerve damage and I bet no broken bones or torn ligaments." He started typing on a computer terminal. "Still, an x-ray wouldn't hurt. I'll put in an order for that and something to ease the pain. As for the party, it might be awhile before you two are back to dancing, never mind the New Year's kiss."

"Kiss?" asked Neil.

Mandy explained, "You're supposed to kiss in the New Year. It's past midnight, though."

Aaron grinned. "It's never too late for a kiss."

"In that case, where's that one nurse? He was yummy looking. So are you, doctor, but I'm getting a straight vibe."

He laughed. "Yeah, you'd be right about both of us. He's probably who'll take you to x-ray." He paused before leaving the room and winked at Mandy. Robert's on duty, though, so no kissing during work hours."

"You're catching flies," Neil whispered when the curtain fell back into place.

She closed her mouth. "He's never winked at me."

"You know him?"

"He's my new neighbor."

"Oh, my God! Him?" Neil dropped his voice several decibels. "He's gorgeous. Rugged, but refined. Makes me wish he was gay, too."

She crossed her arms. "Really?"

"Maybe not. That nurse was fine. I'd be happy with him."

The nurse pulled the curtain back and pushed the wheelchair forward. "Time for your x-ray. Is that pill I gave you working, yet?"

Mandy spoke first. "Yes, because between the alcohol and meds, he's been chatty."

Neil leaned against her as if needing comfort. "I'm always chatty."

"Just giving you an out in case you embarrass both of us." She eased back, letting the nurse take over.

"I won't do that, Mans, I love you."

She grinned at him, and then at his nurse. "I love you, too, Neils."

"I'll take good care of him."

Mandy took that as a cue to wait, okay with missing the radiation. Suddenly tired, she sank into a nearby chair and retrieved her cell phone. A dozen texts waited for her to answer and she spent the time reassuring everyone with a reply. Neil would survive just fine.

"We're back!"

She looked up as her employee entered the room, pushed in the chair by his nurse. "How did it go?"

"He did great," replied Robert. "A trooper."

Neil sighed. "The side angle was terrible."

She stood and went to the nurse. "What's next?"

"The radiologist will look at them and report back to the doctor."

Mandy snickered at Neil's grin at her, and she confirmed, "We're to stay put until then?"

"Yep. He said you'd need a prescription. I'll go check on that right quick."

When he left the room, she leaned over to Neil and asked, "Did you get a number?"

"Not yet, but I'm working on it." He grinned. "What about your doctor?"

"Mine? He's my neighbor, not my doctor."

Neil leaned back on the bed and closed his eyes. "He's your something. That's for sure."

Mandy opened her mouth to rebut his argument when Aaron walked in. She didn't want anyone as more than a friend. Not so soon after Geo. "What are his chances, Doc? Will he live?"

"Yep. Give him six weeks, and he'll be dancing on tables again. Sturdier ones, I hope." Aaron moved closer to the bed. "Nothing is fractured or torn. It looks ugly and probably hurts enough to feel broken." He smiled at Mandy. "His discharge papers are at the desk, and Robert's getting the meds and chair. Does he live on the ground floor?"

"Yes."

"Good. I'd hate to see him climb something like our stairs. So, RICE it, rest, ice, compress, elevate. I've included instructions in your papers. Stay off your feet as much as possible and let it heal."

Neil held out his hand for shaking. "Thank you, doctor."

Aaron grinned and shook his hand. "My pleasure."

Robert came in with a chair and a small paper bag on it. "Ready?"

"Take care, guys," Aaron said before slipping from the small room.

As soon as he was out of earshot, Neil sighed. "That man is dreamy."

Mandy gasped. "Neil, you need a muzzle."

Robert lifted the patient into a wheelchair. "He's single, but would be interested in your friend more than you."

He nodded. "I figured. Too bad we can't set them up, they'd make an adorable couple."

Mandy put her hands out as if to stop both of them from going any further. "I'm sorry, it's the meds and the margaritas making him say crazy things."

"Hmm. I've heard worse." All of them paused at the inner desk. Robert gave Neil a clipboard. "Here's the paperwork, when you've reviewed and signed, you'll be free to leave."

He blinked several times "Oo, my head is swimming."

"Do you mind if I read it to you?" When he held the papers out for her, she scanned the documents. "You're satisfied with the treatment, realize they've done everything possible, and you're leaving of your own free will? Also that you'll comply with the discharge instructions?"

"Yes. All of that."

"Okay, then sign and I'll get you home."

Neil signed on the highlighted line and handed them back to the nurse. "I could always call you if I need more medical help."

"You could, or you could let me call you when I'm not at work," offered Robert.

"That sounds even better." He leaned his head back and asked her, "Mans, do you have a business card to give the man?"

Mandy sighed and began digging through her purse for one. "Call this number, ask for him, and you're good. Come on, Casanova. Let's get you home with an ice pack so I can go to bed, too. This

Holidays

is turning out to be a very long day." She led both of them out of ER. With a good amount of labor, Robert got Neil in the car. If she didn't know better, she'd think Neil was faking his helplessness. They both waved goodbye to the nurse as she drove out of the parking lot.

He sighed, staring out at the passing city. "Your doctor's not Geo."

The hairs on the back of her neck rose. "No. He's not."

"He's gorgeous as hell." Neil sighed again. "You should jump on him while he's available."

She glanced at him, trying to not laugh at his melodrama. "Aaron's a decent neighbor."

"You'd said you did laundry with him. Did he separate the towels from his scrubs?"

Mandy laughed. "Yes."

Neil turned to face her. "What car does he drive?"

She grinned, wondering when he would turn on the overhead light and interrogate her properly. "Gosh. I can't tell them apart. Something recent enough to be round but not a box."

"You didn't recognize the make, good. His vehicle doesn't define him. Ok, from what I can tell, this guy is a catch.

After meeting him and you filling in the blanks, if he's not a mass murderer, I say date him."

She laughed and shook her head, not quite agreeing. "Just like that?"

He gave her a heavy-lidded look. "You weren't married that long, sweetheart. You have to remember how it goes."

"I know. I also know how it went. Geo felt right, and Aaron? I'm not sure…."

He clapped his hands. "Oh! He feels right, too?"

Her heart skipped a beat. "Yeah. A little."

"What happens if you find out he's is interested in dating you?"

Panic jumped around in her stomach, and she swallowed. "That's what scares me."

"Sure, I understand. No worries, okay? He's a regular guy, you two can be friends. See how it goes." Neil shrugged as she pulled into his driveway. "You could date around while not dating him. Then when you're ready? Voila! There he is."

"I'm not interested in dating around. The whole idea makes me queasy."

"Come on, Geo isn't worth that much sacrifice."

Holidays

She got out and went to his side of the car. He opened his door, and she said, "Yeah, he's not, but it happens."

"I can't believe Dr. A is single." He blinked his eyes, trying to focus on the keys in his hand. "Wonder if he's ready to settle down, yet."

"Damn, Neil. You're thinking about Aaron more than your nurse." She helped him into the house. Mandy had been here before, and the place was still as lovely. He needed to go shopping with her sometime. All she had now were thrift store items and could use some advice. "What happened to that one guy you were in love with last week?"

"I've grown since then."

She laughed. "Sure you have."

He sank onto the sofa. "I can sleep here tonight."

"Okay. Do you want a pillow, blanket, and ice bag?"

"Are you serious? You'd do that for me?"

"Yeah, of course."

"Thank you so much. Pillow and blanket are in my bedroom. Just get whatever, and I have plastic bags in the cabinet, ice in the freezer. I love you."

"Not a problem." She went to his bedroom, almost as messy as Aaron's. She dropped the bedding off on the sofa and went to the kitchen. Soon, Mandy had him a bag of ice, wrapped in a cloth napkin. "You have a great setup in there."

"Thank you. My kind has impeccable taste."

"Right, your kind." She helped to get the ice against his ankle. "Can I lock your door before closing it?"

"No, it's a deadbolt."

"Ok, let me have the key, and I'll slide it under the door."

"You're so smart."

"Thank you. Good night and sweet dreams."

He didn't answer, already conked out. Mandy stifled a chuckle and remembered a pen and notepad set in his kitchen. She wrote him a note to rest, stay off his foot, and not come in tomorrow, putting it where he'd be sure to see and read.

She did as he'd suggested, taking his key off the ring and locked his house. Sliding the key under the door took extra prodding from her car key, and she hoped his idea worked. She drove home, not seeing anyone else out on the roads. When she entered the apartment complex's parking lot, Aaron's car was in the usual spot. How had he beaten her home? She parked next to him and started up the stairs.

Holidays

"You made it."

She smiled and looked up at him. "Yes, the patient wasn't difficult and is already sleeping it off."

"Good."

He stepped back to let her pass, and she asked, "Do you race other patients home to make sure they're safe? Or am I special?"

"I was at the end of my shift when you two came in."

"Ah, so finding you at my doorstep is a happy accident." She unlocked her door.

He asked, "Would you want to come in for a bit?"

"No. I'm exhausted. Tonight was completely unplanned." Mandy stepped inside her home. "My flannels and bed sound great right now."

"Sounds good." He hesitated for a couple of seconds. "I might need to chat with you about next week if you're interested."

"This seems important." She held her door open wider. "Come over and keep warm while you tell me what's up."

"Okay." He stepped in, closing the door behind him and turned the deadbolt.

Her pulse rate jumped at being locked in with him. Not that she was afraid or thrilled to be alone with him. Mandy slipped off her shoes, sighing in relief at her toes' freedom.

"Do you wear those at work?"

She loved his frown, almost as cute as his smile. "Only when I don't have clients. Otherwise, it's padded soles all the way."

"Good."

"Excuse me while I slip into something more comfortable and ugly. My kitchen's open if you want something to drink. I think there's at least one beer."

"If you're sure, yeah."

"Go. Drink my beer and make me buy more." When he laughed, she disappeared into her bedroom. Mandy changed out into her nicest flannel pants and t-shirt. After resisting the urge to wear anything dressier, she went back into the living room. "So, is everything good? Nothing wrong with Neil, no complications from your own injuries?" She sat on the sofa with him, suddenly aware of how small it was. He had fixed them each a glass of water.

"Nothing like that. It's just…." He fidgeted and took a drink. "I'm going back to Vancouver tomorrow, and will be there for at least a week. I wanted to tell you. In case you noticed I was gone and wondered why."

Holidays

She smiled. He thought she'd miss him? He might be right. "Does this mean you need a ride to the airport?"

"No, I'd planned on Park'N Go."

Mandy wondered how neighborly did she want to be to him. Enough to risk driving around the terminals? "I can drop you off, no problem."

"That'd be great. I'll use the money I save on parking to take you out to dinner or something. A place nicer than Timmies."

"I don't know if that's possible."

"True." Aaron leaned against the back of the sofa and took another drink. "You're a friend, and when I saw you in the ER tonight, I was glad you weren't hurt."

Her heart thudded a little harder, and she hoped Robert hadn't said anything to him after they left. "Thanks, that's sweet."

"Well, so, I couldn't leave and be gone without saying goodbye."

"You're not coming back?" She took a drink, her throat suddenly dry.

"I am, as soon as possible. It's why I've been taking every shift I can and building favors." He leaned forward to set down his beer. "I'll be testifying in court, and no one knows how long that will last."

Court? Great. A criminal. Only, what province let serial killers roamed free? Not even the territories did that, did they? She was overreacting and shook it off, asking, "Are you in trouble?"

He grinned, chuckling. "No, not me, and it's why I don't enjoy talking about my family."

"All right. You can leave it at that, then." She put her glass next to his drink.

"I could, or I could tell you everything and let you decide if I'm worth your patience. I know something about you and your ex-husband. More like I know you have one. You get a scared look on your face every so often. I think it's similar to the one I get when talking about my younger brother, Brad." Aaron paused for a moment. "He tried to kill me, and I'm testifying against him in a few days."

"Oh no. I'm sorry." No wonder Aaron had run away and didn't want to mention the guy. "He's why you're injured? You're just now walking without a limp, and no one has touched your hair. You'll need a man bun before long."

His jaw dropped, and he laughed. "He's why, and I'd rather you drive with one hand and hack at my hair with the other instead of my having a man bun. Not going to happen."

She smiled despite the horror she felt for him. "I can't imagine Marty doing anything like that."

Holidays

"You're actually pretty when tired. Not many people are." He tucked a stray lock of hair behind her ear. "Why he did it is a long story for later, when it's not so late, and you're not so sleepy."

His thinking of her after dropping such personal news warmed her heart. Mandy said, "Come here, I need to give you a hug." As soon as his arms encircled her, she knew this was a mistake. He felt too good against her. His warmth, the soft fabric of his sweatshirt, how his skin smelled, intoxicated her. If Mandy stretched at little more, she could kiss his neck. She shivered and his hold tightened.

"I'm telling you my problems, and you're not only exhausted but freezing, too."

"I don't mind this part. You're wonderfully warm."

"Yeah, but I can't stay all night." He relaxed and pulled back. Aaron stared into Mandy's eyes. "I could change my mind about that." Looking at her, he smiled. "I shouldn't, but I could." He leaned in and gave her the briefest whisper of a kiss. "And when you're ready, I might."

"Well. Sure." Mandy couldn't breathe, her lips still tingling from his touch. Every part of her body wanted his. More to herself than him, she said, "I don't want to date anyone or another serious relationship."

"I understand. My check engine light came on. Marty says hello, by the way." He let her go as if reluctant to end their hug. "Your brother's a great guy. Protective and persuasive, too."

She examined his face. He had a wary expression, and she could guess what her over protective big brother might have said to him. "Uh oh. I might have to refute some statements of his."

"No, he's great. If Brad were that loyal, I'd still live in Vancouver."

"I don't know what to say. I'm glad you're here but not how it happened."

"Me too." He took her hands in his, caressing her manicured nails with a small smile. "Thing is, I don't want a relationship, either. Not now with you. Now is wrong."

"It is?"

"It is." Aaron stared into her eyes. "I'm the permanent type, not the rebound type of guy. I don't go into relationships halfway or halfhearted. You're not ready for permanent, and with good reason."

"I don't know if I ever will be." As she said the words, Mandy saw first disappointment, then resolve in his face.

"Fair enough. Let's be friends because we're already neighbors and see where that goes."

Holidays

"That might be ok, too." She returned his grin. "We have time."

Laura Stapleton

Betrayal

Laura Stapleton

Betrayal

When a family friend of Mandy Hays washes up on shore, everything points to homicide. But how, when he was alone on a fishing trip? Her sexy neighbor, Dr. Aaron Nicholson, knows much more than he can say. As the evidence piles up, all of the victim's family and closest friends seem guilty.

Laura Stapleton

Text Copyright © 2016 Laura L Stapleton

All Rights Reserved.

Covers by Cheeky Covers.

No portion of this book may be reproduced, stored in a retrieval system, or transmitted in any form or by any means, mechanical, electronic, photocopying, recording, or otherwise, without written permission from the author or publisher.

Names, characters, and some incidences are imaginary and complete fiction.

Betrayal

Acknowledgements

Huge thank you to Crystal St. Clair for being the best Literary Service provider ever. Mandie Stevens is probably how you heard about this book, her promotion company is amazing. Dirk Stapleton does the minutia work for his usual wonderful self and me. Dr. Christopher Harlan is not only the best family doctor, but he also fills in where Google can't, and that's invaluable.

Dedication

This is for all my aunts and uncles. I'm so grateful and lucky to have their support in what I do.

Laura Stapleton

Chapter 1

"What makes you think he was murdered?" Aaron Nicholson swiped to the next page on his tablet. "Does it say that in the newspaper?"

Mandy Hays took another slice of bacon from the center dish. "It's Craig Walker. I've known him for forever. Dad does his taxes, and Craig's a careful guy. He wouldn't just fall overboard."

He frowned. "The guy never made a mistake, tripped over his own feet?" Aaron ate the last bite of his toast.

"Maybe. Probably." She finished reading the story by skimming the paragraph and then reread the first few sentences to make sure this was the same Craig Walker she knew. "It doesn't mention a life jacket. He always wore his, so I think someone else had to be there and killed him."

"Hmm. I'm sorry he's gone." Aaron shifted in his chair. "Would you like more coffee?"

"Yes, please." She lifted her cup as he stood and stared at him. His face seemed bored as if a mask evened out those handsome features. Her breath always caught when his blue-grey eyes met hers, and she smiled when he looked at her again. They had been next door neighbours, what, five months? Long enough to know this expression by now. Mandy folded the newspaper and set it aside. "You know all about what happened, and now you're hiding something. I can tell when something is up with you. What is it? What do you know?"

"Nothing." He went to the counter and faced away from her. "Never met the guy."

Yep, he was a horrible liar. Aaron must have been the ER doctor when Craig had been brought in. His forced disinterest had fooled her a couple of months ago with an already forgotten topic. She got up and peered at him. "Did he die of natural causes? He was a good friend of mine, Aaron. Give me a tiny hint?"

He handed her the mug. "No."

His refusal told her more than a confession. The firm mouth, squinty gray eyes? A quarter would bounce off the tension in his shoulder muscles. "So he *was* killed! I knew it. People like him can't just die." She followed him back to the table. Mandy sat when he did and leaned forward to examine his face for clues, elbows on the table. "Craig could swim, loved the ocean, fishing, and was a huge safety nut. I'm not surprised this is considered murder."

"Nope, you know nothing." He

Betrayal

glanced at her and grinned. "I meant nothing about Mr. Walker."

"Good catch." She leaned back, crossing her arms. So did he. "All right. I'll just talk, and you listen. You'll tell me everything with your face." She enjoyed his scowl. He didn't stand a chance. Tighter lipped men had cracked under her questioning. When a guy came into her salon for a Fifteen Dollar Friday discount, she had him give her more than an "I don't care," about his haircut. "We'll have to play high stakes poker sometime. I could use the money."

He kept focusing on his tablet while chiding, "Ha! You wish. I'm the best."

"Ok, sure." Mandy watched his face, waiting for any muscle twitch. "Craig is, or was, an avid fisherman." Getting the tense wrong reminded her he really was gone. She paused, looking at her unfinished bacon. All his family had to be devastated, and did her father know, yet? Probably. He read the paper every morning as well.

Aaron took her hand and squeezed. "I'm sorry."

"Thanks. It's just sad. Poor guy. He had plans for retirement and had told everyone last year at the barbecue that he planned to live on his fishing boat full time."

He took a sip. "What do you think

his wife would say about that?"

She rested her chin on her hand without taking her eyes from his. "Sabrina would have been okay with it, but Debbi? She'd not like it."

Aaron frowned, setting aside his device to eat another toast with jelly. "Who's Debbi?"

Mandy grinned. "His second wife." He glanced at her barely long enough for her to catch his surprise. "You didn't know that? Gosh, I thought everyone did. Maybe she's not relevant to his death." No reaction showed from him, so she shifted tactics. "Or maybe she is."

"Nice try." Aaron took a bite, his attention more on her than his emails and breakfast. "How recently did this wife exchange take place?"

She gave him what she hoped was an evasive shrug. "I don't know if I should say. Not until you start answering my questions."

He waved a hand in a goodbye motion. "Doctor-patient privacy means I can't and won't answer anything, sweetheart. You know that."

She smiled at him, his endearment doing funny things to her heart. His tall, broad-shouldered frame took up all the space in her apartment. He seemed normal sized at his own place, but he'd been sparser

Betrayal

with the décor in his home. His place felt strong, manly, and sexy, like him.

Mandy needed to ignore the flutters for a moment and concentrate on this Craig tragedy. She shook the romantic daydreams from her head. "You're his doctor, though. Interesting. In that case, I don't expect you to help find his killer."

He laughed outright. "You're on the police force now? Neil and the gang will miss you at the salon."

Not wanting to reward his teasing with her attention she said, "Let's go back to how you think he's still married to Sabrina because I'm certain all the legalities were handled by now." She stopped just short of saying anything about her father's accounting business and how dad would have mentioned any loose ends to Craig by now. If Shawn Hays signed the preparer's signature on a tax form, it was accurate. She tried to be as precise when cutting or colouring hair at her own business. Hair had its own ideas.

Aaron narrowed his eyes at her before returning to his meal and electronics. "No idea."

"Of course not. You didn't even know they were married." Her face tilted to the newspaper, Mandy kept her attention on his reaction. "It's fine. Don't tell me. She's coming in next week for highlights."

He glanced up at her, his eyebrows raised before frowning. "Which wife? His ex?"

She read her newspaper as if unconcerned, wanting to make him wait. Her face warmed a little under his scrutiny. His expression softened and that half smile of his ratcheted up his attractiveness, in her opinion. She hated being a pushover, but couldn't resist replying, "His second wife, Debbi. She might cancel, but I doubt it since she's high maintenance. Sabrina cuts her own hair and lets the sun highlight."

"Cut it herself?" He shook his head. "Brave woman."

Mandy folded up the news and set it aside for later recycling. "She's actually good. I have to give her a shaping every six months, but she's not the disaster I've seen with others."

"So he went for the radically different trophy wife, huh?"

She squirmed a little under his full attention. "You'd think so, but no. They're a lot alike. Debbi is a younger, vainer model of Sabrina."

"Why did he swap them out?"

"You're a man asking me this?" She pushed her ex-husband out of her mind and forced a smile at Aaron. "Isn't this just what

Betrayal

guys do when they hit forty?"

His expression softened, and he reached for her hand, giving it a squeeze. "Did your dad? Mine didn't. Not every man does."

Aaron's touch warmed her skin and her heart. She put her hand over his. "Fair enough. Maybe not every man dumps his wife when she gets, well, dumpy." She took a drink of coffee to keep from saying anything more. Remembering all the women her ex dated during their marriage left Mandy's ego flattened. None of his cheating was her fault, she'd stupidly trusted him. "Sometimes, couples have good reasons for splitting."

"Your ex is a lot younger than Craig, I'm guessing?" After she had nodded, he continued, "At least Walker had the fear of impending geriatrics to motivate him. Your ex was just an idiot."

Mandy laughed. "Tell me how you really feel, because you seem to be holding back."

He slid his hands from hers after a final squeeze. "Discounting your ex completely, I think anyone dropping a forty for a twenty is not a good idea no matter who the new wife is. It's costly, traumatic for the children, and shows a weakness of character."

She tried to ignore the sudden rush of affection for him. It'd be so easy to fall in love with such a sweet man. Mandy wanted to lighten the mood or she'd cry like a sap. "Says the young single guy." She reached over to tousle his hair. "Or have I missed the gray in this mess?"

He combed his dark hair with his fingertips. "Hope there's no gray yet, but true. I could feel differently at Craig's age. Still, I'd have to be sure enough about both women to make the change all across the board."

She drank the last of her cooled coffee. Divorcing her ex, Geo, three months ago had meant losing her home with him, downgrading to a car with lower payments, and taking a loan out on her styling salon to pay the lawyer. She'd never known someone to come out ahead on a divorce unless they married into money. "Do you think he remembered their life insurance policies? The first thing I did was remove Geo from mine. If Craig didn't, either woman had the motive to kill him."

"I might want to file that bit of information away for later. Just in case you remarry."

Her pulse jumped at that. No marrying anyone. Not yet, and not even if they were an easy going, good looking,

Betrayal

breakfast date most days. She had to deflect this topic somehow and went for something he avoided. "Yeah, because I'm sure you'll be in Halifax for good by then."

He grinned and leaned back in the chair, hands behind his head. "You don't know. I might."

She wasn't going to let herself be happy in him deciding to stay here instead of moving back to his home in Vancouver. Wanting to steer the focus away from their future, Mandy concentrated on the lack of one for the victim. "True. Who knows what could happen? One day, you're out fishing on a great boat, the next? Two friends are debating over who gets your life insurance."

"I need a great boat. A guy in Walker's situation should have had two policies, one for kids with his former wife, the second for the new wife and maybe new kids.

Mandy used a napkin to brush all the crumbs from the table to her plate. "Way more trouble and expense than what it's worth."

"Yeah, just keep the first wife and be done with it. No mess, no traumatized kids, no heartbreak."

"Unless something horrible is going on."

"Right. Every couple is different.

Sometimes two good people can't be anything but bad together." He leaned forward and stood. "Maybe Craig's new wife being younger is a happy accident for him. All the guys his age high five him for the younger woman when really? He's in love, and nothing else mattered." Taking her cup and their plates, he added, "Want more coffee before I leave? I'm topping this off."

She gave him a smile. "Thanks. Half full, please." Aaron's keeping a first wife instead of chasing the next shiny woman seemed about right to her. Judging by the car he drove, she guessed he kept things until they fell apart. Even now, he wore a high school sweatshirt. Who past the age of thirty did that? She glanced down at her own university shirt. At least she'd advanced in attire.

He came back and handed Mandy her cup. "I'm sure someone is looking into how and why he fell. Even if he was a mountain goat, the guy probably tripped on something and went over. No big deal." He went back to refill his own drink and then peeked around the corner. "I mean, not murder. That's always a big deal." When she started shaking her head at him, he grinned. "You know what I mean."

She had chuckled at his shamed face before he disappeared back into the kitchen.

Betrayal

"I do," she said loud enough for Aaron to hear.

He set down the cup and put on his leather jacket. "Time for work, so you're done fishing for now."

"No more details?" She tried a puppy dog expression with him until he laughed.

"Nope. Our friendship has its limits." Aaron grabbed his tablet.

"That's a shame, big boy." She patted the empty chair beside her. "Get comfy and tell me all about how far I can go with you."

He zipped up. "Nice try, but no. I'm not falling for some smooth talking woman again."

She paused before taking a sip. The man had mysteries wrapped inside of puzzles. He knew something about her divorce with Geo, yet, she'd heard little of his love life. "Again? Sounds interesting! Call in sick, and sing me your song of woe."

Aaron gave her a grin before tapping the end of her nose with his tablet. "We both know better than that. I have patients, and you have clients." He took and lifted the cup. "I'll bring this back washed."

She frowned. "I suppose, Mr. Responsible."

"You fix dinner tonight, and I'll take you out on Monday."

"All right. Go already." She frowned at his chuckle as he left her apartment for his, both of them knowing her bad mood was a ruse. His leaving left the room feeling empty. She missed him already. Mandy closed her eyes, feeling but not giving into the beginnings of a crush on the guy. She kept waiting for the other shoe to drop. Something awful to counteract all the wonderful she saw in him. Like, he hated puppies and kittens, maybe spent all his earnings on video lottery games or even something as awful as keeping a mummy of a former girlfriend in his car trunk.

And she was back to poor Craig. Mandy took her cup to the sink. She didn't want to imagine what his body must have looked like after being out at sea for days. A shudder went through her, and breakfast tap danced in her stomach. Better Aaron dealing with those things than her. Cutting someone's ear during a trim or a nicking a jaw during a man's shave was bad enough when she'd been a new stylist.

She locked the front door before heading to the bathroom for a shower. For some crazy irrational reason, she missed Aaron already and had zero reasons to do so. The guy lived in the apartment across from hers. Five feet separated their front doors. When his schedule allowed, he or she fixed

Betrayal

breakfast for the other. Yet, she looked forward to dinner with him this evening.

Mandy undressed, wanting her mind to change the subject. Otherwise, getting naked and soaped up when Aaron might be doing the same next door teased her too much. Maybe she needed a one-night stand with him to get this out of her system. Even the idea of asking him to her bedroom left her breathless at the possibility he'd agree. She stepped into the warm spray. One raunchy, casual sex fling and she'd be good. No more thinking about him and how he'd feel against her.

She sighed, standing under the hot shower. No more idle wondering how hairy the rest of his chest was, or if it matched what little she'd seen exposed at the base of his throat. After that, she'd like to see if his body's scars matched the slight one on his forehead.

"Enough of the guy," she said aloud to derail her train of thought. The salon had taxes to pay, inventory to check, and now interviews for new stylists. Space had opened up last week, and while four booths paid the rent, five paid for the extras. She could get a higher quality of product for the clients, maybe better style for the entire place. The customers they'd had were great and deserved her best. She and everyone in her employ had a good business going and knew it.

Turning off the water and stepping out, she heard his door shut through her open bathroom door. Mandy wrapped her hair and dressed. The big question in her mind was, would he care if she saw someone else? Aaron gave off such mixed signals. He'd flirt one day and be too busy or preoccupied to reply to a text.

Her hand shook a little as she applied eyeliner. No one appealed to her as much as he did, but who knew? The next guy in her stylist's chair might be her Mr. Right. Or Mr. Right Now For Sexy Times. Either was good, she tried to convince herself, except, neither one was. She wanted Aaron to be her rebound guy.

Mandy paused, not happy at how appealing she found him. She took a deep breath and continued putting on makeup. Dr. Aaron Nicholson was her neighbour and off limits. She liked her drama free life and an intimate sleepover with him? Nothing but trouble if the relationship didn't work out. Their friendship now was great. A failed romance meant the end of their comfy times hanging out together.

She drove to her business in the strip mall on the Dartmouth side of Halifax's harbor. Mandy parked in her usual spot,

Betrayal

marked with a sign one of her stylists, Neil, had made her. Coming in from the back, a peek of everyone working and the waiting area full of clients pleased her. The place smelled good, like her favorite expensive hair spray. The local easy listening station played over the speakers. Not too loud, not too soft.

"You heard the gory details, too?" asked Edie.

Mandy almost stopped to respond. Her assistant manager's client beat her to it by saying, "Yeah, she shoved him over the side after conking him in the head. It's how he got the cracked skull."

Mandy leaned against the wall. No wonder Aaron hadn't said anything more. Her own head ached in sympathy for what Craig must have endured. When her eyes started to sting, she blinked. There'd be plenty of time to cry later.

The stylist paused in snipping off the dead ends from the woman's hair. "I didn't know that! Does that mean he didn't drown?"

The woman in the adjoining booth leaned over. "You know he had to. He couldn't have been hit with anything hard enough to kill him before he hit the water."

"I don't know." Edie gave her client a large hand mirror. "If Sabrina hired someone, a burly new boyfriend perhaps, he could do the job."

Mandy shook her head at the gossip as she opened her office door. She'd have better luck stopping the ocean waves than curbing chatter about Craig Walker's death. Or murder, per popular consensus, it seemed. She hung up her coat, putting her purse away before powering up her computer and signing into their homegroup.

While waiting, she rested her elbows on her desk. Aaron knew a lot more than he'd said and while trying to pry it out of him was wrong, she couldn't help herself. Mandy grinned, thinking about her stylists and their inquisitive natures. Wanting to know more was an occupational hazard.

She focused on bills and payroll instead of the topic of the day. The position of her desk allowed her to see in the mirror as new clients walked in. Each person entering distracted her because they might know more than she and her staff did about poor Craig. A glance at the clock disappointed her. This late in the morning and her to do list mocked her. She stood and closed the door soft enough to not attract attention. Catching up on Craig's death could wait until she finished financials.

Her stomach growled a couple of hours later. She stood and stretched, judging

Betrayal

now was as good a time as any for a break. Mandy went into the main salon. "So what does everyone think?"

Edie offered first, "Accident."

"Murder," replied Barb.

Angela added, "For hire!"

"Yeah, but by who?" asked Mandy. "Do we have anyone as a suspect, yet?"

Neil limped over to her. "You had to start it again, didn't you? I almost had them calmed down."

"Sorry, but it's fun," she said, his sprained ankle getting her attention. He'd healed a lot in the three weeks since injuring it. Every time he had spent too much time on his feet, Neil favored that foot. She went to the appointment program on the front computer to check his work schedule. "You're done for the rest of the afternoon, right?"

"Yes, no more fun for me."

She grinned and closed the calendar. "Good. I'm running out of things for you to do on your butt, but you still need to stay off of that ankle."

"It's feeling better. How is Dr. Hottie, anyway?"

Mandy tried to give him a frosty glare. Her employees loved to tease her into a blush and Aaron was the quickest way to do it. "Dr. *Nicholson* is fine. We meet up around once a day. He needs to get out more often because I think I'm his only friend."

Neil wrinkled his nose and shook his head. "Really? You might be the one who needs to get out more."

His disagreement surprised her. "Don't think he's lonely?"

He shrugged, not looking her in the eye. "Not him. He's fine, as in super fine. I'm sure all the nurses, except the one I'm dating, are chasing him."

She narrowed her eyes at him. Remembering some of the women working at the hospital, Aaron had a great dating pool to dive into. "What has your nurse told you, exactly?"

"Nothing about Dr. N," he replied with a grin. Neil gave her a searching stare before easing down into the empty booth chair as if he were a client. "Give me a minute and I'll have some answers." He began a furious texting on his phone.

Mandy shook his shoulder to distract him. "You're not texting Aaron, are you?"

He laughed. "No, I'm past grade school. Just asking my guy if your doctor's interested in anyone around there."

Already embarrassed at the thought of Neil's boyfriend asking Aaron anything about her, she glanced around to see who listened in on their conversation. "No, don't.

Betrayal

He and I are just friends. That's it."

He paused the staccato taps on his phone. "This is interesting. Tell me more."

She laughed. "Nope. There's me, there's you, there's the line I'm not crossing."

"Fine. Be that way." His phone chirping distracted him. "He says Dr. N hangs out with all the nurses, no discrimination. Aw, that's nice. He can't tell me if or who your guy is dating."

"Good. He's discreet at work, much as we should be." She gave him the evil eye for emphasis.

"Us? Discreet?" Neil batted his eyelashes at her. "Sweetie, I didn't know you cared."

"Ha! You know what I mean, darling." She cuffed him on the shoulder, grinning when he laughed.

He put away his cell phone and spun around in the chair. "I do. So, what's my job this afternoon? Laundry?"

"Yep. I'll even bring the baskets here so you can fold and chat at the same time." She tapped him on the forehead instead and headed to the back room.

"This is why I love you, darling." He yelled back, "Love you more if you bring a drink."

"Eh," she called out while checking

the dryer. Mandy dreamed of the day where she could afford a laundry service. With her business this size? It was more a wish than a possibility. She brought the full basket of towels and a diet soda to the front for Neil.

He was already engrossed in conversation about the two wives of the dead man. Or, as her stylists argued, one real wife and one replacement wife. The switching for a better model comments they made hurt. Her ex-husband had used those exact words about his dumping her for his girlfriend. She didn't react or interrupt their talk. None of them knew why she and Geo split up, and Mandy wanted to keep it that way.

She straightened the magazines up front, tossing the older ones. The tension in her shoulders eased when the conversation shifted. She tuned out the talk about last night's hockey game while turning the product labels all to the front. With her defenses down, Mandy could mull over what happened to Craig. She'd been straight with Aaron. Her friend was the last guy she's suspect to have fallen overboard and drowned.

The Walkers and Hays had been friends for ages. Long enough to know how first Craig, then his daughter knew how to fish almost before they could walk. Debbi

Betrayal

came in for a weekly wax and blow out at least. Mandy went to the computer, wanting to double-check the appointment calendar and see if her every Friday at two was there.

"She canceled."

Mandy glanced over her shoulder at Barb. "Oh?"

The older woman walked up to the computer. "Yeah, around eight this morning."

"She didn't just leave a message, but waited until we were open? Interesting."

"It's why Angela put all her money on Debbi hiring a hit man and thinks she didn't want to break a nail while beating Craig to death. Edie is still betting on Sabrina, while you know Neil. He's betting on a secret male lover."

Mandy frowned at that, knowing how Debbi bragged on her new husband at their wedding reception. "You're wrong, Neil."

"No one can prove it," he called back to her.

She stared out at the gray day across the harbor. "I'd be more suspicious if Debbi hadn't canceled."

"That and if she weren't pregnant," added Barb

Her jaw dropped. This was a bombshell no one had mentioned or even hinted at before now. "She's pregnant? How far along?"

"Just a month," replied one of Edie's customers as she came up to the register. Barb and Mandy moved aside so the stylist could ring her up.

Edie added, "She had the home test last week before she came in and said no more hair color for her. It might harm the baby."

Both women nodded, saying at the same time, "Ah."

She shrugged. "She was all right with a manicure. Acrylics, I suppose, aren't as inorganic."

Mandy shook her head. Now the tragedy deepened. Craig had never met his youngest baby. She sighed. They'd need to help Debi keep chemicals away from the small fry. "Next time she comes in for a mani, put her in booth one and with a little fan, okay?"

Barb winked. "Closest to the door, gotcha."

She went back to the appointment program, clicking ahead a couple of weeks. "She's still on for the Friday after."

The stylists crowded around, as did Angela and her customer. Barb added, "It'll be interesting to see if she cancels on that, too."

Betrayal

She nodded. Putting herself in Debbie's place, Mandy would have canceled everything forever if Geo had died. Or, she would have done so before the divorce. "I suppose she's on auto pilot."

"Probably," replied Barb.

Her phone buzzed in her pocket, so she peeked at the text from Aaron. She smiled at her pulse jumping when seeing his name. They were just friends. No reason for her to get excited at all.

Having a rough day. Still on for dinner 2nite?

Yeah! You buy or I cook?

Hows your day been?

She laughed, knowing what he wanted, and texted back. *Good and I can cook for u.*

:D

That stinker conned her into dinner at her place every time. He'd never cooked for them, so maybe it was just as well. He might be the type to ruin a Kraft Dinner. She glanced up to see her manager, Fiona, stroll in. A quick check of the clock reaffirmed how they were that far into the afternoon. "Hey there, Fee."

"So is the topic of conversation Craig Walker?"

Everyone in the salon nodded. Neil added, "We've talked it to death, but if you know anything new, we're listening."

She shrugged out of her coat and other cold weather gear. "Gosh, I heard at Timmie's that he was all cut up. Like he'd been in a fight to the death before they found him." Fiona took off her earmuffs and looked in a mirror to repair her hair. "Very nasty head wounds."

"Bad enough that a woman couldn't have beaten him to death?" asked Angela.

Mandy saw everyone lean toward Fiona for the answer. She didn't want to indulge in gossip, but couldn't help her curiosity. Fee milked the delay by checking her lip gloss before saying, "If she had something very sharp, yes, a woman could have done it."

That did it, Mandy decided. She'd have to cajole some sort of answer out of Aaron tonight. After a beef stew and chocolate cake, he'd spill whatever secrets she wanted to know about any possible foul play. She had to admit the police did have better resources and skills. Even then, she couldn't just stand by and do nothing. She owed it to Craig and his new little family to help.

Aaron paused at the mailboxes to retrieve his junk mail. Mandy knew he was late. He'd texted a couple of hours ago,

Betrayal

warning her how car wreck victims kept him there. He started up the stairs, his feet and bad knee aching. At the top, he glanced at his apartment door. If not so late in the evening, he'd take a quick nap before seeing her. The cold breeze carried the smell of food to him, giving Aaron new life.

Mandy opened her door and peeked out. "Finally! It's good to see you."

The warmth hit him, and he let the heat soak into his bones as she moved back to let him in. He kicked off his sneakers, making sure they stayed off the carpet. "Food, beer, hug, and not even in that order." Aaron saw her hesitation on the hug before she complied. Her body was stiff in his arms for a moment before she melted into him. He appreciated her body's acceptance. His muscles relaxed in response. He pressed his lips against her hair, saying, "Thanks. It's been tougher than usual today."

"Was the accident that bad?"

He let her go and pulled off his coat, hanging it on a hook next to the door. His scarf and toque followed. "Very, and while I could talk about it, I'd rather not until later." Aaron swallowed the rising bile when thinking of the family brought in and their condition. He sat down his mail before settling into the chair. "Maybe after dinner.

Or tomorrow. Tomorrow might be good, too."

"Ah. I see. That terrible. I'm sorry." She disappeared into her little kitchen before returning. "You're not in scrubs, though."

"I changed out at the hospital. Clothes were a mess and turned me into a walking biohazard." Aaron took the bottle of beer she brought him. His hands were a little shaky, but better than back in ER. Fatalities in car wrecks with entire families and their children dead in an instant bothered him more than anything else. There'd been nothing any of them could do by the time the victims arrived. Days like this made private practice look better than usual. He sat up, giving Mandy a reassuring grin when she sat a bowl of stew in front of him. "Thank you."

She took a seat opposite him. "You're especially welcome since you're taking me someplace nice for dinner tomorrow night."

"Oh?" He paused the spoon halfway between mouth and food. "Are we calling it a date?"

She shrugged off his reminder. "It's not a date, but payback."

"Ah." Aaron almost quipped about Mandy's cooking being equal to an expensive dinner out. The beef melted in his

Betrayal

mouth, convincing him anything was worth this. He wanted to eat, not talk. Breakfast had been too long ago and vending machine peanuts only went so far. The day's tensions faded more with each bite he took.

He glanced over at Mandy, really looking at her now. She must have changed clothes when getting home tonight. Aaron couldn't imagine her in a fancy salon wearing a red flannel shirt, one begging to be undone by him every time he glanced at the top buttons. Her skin tempted him to trace a finger down the hollow of her throat. He wanted to press his lips there as well and find out if she were as rose petal soft as he imagined.

Aaron glanced up into her eyes and nodded at her raised eyebrows. He grinned, knowing he'd been busted staring at her. "Very good. I'll need to find a place to take you that's equal to this."

She laughed. "Sure. There's a King of Donair's up the road from your hospital. You can take me for lunch there sometime."

"Only if they serve champagne."

"Oo, big spender." She winked at him. "You're treating me to champagne for serving you beef? What would you want me to make to earn lobster?"

He took a drink. Aaron toyed with kidding around but figured Geo had done enough damage to her self-esteem for a while. "I'm serious. If your chocolate cake is half this good—"

She pouted and stabbed at a potato. "You saw? The cake was supposed to be a surprise."

"Consider me surprised. I saw it when you got my beer and hoped you'd wanted it for dessert tonight." He liked how the irritation in her expression faded into a smile. Aaron took her hand as she tapped on the table, squeezing her fingers in a mini hug. "Trust me, I'm happy enough for anything you want tomorrow. My treat all the way."

"If you insist…."

When she looked up at him through those long lashes, his heart skipped a beat, and he grinned at the cliché happening to him. "I do."

Mandy nodded at the pile of mail he'd brought in and placed on the table. "Any catalogs? Or are you still too new to get decent junk mail?"

Change the subject, hmm? He turned his attention to the stack beside him and let go of her hand. "There's a couple of them addressed to prior occupants. I didn't even look." He shuffled through everything, setting aside the food mailers and charity requests. One last envelope remained. He

Betrayal

folded the bill for his storage unit in Vancouver and put it in his pocket. When seeing her watching him, he said, "It's a bill. I have most of my stuff in storage back home."

She grinned. "Don't you know? Envelopes with windows get returned to sender. I do that for all the ones I get."

"Ha!" Getting the joke, he chuckled. "And then they sell my kayak? Nope, but if they sold the ratty old sofa, I'd be ok with that."

"Hmm."

He didn't add anything despite her unasked questions. He knew Mandy wanted to know how long he'd be living here. So did he. Aaron liked Nova Scotia, enjoyed how different it was from home. But was an infatuation with a place enough to make it permanent? He wasn't sure. Until things changed between him and his asshole of a brother, he didn't mind the extra cost paid to keep his bigger things in British Columbia. He almost enjoyed going back every few months even if it meant testifying about his own brother trying to kill him.

"I heard something interesting in the shop today." Getting his attention, she continued, "Fiona came into work telling us all about Craig Walker's injuries. Seems he'd been bashed around on the head and shoulders with something sharp."

"Damn." Severe lacerations were exactly what the authorities wanted to keep from the public. A suspect confessing facts only the police and the killer knew made a conviction a hell of a lot easier. He tapped the spoon against his empty bowl. Why did confidentiality exist if people around here ignored it? "Who told you this, again?"

"Fiona at the salon. She heard it from somewhere."

He shook his head. Anyone mentioning how cut up Craig had been now couldn't be suspect. Not now that everyone in town knew what exactly had happened. Aaron pushed the bowl away from him, not hard, but firm, trying to not be angry. "All right. This is exactly why I don't tell you anything. Even the dead deserve privacy until all the facts are in." He glanced at her and caught a flicker of something like she'd bit into the bitter part of a walnut. That expression on her face meant he'd said something touchy to her feelings.

She had a thing about being nosy and he'd forgotten. Every time people mentioned gossip, beauty salons, and her, Mandy got her back up. Someday, he'd like to see her truly angry, but not now. Not when he was furious, too. He took a deep breath and tried to smile. "I'm sorry about losing my temper.

Betrayal

If I'd known she'd blab to people, I'd have gone ahead and told you."

"It's okay." She shrugged. "Of course, if you say don't tell anyone, I won't. I figured with the medical stuff if you wanted other people to know, you'd tell them yourself. Believe it or not, most stylists don't gossip more than any other professional. I think Fiona would gossip in solitary confinement."

Her pout didn't soften, so he tried humor to lighten her mood. Aaron wanted her quiet happiness back. "So if I want to spread the word about something, tell her? Gotcha." He drained the last bit of the bottle and set it in front of her. "You should have her announce your specials at the store and save your advertising money for important things like beef and beer for me."

"You got it." Mandy stood with a smile, taking his dishes. "I'm going to ignore that whole girl thing, too. You're just now walking without a limp."

"Not when the weather turns cold." He stretched, flexing the foot of his bad leg. The injury was one of the several leftovers from when his brother shoved him off a cliff last Thanksgiving. Aaron would have preferred a container of cranberry sauce, but then, his brother probably preferred to be a free man. "I had a tough time getting up the stairs."

She paused. "Oh no, really? You've been improving until now."

"Yeah, the only cure is chocolate cake and ice cream. Vanilla, if you have it."

Mandy disappeared into the kitchen. "I don't. In fact, what I do have is a nice walk. A long one off of a short pier."

He opened his mouth to retort something before remembering there was cake on the line. He settled for merely thinking a smart-assed remark. Little jerk. Mande needed to be glad she was cute. "No thanks. It's turned cold this evening, and I'm allergic to frostbite."

She came back and slid into the chair next to him, her hand on his shoulder. "I was thinking... We could go for a walk down at the yacht club."

"Why? I did mention frostbite, right?" Halifax seemed warmer than Vancouver, but still. Cold was cold, and he'd rather eat dessert than freeze.

"We could grab ice cream on the way back here." She traced a circle with her fingertips. "Craig's boat is probably at the club, and we'll be driving around anyway. Couldn't hurt to check it out."

He glanced at her hand, then into her eyes, letting her know she wasn't fooling him. She wanted to snoop around. Not that

Betrayal

he blamed her, but detectives existed for a reason. "Why should we stop and walk around a marina when we could come back here and freeze to death eating ice cream?"

"I don't know. It's just something about what Angela said about the whole thing." She bit her lip in that way that drove him crazy. "Craig was supposed to be alone on the boat, yet, was beat to death. There were a few cuts on his shoulders and back like he was trying to get away. But again, he supposedly rode out to fish alone."

Walker hadn't worn a life vest, either, and Aaron wondered if Mandy knew that. He did not want to go anywhere tonight, barely wanted to walk across the hall to go home, but she had started the wheels turning with her questions. "Okay, your curiosity is contagious. We can check out the boat from the dock, see if anything on the railing is broken, but that's it. We're not law enforcement, and anything we see goes nowhere else but us. I don't want to learn later how we messed up a conviction."

"Yay! I'll go get my snow boots."

Aaron stared at her. She had yet another pair? He shook his head and went to his own shoes. He'd not been entirely joking about the cold. Though more likely psychosomatic, his right knee and ankle ached when the outside air dipped below zero. He leaned against the wall and eased his foot up to his thigh to tie the shoe. The left side was easier. He hurried so she didn't see him struggle. The less said about his injuries, the better. He didn't want her well-intentioned sympathy.

By the time he had on his outer gear, she had strolled back into the room and said, "I'll drive since you've been drinking."

"One beer? That isn't drinking," he teased on his way out of the door.

"Doesn't matter since I know where we're going."

"Makes sense." He waited until she locked up before following her to her car. Once seated inside, Aaron smiled. He liked how the interior smelled like her perfume. Sneaking a peek at her profile, he loved how her dark hair curled around her face in defiance of her straightening attempts. She caught him looking when she glanced back while easing out of the spot. A little twinge hit his heart when their glances met.

"I promise this won't take long. We'll be back to the cake before you know it."

"Sounds good."

She put the car into drive. "Thank you for going with me." Mandy gave him a slight smile. "I just want to see if there's any damage. Craig parked his boat near here, or

Betrayal

I'd never even think of being out right now. I'm not that nosy."

He reached over and squeezed her shoulder. "I know you might not believe me, but your curiosity about things is one of your better qualities."

She frowned, slowly braking to a red light. "Hmm. You think so?"

The uncertainty and hurt in her eyes hadn't faded, so he responded, "I know so. It's great when someone wants to learn."

Mandy looked at him. "Even if they're not supposed to?"

Changing her mind might take more than a few random compliments. "Okay, being intrusive is not so great. Especially when there's cake at home."

"Thought so." She pulled into the yacht club parking lot. A couple of high-end vehicles were parked there, dusted by the new snow trying to fall. "Just a quick walk to see if there's damage. Pretend we're a couple out for a moonlit stroll?"

"No problem." He got out, waiting until the doors clicked. They weren't in a bad part of town, but Aaron saw no need to invite trouble. He caught up to Mandy and linked arms with her. "You're saying our excuse is romantic, right?"

"Um, yeah. Right." She tried the small gate and found it unlocked. "I expected more security."

Aaron nodded to the larger gate sized for boat trailers. "Check out the padlock and chains over there. They care about driving traffic out of here, not foot traffic." He let his hand slide down to take hers so they'd go through easier than side by side. Gloves kept them from touching, but he still felt her warmth. An odd sort of emotion settled in his chest. Contentment? Certainty? He couldn't pin it down, but her touch felt like forever to him. He squeezed her fingers and refocused on why they were here and not warm at home. "The shoe prints are faint, but looks like someone left here after the snow began again."

"Ah."

"It's well lit, so I'm betting CCTV saw who walked out." He saw fresh tire tracks from a formerly parked car. They led out and to the street. "And drove away."

Mandy searched the area around them. "Do you think someone's watching us from a security office, or just recording?"

He pointed to one of the cameras. "Recorded for sure, if that's working, and watched possibly."

She paused, pulling him to a stop with her. "I don't know if I like that. Doesn't it bother you? Knowing someone has you on film somewhere?"

Betrayal

"Film?" He chuckled, nudging her. "How old are you, again?"

"They're always watching tapes on crime shows." She faced Aaron, getting close.

"True. So you're not elderly, just act like it." He put his arm around her. "You're also distracting me with this cuddling thing. What are we supposed to be going, again?"

Mandy grinned, pulling away from him, and leading the way down the dock. "Craig's boat is over here."

They passed several sport-fishing vessels, each one bigger than the one preceding it. He'd looked into buying a smaller version once. Pricing for even the used ones went way past his comfort level. He let out a low whistle at the investment glittering under the falling snowflakes in the marina. "With this much money on the water, I'm betting they've reached the digital age in surveillance. A night watchman, maybe, or at least longer recording times in case something does go wrong out here."

She leaned over to him, quiet in the still air. "Do you suppose the security here knows if someone went out with Craig that night?"

He liked the contact and put his arm around her shoulders. "If any evidence exists, I'm sure they do."

With an abrupt stop, Mandy pointed at one of the sport fishing boats. "Stop, Aaron. Someone is in his boat."

"Police?"

"Come on, let's check out who's there. Maybe it's the murderer, cleaning up after himself." Holding his hand tighter, Mandy pulled him along.

He let his feet drag a little to slow her down. Aaron didn't want her to hear him pant. The cold still bothered his healing lung, and he'd be okay with keeping it easy. "Or herself. Remember his wives had a motive."

"Yeah."

Now that they faced getting caught out here for no reason other than snooping, Aaron was inclined to turn around and leave. Especially if a criminal waited for them in Walker's boat. Taking a different direction sounded better all the time. Plus, he had cake and sleep waiting for him back at the apartment. Nothing but complicated explanations and stupid excuses lay ahead of them. "Come, on Mandy. Let's head home and let the police do their jobs. Won't Fiona or Neil tell you all about this tomorrow, anyway?"

She stared at the boat as if mesmerized. "Maybe. I don't think it's the

Betrayal

police, Aaron. It looks like, I'm not sure, but could be Debbi. If she's not guilty, we have to help."

He ignoring for a moment how much he liked hearing her say his name and leaned forward. "Who's Debbi, again?"

"You know, Craig's wife."

"Oh right." He remembered her telling him this morning about Craig's swap for a younger model. Debbi's name hadn't stuck in his mind since Aaron had seen for himself how Sabrina was the next of kin listed.

A little gasp escaped her, and she put her free hand to her mouth. "Oh no! I think she's crying." She tugged at his hand, leading him to the boat's walkway. "We have to help her."

"No, Mandy." He held her fingers tighter, trying to be easy while pulling her back with him. "If she's crying, I don't want to go."

"Oh come on, you big baby. You know how to handle crying women." She slipped out of his hand, almost leaving her glove with him.

He followed, cursing in his mind and not wanting to intrude on Debbi's grief. "Damn it, knowing is different than liking." She turned, giving him a dirty look, so he tried a different tactic. "Mandy, sweetheart, please." Aaron halted. Where the hell had that come from? "I mean."

"Fine." She stopped, letting go of his hand and adjusting her glove. The air around her seemed to freeze with her icy mood. "I know you're desperate for cake. Let's just go in, give her our condolences, and leave. We won't stay long, and you're not playing the love card ever again."

Now she had him confused. He'd not heard that term before now. "Love card?"

"I'll explain later." She walked down the small boardwalk to the side of the boat. "Knock knock? Debbi?"

Aaron followed Mandy. The vessel seemed more like a small yacht than anything resembling a boat. The top bristled with what looked like several antennas. He had no idea why something smaller than a cruise ship needed so much in communications. A canoe or kayak was more his speed than anything like this. He caught up with Mandy as she greeted the new Mrs. Walker. Police line tape hung limply in the still night air. He frowned when seeing fingerprint powder on the boat's railings. Had the cops cleared the place, or was Mrs. Walker and now Mandy ruining evidence?

The woman stood up from a long seat, wiping her face. "Oh, Mandy? Hi. I'm

Betrayal

sorry. The police have been here and gone. Both I and the boat aren't presentable at the moment."

"Can we come aboard, or should we?"

"You can. They gave me the all clear."

Mandy stepped over onto the boat, giving a hand to Aaron and letting him steady her. "You poor dear, we're so sorry about Craig." She went up to the other woman, giving her a brief hug. "We only heard about your loss this morning." She helped him onboard the same way.

"Thank you. It's all a horrible. We had plans tonight, and now, he's just not here anymore." Debbi collapsed onto the vinyl cushion. "I don't know how to even start living without him."

She sank down to sit next to her. "You don't have to do anything right away, I'm sure."

Aaron fought the urge to fidget while standing there. He felt bad for Debbi and wore what he hoped was a sympathetic expression. The opulence below deck kept him distracted. All that gorgeous cherry wood, the chrome, and what he mistook for vinyl had been real leather.

He sat down on Mandy's right side and ran his right hand over the leather his body hid from the women's view. The smoothness seduced him like rich hot cocoa on a night like this. Forget kayaks. He wanted one of these to live in. If it had even a cot, he was gold. Anger in Debbi's voice brought his attention back to the present.

"Sabrina has been here already, that old cow. Ken, too. You just missed him."

No love lost there, and he suspected the first wife had choicer words to describe the second. He'd meant what he'd said to Mandy. He'd never heard of Ken but assumed the guy was a mutual friend of the two women.

He half listened as the women talked. Debbi was stunning and seemed like the typical trophy wife. She was slender, a little too blond, and relied on her eyeliner to look good. A lot of the older doctors' wives were this gal's clones. They tried too hard to stay young and beautiful instead of aging gracefully.

He snuck a glance at Mandy. She wore makeup she didn't need, in his opinion, and her body? Most mornings, he struggled to ignore her soft curves in even softer flannel. Just thinking about it sped up his pulse. He stared at the back of her head as she chatted with the other woman. Mandy's long, dark hair stayed pulled back into a ponytail most of the time. He'd come

Betrayal

over for coffee on days where she straightened her hair into submission.

Aaron didn't know why. He thought her loose curls were beautiful. She probably envied Debbi's stick straight hair and bony body. Who knew why women were never happy with what they had?

Mandy leaned back and out of the way. "Debbi, this is my friend, Aaron, and he's going to check the galley for some tissue paper or a paper towel and a glass of water for you."

He patted her shoulder, grateful for giving him something constructive to do. Plus, it gave him a chance to check out the interior. He ducked under the low doorway leading the way into a tiny but beautiful kitchen. A closer look showed a little bit of wear and tear. He peeked into the bedroom, amazed at how large the bed was. His own apartment seemed shabby now, and he made a mental note on how this whole sports fishing lifestyle needed further study.

Aaron found the paper towels pretty quick. He tore off a couple, liking the nice quality. They would be nice for wiping tears and noses. Now, drinking glasses? He opened a cabinet door. A sticky plastic shelf paper covered the shelves. The liner kept in place the variety of medicines from various pharmacies and for people in Walker's family stood inside. He found a plastic cup next to the meds and picked it up. Not expecting the rattle of pills, Aaron looked inside to find a medicine bottle. "Huh? Weird," he muttered. Space wasn't at a premium in the cabinet enough to stack or stuff small items into the larger ones.

Wondering about the hidden meds, he examined the label, squinting at the drug name and dose, a triptan class of pharmaceuticals. For migraines, he assumed and didn't need to open the bottle. Shaking it told him a couple of pills remained, not enough to kill the guy. This particular drug wasn't something he prescribed a lot, so he didn't have dosages and side effects at the top of his mind.

He double checked the patient name to see which Walker's medicine this was and saw "Cole, Ken." Was this Ken the same one the women had mentioned earlier? Were these illegally sold and if so, why this particular class? This wasn't an opiate. He opened the bottle, noticing the orangey smell first. Aaron shook out a few into his palm. Yep. Baby aspirin, but why in a prescription bottle?

Betrayal

Chapter 2

Mandy glanced down at the galley. She could see Aaron studying something, even watched him video it with his cell phone. He had to tell her everything as soon as they went home, patient confidentiality be damned. She'd not give him a choice and might have to use her ultimate weapon, homemade chocolate cake.

"I forgot to tell you. The water might not be safe. Craig probably didn't flush out the winterizer."

"I'll tell him. Don't worry about it." She hugged Debbi closer, patting her upper back before letting her go. "Aaron? There's bottled water in the fridge. Nothing else is potable."

"Okay." In a minute, he came back with the water, taking the lid off for her. "Here you are." He sat next to Mandy holding out a paper towel.

"Thank you," Debbi whispered before getting a drink. She wiped her eyes with the napkin, taking off the smeared mascara. "I appreciate your help, Mr...."

"I'm sorry. I should have properly

introduced you. Debbi, this is Doctor Aaron Nicholson. Aaron, this is Debbi Penn, Craig's wife."

"I kept my maiden name," added Debbi as if knowing the next question before he had to ask.

He smiled at her. "Of course. I'm sorry to hear about your husband, too. He seemed like a great guy."

"He is, was." She blew her nose before taking a drink. "I've been crying out all my woes and didn't think to ask, what brings you two out here?"

"Um." Mandy looked at Aaron, wondering how far to take this romance act they'd decided on. "We, were, out."

"Out for a moonlight stroll." He patted her shoulder. "She disagrees, and thinks it's too soon for her to date."

"Oh?" Debbi sniffed. "It's not that soon, Mandy. He seems nice."

"He is." She glanced at him, feeling an odd twist in her heart when seeing his smile. "I mean, yeah, we're just out tonight. Like a date."

Aaron put his arm around Mandy as if they belonged together. "Ms. Penn, do you want us to walk you out?"

She crumpled the paper towel into the palm of one hand and used her fingertips to recap the water bottle. "I suppose so.

Betrayal

Sitting here crying won't bring back Craig."

Mandy stood, following Debbi's lead. Aaron did, too. He squeezed her shoulder, seeming to be as nervous as she was. He stepped out onto the boardwalk first, helping Mandy out as well. She gave his hand an extra squeeze in thanks. The other woman turned off lights and secured the boat before letting him lead her onto the dock.

The three didn't talk as they walked down the boardwalk to the main marina building. As they drew closer, Debbi asked, "Are you two coming to the wake tomorrow night? It'd be a comfort to me if you did."

Aaron took Mandy's hand and nodded, saying, "Yes, we'll be there. It's the least we could do."

She wanted to do anything but see Craig dead and opened her mouth to make an excuse. A warning glare from Aaron changed her mind. "Yes, we will."

"Thank you." Debbi hugged both of them. "Goodnight."

They watched until she got in her car. Mandy unlocked the car only when certain Debbi was secure. Inside and out of the other woman's earshot, she asked him, "Did you learn anything?"

He shook his head. "Nothing I can tell you about."

His closed mouth and secrets were starting to wear on her nerves. She'd tried to not ask anything of or about him, but Craig was a different story. She wanted to know if some sicko was out killing men her father's age, not fumble around blindly hoping for the best. "Damn it, Aaron, really? Why do you get to know everything and I don't?" She stopped short of smacking her steering wheel in frustration. "I should have got her the water myself. Then I'd know something."

"Whoa, there, Mandy." He put a hand on her shoulder. "I honestly can't tell you."

His touch irritated her. He could be handsy but not tell her anything? She hated all this hinting at without saying anything. It felt too much like being married to that lying Geo again. The only difference between the two men was Aaron hid behind his medical oath, not a fear of her gossiping at the salon. "Let me guess, it's a doctor thing again? Craig isn't your patient. You owe him no privacy."

He took his hand from her, crossing his arms. "Okay. I'll pretend you're right and agree how I personally owe him nothing." He stared ahead at the road. "What kind of physician would I be if I blabbed this other guy's medicine all over town?

Short answer? Not a good one."

His words hit her where it hurt. Already angry with him holding out on her, now she fumed with him using the word "blabbed" in her car. Geo used that particular word when their arguments grew nasty. If she never heard a man say blabbed, use her occupation against her, or an outright order to keep quiet, she'd be happy. Mandy glanced at him, seeing her own clenched jaw echoed in his. "Fine. Don't tell me, and I'm sorry I asked. I'm persistent because I'm friends with the Walker family, and I don't want either of Craig's wives going to jail."

"I understand."

She kept quiet while wanting to retort he knew nothing. As they eased into her parking spot, Mandy glanced at him again before turning off her car. She didn't want to just leave things unsettled but didn't know what to say. "See you later, then."

He got out of her car, waiting for her to step out, before saying, "It's been a long day for me. I'm headed home and to bed."

"Okay." She secured her car before following him upstairs. Mandy was uncomfortable with talking to him as they both unlocked and went into their homes. Her place still smelled good from dinner. She had cake on the counter, just waiting for a binge.

Mandy pulled off her outwear and boots, setting them aside to dry overnight. A light knock on her door startled her. She peeked through the peephole to see Aaron out there. The familiar thrill of seeing him swept through her. She opened up. "Hi."

He gave a little wave. "Hi."

"Come in, if you want." Mandy opened the door wider.

He stepped in, standing out of the way while she shut the door. "I couldn't even take off my jacket without saying I'm sorry. Sleeping would be impossible if I didn't try to clear up this weirdness."

She smiled. He looked so repentant, and she had to admit, a lot of the blame went to her as well. "Okay. I'm sorry, too. You have ethics, strong ones, and I keep asking you to break them. I shouldn't do that, and I really am sorry."

"I'd like to tell you everything."

"You can't trust me, though."

He held her shoulders, taller than her due to his boots. "Mandy, it's not a matter of trust. I can tell you anything and feel comfortable with that. It's just the patient's right to privacy I can't go against it." Aaron pulled her into a hug. "Didn't you say your mother is a nurse? She didn't bring work home, did she?"

Betrayal

Mandy bit her lip. He had a point. She wouldn't grill her mom the way she did him, "No, and I shouldn't have asked. If I'd been thinking clearly, I'd have heard the medicine word more than the blabber word."

He squeezed her, kissing the top of her head. "That's better. I've learned something tonight about how I feel when we're angry with each other."

"I don't like it," she blurted.

"Me neither. If I promise to never or rarely use the word blabber around you, you'll respect my ethics?"

She nestled into him, liking the warmth and his clean scent. "I am really sorry. I know better than to let my inner busybody take over."

"Shh, everyone is curious. Everyone wants answers, especially when it's murder."

He'd opened the door, and she had to ask. "You know that for sure, now?"

"Don't you have chocolate cake in here? And didn't you promise me some?"

Mandy nestled into him, letting his jacket cover her face and keep her warm. "Yeah, but I like this hug thing we have going on."

He leaned back only far enough to kiss her forehead. "I do, too, but that cake is calling to me."

"Why do I suspect chocolate was your motive for coming over to apologize?" She slipped from his arms and headed for the kitchen.

Aaron followed, leaning against the doorway. "It wasn't. Not at first."

She cut the dessert while giving him a wicked grin. "If I were mean, I'd make you wait until breakfast for a slice."

"You're a sweet, kind, angel, who indulges my every cakey whim."

"Here." She held up a full plate. "Forks are in the drawer behind you."

"I know."

Mandy chuckled at his remark. Of course, he did, their apartments were mirror images of each other. She cut her own slice, taking the fork he handed her. They stood, eating, until she said, "Come on and have a seat. We really should savor this."

"Good call." He settled into his usual chair. "I could probably tell you the meds I found weren't Craig or Debbi's."

"Sabrina's?"

"No. I didn't recognize the name."

"Who would leave their medicine there?" Mandy asked herself more than she did him. She took another bite, thinking. If Craig were Geo, Mandy would suspect another woman, a new one to replace the one he was about to drop. "Craig's mother's name is Martha if that helps."

"It's probably one of his son's friends. Someone unrelated."

She smiled at being given another clue, being, the meds belonged to a male. "Craig also has a daughter, no sons." Watching him lick his fork clean of icing, she added, "He doesn't have brothers, either. The closest person to him, other than first Sabrina and now Debbie, is Ken Cole." Aaron paused, his tongue still sticking out for a moment, and she laughed at his "tell." So it was Ken's medicines? She knew they'd have to play poker sometime, with real money, or at least decent candy bars. Mandy counted on being rich or in a sugar coma by the time she finished with him. "They co-own Bug Off."

Aaron smiled. "Let me guess, pest control?"

"You're a genius!" She scraped up the last bit of icing from her plate. "They've been in business for a while, or were in business together."

"If this were television or the movies, I'd say Ken and Debbi killed him, wanting the business for their own."

"This goes nowhere, of course, but I'm better friends with Sabrina than Debbi."

"How is that a secret?"

"Ok, that part isn't, but few people

know about Sabrina believing Craig and Debbi were carrying on before his divorce. I would have never known about it except Dad and Craig were talking. He was asking Dad what to do about Sabrina's accusation that Debbi seduced him away from her." She licked the chocolate from her fork, a "Mmm," sound escaping her. "Much like this cake is seducing me into another slice."

"You don't think they'd been having an affair beforehand?" He glanced up from his empty plate. "Sorry, if you can't tell me, don't."

"I suppose letting you know wouldn't hurt. It's all true, and you keep confidences. Craig had been frustrated by Sabrina's demands in the divorce. He'd joked about how it'd be easier to either kill her or him than go through the legal proceedings. At least, I'd thought he'd been kidding until this week. Which is crazy that it happened now, a couple of years after the dust had settled. I had figured he was just fantasizing about an easier way out." She wanted to wait until they knew each other better before admitting to some of her more gruesome fantasies about strangling Geo. Mandy paused a little before adding, "Besides, marriage is temporary. Blood stains on the carpet are forever."

He chuckled. "Not if you use

hydrogen peroxide."

Now he had her full attention. What did Aaron know about cleaning up blood that the mystery shows didn't? He had to tell her this, at least. "Does that fool the luminal tests?"

He shrugged. "I have no idea. I just know peroxide gets bloodstains out of clothes."

The second piece of cake didn't sound as good now. She imagined the ER as a bloodbath and shuddered. "Do you have to wash a lot of your things after work in it?"

"No, bloody scrubs go into biohazard bins for laundry service." Aaron took both of their dessert dishes and disappeared into the kitchen.

"I wondered because I never saw mom wash anything bloody unless Marty skinned up something." She heard the dishwasher door shut and the machine groan to life. Mandy loved a guy who knew his way around large appliances other than flat screen TVs.

"Glad she didn't. Besides, I'm talking about my own blood on my favourite shirts." He came back in and began to sit.

"Ah, good to know." She made a follow me motion. "Speaking of that, are you still going to be my date at Craig's wake?"

"If you want me to, I suppose."

"Good. Keep walking." She led him down the short hall to her bedroom.

He followed her into the room. Aaron grinned, looking around like a boy in the girls' restroom. "Why are we in here?"

Her jaw dropped at his suggestion. All of a sudden, her bed seemed too large and inviting to ignore. She swallowed. "I don't know. I'd not thought about that."

He took her shoulder and shook her a little bit. "Don't be afraid, I'm kidding. Unless…." He shrugged. "I'm open to suggestions if you are."

Did he mean it? Her heart beat a little too hard in her chest at the possibility. She searched his face for clues and only found dark circles. Poor guy. He'd probably be asleep as soon as his head hit the pillow.

Mandy smiled and kissed his cheek. "No, get a good night's sleep first, tiger." She turned back to the closet and began searching. "We're here to find something for me to wear tomorrow night. I have nice clothes, just not nice somber clothes."

"If it were any earlier, I'd stay. Unless you're changing out in front of me." He sat on the edge of her bed before laying back, resting on a pillow he'd pulled down and his feet on the floor. "Do a striptease for me and I might find the energy to hang around a while."

She turned to see how serious he was. Mandy didn't want a rebound, and Geo had left her feeling like a dud in the bedroom. She wanted to say no, but her body wanted now. He blinked a couple of times before his eyes closed for good. His face relaxed, and she wanted him to spend the night. And that felt like too much too soon all of a sudden. She gave up on the closet and tried to pull him to his feet. "I don't know if anything can keep you awake at this point, handsome."

He resisted at first by being dead weight in her arms before standing. "So no nudity?"

Mandy led him from her bedroom before she could change her mind. "No, just a goodnight hug and see you in the morning. I'd forgotten you'd had a full day already."

"All right." He stood still while she hugged him.

"Good night, Aaron," she said against his chest. He appealed so much that all the baggage a real relationship had seemed like no problem all of a sudden. She rested her cheek on his shirt, wanting more from him than a rebound or friends with benefits. "Thank you for going to see the boat with me, and for eating some of my cake."

"Totally my pleasure." He gave her a little squeeze before letting go and grabbing his coat. "Especially that cake part. Not so much on missing the undressing you were supposed to do. I wouldn't mind inking that in on my schedule later."

She grinned, feeling shy all of a sudden. "Okay, I'll have to check when I'm available."

He paused in putting on his boots. "Whenever is fine with me." Aaron knelt and started tying his laces. "Do you happen to know what type of car Ken drives?"

"That's a strange question. It's something German. Why?"

"Did you notice the new car in the lot as we were leaving the marina? It drove over the previous tire tracks and parked in the same spot."

She searched her memory and recalled what her friend had said. "Oh, so maybe Ken came back to see Debbi and saw us there, too?"

"I did, but now I don't since the car was a truck."

"With no Bug Off on the side?"

"No. Nothing there and not as important as I'd thought after all. See you tomorrow?"

"See you then." She waited until he disappeared inside his home before closing

Betrayal

and locking her door. Mandy breathed in deep, enjoying how she smelled like him. Her pillow probably did, too. Nice.

"Calm down, girl," she whispered. He'd been friendly and a little forward in her bedroom. Didn't mean he found her irresistible. Geo had taught her most regular guys took advantage of an opportunity whenever possible. Who gave the advantage to them didn't matter. She put away the cake and turned off the lights on her way to the bedroom.

"Boss!" Neil peeked into her office. "Debbi is here, and she's asking for you."

"Really?"

"Yes, ma'am."

She went to the front with him, and as he said, the second Mrs. Walker stood there with a watery smile. Mandy held out her arms, saying, "Hello, Debbi, it's good to see you again."

"Oh, Mandy!" She ran over and hugged her. "I'm so glad you and Aaron came to see me last night. It meant the world to me that someone cared."

"Of course, someone cares. A lot of people do." Over the other woman's shoulder, Mandy glared at her employees and mouthed the words, "Back to work."

Pulling away, Debbi said, "Can you

give me a trim? You do take walk-ins, right?"

"I do. Have a seat." She led her to the vacant booth, pocketing the shears Edie handed her. "Do you have anything else in mind?"

"Why?" Debbi lifted her chin. "Do I need a wax?"

"Not that I can tell. You look perfect."

She sniffed as if getting teary eyed. "Thank you. This is just so hard. I never expected to be a widow." She took a tissue Neil handed her. "I mean, maybe someday. Just not when both of us were so young."

Mandy frowned at how everyone made a face and looked away as if they didn't want to say anything about the much older Craig. Instead, she smiled in reassurance. "Of course, you didn't."

"I'll be glad when all this is over, but I guess it never will be." She paused while the apron went around her neck. "There're so many details, and I'm overwhelmed. Craig kept everything in the lockbox. I know I need to go there and review life insurance, the will, all that stuff, but when I do, all this will become real."

"Oh?"

"Logically, I know he's gone, but in my heart, it's as if he's on a business trip and due back any minute. Sounds silly, but pretending keeps me from crying all the time."

"I'm so sorry, Debbi." She put a hand on the woman's shoulder and reached for a box of tissue paper. "I can't imagine how you feel. Craig was a great person and his loss breaks my heart."

Debbi sat up straighter, taking a tissue. "If I cry, my contacts will cloud up too much for me to drive my way home. So, enough about my problems. Tell me all about your new friend."

Mandy glanced around her. In the mirrors lining the walls, most of her stylists' scissors or combs hovered over the clients' heads as if waiting for her next few words. She tried to think of a good response, not an incriminating or dishonest one. "Oh. Well."

Neil edged closer. "Yes, tell us all about Dr. Hottie."

She narrowed her eyes at him. "He's from British Columbia, Vancouver exactly. Not close to his family at all, from what I've gathered. He's a doctor and likes chocolate cake."

"So don't we all," said Barb and everyone agreed.

Debbi gave her a sad smile. "That can't be all there is to him if you're out together in the evenings."

"We're neighbours. He lives across from me, we have coffee together most mornings, and before you ask, I go over there, or he comes to my place. No hanky panky." She ignored Neil's smirk and Fiona's chuckle. "Besides, it's easy to hang out after work when his shifts allow and just as easy to go back to our own beds."

Debbi narrowed her eyes before examining her manicure. "Ah, so there's no affection. That's a shame because it seemed like you two were good friends."

She smiled, recognizing a fishing expedition when she heard one. "We are, and it might be more than that when we're ready. He's a great guy, and I enjoy being around him."

Her lone male stylist led his client to the computer register and quipped, "His gorgeous looks have nothing to do with that, I'm sure."

"Really, Neil? He's more than his appearance."

Fiona passed by them on her way to the front for a walk in client. "If he's a doctor, He sure is. He has a brain, too."

Mandy smiled. The guy was attractive, smart, and more. "Aaron's just a nice person all around."

"Have you been on any dates, or is it all movies and chill at your house?" asked

Debbi.

She kept the smile on her burning face, at the implications. "Some sort of dates and no chill."

Neil nudged her on the way to his chair. "Are you sure he likes girls? He might be on my team."

Mandy laughed. "He's made comments a time or two. I'm pretty sure he's into the ladies. I want to take my time with him. Maybe let the ink dry on my divorce papers."

"Good point."

Debbi seemed just as disappointed as she was. Mandy checked the woman's hair for an even cut. "Between my divorce and him not being sure about living here permanently, I'm not letting myself get attached just yet. He'll end up going back to BC, and I'm staying here." She gave her a hand mirror.

Debbi nodded, checking the back of her head. "I understand. This is home, your business is here, and so is your family." She stood, retrieving her purse. "How much do I owe you?"

Not wanting to add to her recent and unexpected expenses, she replied, "Don't worry about it."

The other woman held out her credit card. "Are you sure? I don't mind."

Mandy waved a hand. "Think of it as a favor to me, honestly. Talking about Aaron was fun. Helped clear up a few crazy ideas I had about him."

Aaron and Mandy stepped into the funeral home. The foyer held several people, all lined up for the viewing room. He glanced around, impressed by how lovely the place seemed. The blood pounded in his veins, and he knew keeping his mind occupied on the décor hadn't fooled his heart.

The only times he'd been inside funeral homes were to send off his parents and grandparents. Paying respects to a stranger instead of a relative didn't ease his anxiety. Memories of saying goodbye to people far too soon crowded his mind.

He suspected no one else liked the place, either. Especially the guy in the casket. Aaron hoped whoever had Walker's criminal case made an arrest soon. He swallowed his collar suffocating and glanced around at what others wore. He asked Mandy, "No one else is wearing a tie?"

"No, so take it off." She watched as he began loosening the silk. "That's not a clip on? I'm impressed. Very sexy."

"Really? I thought you liked my ratty

sweatshirts," he kidded with her and began cinching up the tie again. "Should I leave it on for you?"

She punched him in the arm. "Be serious. Whatever is more comfortable for you is fine with me."

He enjoyed her slight smile despite her attempts to be somber. People around them were talking and mingling with others. This was much more of a quiet party than any other funeral he'd attended. Maybe that was the difference in a true funeral and a wake. "I'll ease it up a little. Don't want to be disrespectful, but do want to breathe."

"I wouldn't worry about it." She patted his shoulder. "You're one of those guys who'd look good in anything."

Her compliment pleased him, and since this was the wrong place to wear a goofy grin, he focused on being a little more somber. He glanced over at Mandy. She'd pulled her hair up into something chic and while he loved her curls, this view of her neck had its appeal. He leaned over to her and whispered, "You smell good."

"Thank you. So do you."

He waited for a while to see if she had anything to add. Aaron hadn't wanted to fish for compliments at first. But now? He enjoyed hearing what she thought, especially the good stuff, so he had to continue. "You ended up buying a new dress, I see. Looks nice and looks good on you, too."

"This? I had it in the back of the closet for ages. Lucky, it was there because I had no time for shopping today." She leaned forward, squinting down the hall. "I've never been to one of these or a funeral, have you? I wonder if they have food here."

His mouth went dry at the sudden reminder of how many funerals he'd attended. Thinking about death was one thing, saying aloud what had happened was another entirely. He didn't know how to tell her without sounding melodramatic or like a one upper. He took a breath or two, deciding simple had to be the best way. "I've been to three funerals, and none of them had food until the reception after. This is my first wake."

"Funerals have receptions?"

He stared ahead to the closed casket. "The ones I went to did."

"Ah." She linked arms with him in a comforting move. "Did you know the people, were they patients of yours?"

Aaron kept his voice low. Say it as fast as ripping off a band-aid, be a guy about it, he thought. "My parents had the same funeral, and the two grandparents that I had known each had their own." He gave her a slight smile, anticipating her curiosity.

Betrayal

"We'll talk more about it later, I promise."

Mandy stared up at him. "Oh, Aaron. I'm sorry. I didn't know."

He put an arm around her, giving her a squeeze. "I didn't expect you to." He nodded ahead to the small group of the family next to the casket. "See? There's Debbi. We'll focus on her right now and afterward, I'll take you to dinner." He glanced over at her and saw her eyes shimmer with tears. "Hey, none of that. You didn't cross a line. It was a reasonable question considering where we are, and you're not nosy, I promise." She sniffed, and he added, "Dinner, and I'll tell you everything, okay?"

"It's not that." She took his arm in a hug. "I didn't know about your parents."

He took in a deep breath. "Mine too, but later."

"Okay." Mandy turned to her friend and hugged her. "Hi, Debbi. It's good to see you, and again, I'm so sorry for your loss. It's just terrible."

The widow gave her a squeeze before letting her go. "Thank you. I'm glad you're here. Hello, Dr. Nicholson." She gave him a hug as well. "Thank you, too. I know Mandy and all of us will miss you when you go back home."

He patted her back before going back

to a polite distance. Home? What did she know that he didn't? "Thank you. It's nice to be wanted." He glanced at Mandy and saw her give him a wan smile. "Don't count me out just yet. I have a commitment to the hospital, so my going away party can't be anytime soon."

Debbi took his hand. "That's good to know." She gave him another hug and pulled away, yet holding on to his hands. Turning to her right, she said, "Ken, here are some friends of mine. They've come to pay their respects." She let go of Aaron to put her arm around Mandy. "You know Mandy, of course, and here is her new friend, Dr. Aaron…." She glanced at Aaron to fill in her sudden lapse.

Nicholson."

"Right, I'm sorry for that. And this is my husband's," she paused while putting a hand to her mouth. "Sorry. He's my former husband's business partner, Ken Cole."

Aaron shook his hand with a grim smile and wondered how to ask Cole about his migraines in a discreet way. "Nice to meet you. Wish it were under better circumstances."

"Likewise, doctor." He addressed Mandy. "Dear, how are you? I heard about you and Geo. A damned shame, he was a great guy."

Betrayal

"Thank you, and you're right, he was. But now he's someone else's great guy. You know how that goes."

Aaron hoped his ears growing three sizes so he could hear better hadn't been obvious. He'd learned more about Mandy's divorce from this one introduction than he'd found out in three weeks. He wanted to linger, let Cole talk, and listen in on more about her. Even better, he might learn more about why Ken would leave behind baby aspirin in a migraine medicine bottle on someone else's ship.

He'd chatted with a neurologist at the hospital, refreshing his memory about the drug. Serious stuff and Ken seemed to be borderline too old and too heavy to be a good patient for it. He wanted to get a better look at Craig, but Debbi and Ken blocked his view. He had meant to listen in as the two caught up and learn more about Mandy's love life.

"....and I thought there'd be lots of time alone to watch movies and read. Not so. The next day, I met Aaron and we've been thick as thieves ever since."

He kept a smile on his face despite the urge to let loose with a damn it or two. He'd missed all the facts Mandy wouldn't tell him about her prior marriage. She wasn't the only person in this relationship needing to know more than the other wanted to say.

"That's good. He'll keep you from being all sad about Geo and his new wife," Ken said.

"New wife? Oh, he married her, huh? I didn't know."

Seeing the hurt on Mandy's face, Aaron put an arm around her. He wanted to smack the other guy on the head to get him to shut up about Mandy's ex-husband.

"Well, damn. I thought you knew." He shrugged. "But then, why would you? Divorce being what it is and all."

Aaron found a good excuse to leave at the far end of the room. "I see someone else we need to console, Ken. If you'll excuse us?"

As soon as they were free of him, Mandy said, "He remarried so soon?" She shook herself. "Sure, she's pregnant, so of course. It's part of why I left him, to begin with." She looked up at Aaron. "Makes sense, right? If you got someone pregnant, you'd probably marry her as soon as your wife signed the papers. It would be the right thing to do."

She looked so lost, small, next to him. Her eyes shimmered with tears, and he wanted to go back and punch Ken. He began, "Look, I—"

"Mandy!" An older woman, frail,

Betrayal

came up and hugged her. "Thank you so much for being here for my son."

"You're welcome, Mrs. Walker. I'm so sorry," said Mandy over her shoulder.

"Thank you. It's a terrible thing." The elderly lady let go of her and looked at Aaron. "Hello. I suppose you know our Miss Hays?"

Mandy smiled at her and took his hand. "Mrs. Walker, this is a friend of mine, Dr. Aaron Nicholson. Aaron, this is Craig's mother, Mrs. Walker."

He gave her a smile and extended his hand. "A pleasure to meet you, ma'am."

She took his hand and pulled him into a quick hug. "Thank you, though this is a horrible time, right?"

The contact surprised him, the woman both frail and strong in his arms. He'd wonder why later, and said, "It is tragic, ma'am."

She let go of him to take Mandy by the arm and led her away from the larger crowd, leaving him to follow. He had planned on following as they left Craig's visitation room, but Mandy grabbed Aaron's hand in a solid hold. Keeping up with her, he gave her fingers a reassuring squeeze. She returned his little hug. All three walked out into the larger room, the cold air both refreshing and a bit difficult for him to breathe.

"I'm happy to see you two, but everyone else?" Mrs. Walker leaned in to say, "If you could make that Debbi woman disappear, we'd all be better off."

Mandy gasped before saying, "I'm sure no one wants that."

The older woman frowned, pushing her glasses up to the bridge of her nose. "I do, but she's pregnant. Now, I have to keep on her good side to see my future grandchild."

She put her arm around Mrs. Walker. "That's happy news, right?"

"Not from her it isn't. But that's not what's important." She stopped, glanced around the three of them to see who listened in on their conversation. Seeming satisfied they were alone, Mrs. Walker continued. "I know how you hear things in that salon of yours."

Aaron felt her arm muscles stiffen. Everyone she knew assumed she gossiped? No wonder Mandy was so touchy about the subject. He tried to remember when she might have chatted about other people's personal lives. She'd never done so in front of him when they'd been at Timmie's, the grocery store, or laundromat on Saturday.

Mandy gave her a thin smile. "Not as much as you'd expect."

Betrayal

Mrs. Walker raised a bony finger. "Still, I know Debbi has a standing appointment. I'm relying on you to keep me informed if the police think Sabrina killed my boy."

"No one I know on the force comes into my place for their hair."

"They should. You're talented." She squinted at Aaron. "You're due for a shearing, too."

He grinned. "I agree, ma'am."

"I know someone down at the station house, but don't hear everything going on in town. Let me see if I have his latest number." Mandy retrieved her phone.

"Well, start calling. Someone who wanted to murder him and pin it on Sabrina cut up my son. I feel it in my bones. She'd never hurt my poor Craig. She still loved him despite that witch's luring him away. We had a long talk, and she admitted she'd hoped he'd tire of Debbi and come back to her. Say you'll help me find who really killed my child."

Aaron's eyebrows had raised at that before he remembered to be discreet. Walker had to be fifty-five, hardly a child. He looked at the man's mother. When did people stop considering their offspring as children? Did they ever?

The elderly woman's eyes squinted

as she pointed a finger at him. "You're thinking something. What is it? What do you know?"

He felt like a bug pinned to a mounting board and just as helpless. "I don't know anything. I'm just thinking about Sabrina's situation." He glanced at Mandy, knowing she didn't buy his excuse. All that mattered right now was Mrs. Walker believing him. "Is she here, or is she too upset?"

"No, she's at home with Shari, my granddaughter. They didn't want to have a fuss with Debbi here. Sabrina thought it best to avoid any situations."

Mandy interjected, "That was a wise move. Mrs. Walker, I'll keep an ear open for talk about Sabrina and call my cop friend. No guarantees he can tell me anything, but I'll do what I can." She hugged the elderly woman.

"You're a good girl, and you've found a much better man than that rascal before." She motioned to Aaron, giving him a hug too. "Take good care of her, she's a treasure."

He glanced up at Mandy and grinned at her horrified expression. "I will, Mrs. Walker. She's a great gal."

She let him go. "Good boy. Now, scoot and let others try to console me."

Betrayal

"Yes ma'am," said Mandy and Aaron at the same time.

He took her hand and led her out to the foyer. In a quiet voice, he asked, "Are we done here?"

"I think so," she replied in an equally low tone. "Did you want to talk to Ken about anything else?"

Aaron snickered at how she wagged her eyebrows and struggled to keep it serious. "I can't without being awkward."

"What? Don't tell me you found Viagra! Oh my God! Do you think that killed him?"

"No. Shhh. I didn't find anything like that." A little louder, he added, "You are so dressed up, how about dinner at a place with cloth napkins?"

"You fancy talker, show me the way." She leaned in, saying, "You're paying, right?"

"That was the deal." The night air constricted his healing lung. Aaron didn't feel the actual shrinking as much as grew breathless as they walked down the long sidewalk. He glanced up, noting how bright the stars twinkled. Early tomorrow promised to be bitter. He'd need a scarf to keep breathing on the way to work.

"You do know I'm kidding. Splitting the check is fine, too," Mandy said as he took her hand, helping her step over a frozen puddle. "I'm glad you think my cooking is worth taking me out for. This is something like our first grown-up dinner out to a nice place."

"Good, because I left my sippy cup and bib at home." Liking her smile at his teasing, Aaron opened then closed the door for her. Sliding into his own seat, he started the engine, driving to a place on the wharf he had found while exploring a historic part of the city. Dinner might cost him an arm and two legs, but she was worth it. He glanced over at her, not sure which he preferred, the somber and stylish or the casual and cute version of Mandy. "We have a couple of topics for dinner tonight."

"Oh?"

He returned her grin. "Yes. The first is why Debbi thinks I'm leaving Halifax."

She laughed. "You're not in Halifax now."

"All right. You got me. Let's try, why I'm leaving Dartmouth soon."

"And second?"

Aaron glanced over to see her serious expression in the red stoplight's glow. He didn't know what to think about her change in attitude. She had to know he needed to go back home. He set that topic aside to mull over later. Now, he wanted to know her thoughts about the death. "Second is how you expect to help Mrs. Walker and Sabrina."

"And that's it?"

He fidgeted and wanted to say yes, that was all. He'd be lying because Aaron also wanted to know more about her divorce and this idiot Geo. He wanted to tell her the guy had no taste if he could give up someone like Mandy. But if he wanted to know more about her, he'd have to share more about his brother.

Aaron debated saying anything about Brad, wanting nice compartments in his life. His brother leaving him for dead belonged in the Vancouver box. Mandy and how he felt about her in the Halifax, or Dartmouth box. Before he could rethink his decision, he said, "No, that's not all. I'll tell you everything about my parents and grandparents."

"You don't have to, Aaron. I'll understand if you don't want to talk about it."

She didn't know he planned on leaving out most of what Brad did to him for the moment. Maybe forever. He slowed to a stop at the next red light and looked at her. "My parents died in a car wreck when I was twenty-five. I clung to our maternal grandparents until gram died two years later and grandpa a year after her. Our paternal grandparents had already passed, so we never knew them." He saw the green light reflected on her and turned back to driving.

After a few moments, she asked, "That explains why you could pick up and leave, but don't you miss your brother? Marty and I give each other grief even if we don't talk every day. To move across the country would be tough."

"It was, but you two are a lot closer than we are. I don't miss Brad. We had a huge fight that banged me up pretty bad. My knee hurts when it's cold, I get headaches sometimes, and my lungs are still healing from my ribs puncturing them."

"That's horrible." She reached out and squeezed his arm. "Did he run over you with a truck, or what?"

He chuckled. "No, but some days it feels like he did. When nothing hurts for a day or two, I'll forgive him. So, that's the first topic all talked out. And see? We're almost to the restaurant." He grinned at her. "We'll need to discuss the next time you're planning to bake a cake."

"No, that's not going to be one of the topics tonight. I have cake left over, and we're supposed to be figuring out how to help Sabrina. It's easy to say she killed him out of revenge, but I don't think so."

Betrayal

He navigated the narrow streets to the wharf. "I agree and don't think Debbi killed him, either."

Mandy laughed and punched his shoulder. "Is it because she's young and pretty?"

"No." Aaron made a face at her. "You're young and beautiful, and I don't suspect you at all."

She let down the sun visor and preened in the mirror. "You think that about me? Really? I like it."

He snapped his fingers and chuckled when she grabbed his hand to make him stop. "Stay on topic. She's pregnant. Now would be a bad time to kill a guy when she's not his next of kin. Tough to get the life insurance she'd need to raise a child."

She turned her head toward him, her eyes narrowed. "She's not his next of kin? How do you know? Have you seen his death certificate?"

"Hmm?" Aaron bit his lip acting like the parking lot took all of his attention. Too late to walk it back or pretend he'd said something else. Besides, next of kin wasn't medical information subject to privacy laws, was it? He turned off the car's engine and looked at her, wondering how to lie.

Laura Stapleton

Chapter 3

"Don't bother saying anything. I know that expression on your face."

"So soon?"

"It's been a few weeks. I've learned your "I know but can't tell you" look by now." She got out of the car with him. "Wait. We're not going here, are we? It's an overpriced tourist trap. Suckers and people too rich for their own good eat here."

He opened the door, ushering her inside. "I'm neither one, so I must be a guy out with a beautiful woman he wants to show off."

"Ha! Should you be driving without your glasses?"

Aaron grinned. "I have perfect vision." He turned to the host. "Two, please."

"This way, and to drink?"

She went ahead, following the guy to their table. "Water please."

"That's it? No wine?" Aaron asked.

"No, I'm more thirsty than anything else."

He turned back to their waiter. "Hot tea for me, please."

Mandy panicked at the prices. Her frugal father would hate it here. Even the appetizers were outrageous. "What are you getting?"

"The lobster looks good."

"No. It's robbery here. How about we just get drinks and go somewhere more affordable?"

He laughed. "I'm getting dinner tonight so you can stop worrying."

"I don't want to spend your money, either."

His eyebrows raised. "Appreciate that, but let me treat you this time. I eat enough ham sandwiches and food from your place. You and I both deserve this."

She kept her mouth closed to keep from blurting out about how he deserved to keep more of his money. Instead, she picked something good but not outrageous. "Crab Crusted Haddock, please."

The server nodded. "Very good, and for you, sir?"

"The lobster, please." Aaron took her menu and gave both to the waiter.

"Excellent choice." He scribbled a note before leaving.

Aaron leaned forward. "If you ask nicely, I might share a bite or two."

She grinned. "You could give me those yucky claws. No one likes those."

"Nice try, sweetheart, but no."

Mandy took a sip of her water,

Betrayal

enjoying his laugh. Despite the cost and slight feeling of being ripped off, she liked the luxury of the restaurant. Dark woods and low lighting gave the place a romantic atmosphere. The windows, large and along one wall, showcased the harbor and lights. If not for an island, she'd be able to see her salon and the Walker's yacht club marina. "I don't suppose you could spill anything on Craig's death certificate."

His face blanked into a bored expression. "No. I'm not even admitting to seeing the document."

"So one blink for yes, two blinks for no?"

He laughed. "Not even that. You're persistent." Aaron waved a hand as if warding off her next comment. "And no, not annoyingly so. You're making me think about details."

She fidgeted in her seat before grabbing her napkin and removing the silverware. "I suppose that's good."

"It is. I can't tell you anything, but I can tell the police or official medical examiner if I think of something relevant to the case."

"Without violating Craig's privacy." She placed her cutlery in their places.

He mimicked her actions and laid the napkin over his lap, too. "That's a tough one, maintaining that while making sure he gets justice."

"Yeah, I'd imagine so."

"So, since Craig is off limits, is this Geo guy not a topic for discussion? Because I sense his getting married was a surprise to you."

She stared past him at the harbor lights. How to tell him anything without sounding like a whiner? Mandy took a breath, opting for the direct approach. "You know how you're expecting something bad to happen, and then when it does? You're surprised at how bad it hurts. Why is that?"

"Good question."

Her stomach flip-flopped at the thought of Geo marrying that woman. "Before we even dated, I had heard he liked the ladies. Because I'm friendly to the point of being almost flirty, I thought he was the same since he married me."

"He took the sociability too far?"

"Very much so. We ran into someone Geo knew but that I didn't and the guy asked which day of the week I was. Turns out he owned a no-tell motel."

"Oh, bad."

"Yeah. There was a bit of a fight that evening. We'd patched things up in time for me to learn he'd gotten someone pregnant." Mandy took a drink, wishing she'd taken

Betrayal

Aaron's advice and ordered wine. "She's gorgeous. He's handsome. Their kids will be beautiful if he can stay with her for very long."

He took the drink menu, opening and sliding it toward her. "I'm sorry about all that. You didn't deserve that. No one does. Order us something you like. I'm in the mood to try something new."

"Thank you." She smiled at him before running down the list of house wines. "So, that's my sob story. I don't like telling people because I don't want the pity, and quite frankly, it makes me look stupid."

"How so?"

"I trusted him. Threw him out for cheating, took him back, and had to throw him out again when the gal's test showed positive." She glanced at Aaron, seeing the question on his face. "Or rather, I threw myself out. That's why you and I live across from each other."

"If I said I liked the guy already, you'd probably get angry. But honestly? I love him. His loss is my gain." He waved over their waiter. "Two glasses of whatever she wants, please."

"The house Riesling is excellent," she said. The server nodded, and Mandy closed the menu. So he loved Geo, huh? She wasn't quite sure how to feel about that.

Glad to have made Aaron's day, or pissed because who cheered on a divorce? "So you love him because he cheated on me?"

"Oh. Yeah, no, not at all." He waited until the server was done pouring their wine. As soon as the guy's back was turned, Aaron took a healthy sip before continuing, "It's just, I didn't know what to expect moving here. I have an erratic schedule that makes it tough to have a social life, even if I make friends pretty easy." He shrugged. "If anything, I tend to rely on you too much for friendship. You might want to have a life besides hanging out with me."

She laughed, enjoying being important to him. "Nice save. I had a feeling you liked me having freedom more than having a broken marriage." She wanted to tell him how she felt without getting mushy. "I get enough of other people at the salon. My door is never closed, and like earlier today, I'll come out into the main area to give cuts or other treatments to clients."

"Oh?"

"Yeah, Neil had a very good time teasing me about you. He has us dating and says if I'm not going to claim you, he would."

Aaron laughed. "Nice to be wanted, but no. Neil is handsome, but not my type. I like the ladies, or more accurately, a lady."

Betrayal

Her fork had paused halfway between the plate and her mouth before she set the bite back down. Did he mean her, or was someone else the reason behind him keeping his furniture in Vancouver? She swallowed a sip, wanting to be confident he wanted her. "Oh? So there's someone special in your life?"

"Sure there is. Has been since almost the day I moved here." He grinned and took hold of her hand resting on the table. Giving her fingers a squeeze, Aaron added, "Why are you surprised?"

"I was under the illusion that although you left British Columbia, one day you'd go back home to stay." She put her fork down and withdrew from his touch.

He wiped a corner of his mouth with the napkin before answering. "You mean a lot to me, Mandy. I enjoy spending time with you."

The unsaid part of his speech hung in the air between them. "But?"

"There's no but. It's and, as if *and* if I didn't have a mess to clean up back home I'd concentrate on you and here a lot more." Aaron leaned back and stared out of the window behind her. "Do you want me to be brutally honest?"

"Always."

His gaze shifted back to her. "I was

running away, plain and simple."

"I see." She wanted to ask more, pepper him with questions, but stayed silent, hoping he'd continue on of his own accord. She considered and rejected several before deciding to ask, "So you chose the flight option out of fight or flight?"

He chuckled. "There's freeze, too, but yes. I wanted to flee but not for forever. At some point, I'll have to go back and mop up what Brad did." He paused when the waiter came by, discrete in dropping off the check.

Aaron took it without letting her see the amount. The total had to be horrendous. His dinner probably cost double what hers did, and that was too much. She waited until their server left before commenting, "Most kids return home not too long after they run away. You're still running BC plates on your car, so I assumed your lease was a month to month."

"It was until yesterday. I changed it to six months for the savings."

"And I'm being treated as a result?"

"Yes, in a way." Aaron signed his name with a flourish, taking a little time to add in the tip. "You're being treated because you deserve it, not just because I have a little extra this month. I can't think of anyone else I'd rather celebrate with tonight."

Betrayal

His words and the way he looked up at her through his lashes, as if he desired her, left her speechless for a moment. When Aaron went back to settling up, putting away his wallet, she recovered and said, "That's nice. Thank you."

"My pleasure." He stood when she did, helping her with her coat.

She waited until he had his coat on before following him out of the place. A gust of wind spat wet snow at them. She skidded, and he put his arm around her shoulders, guiding her to the car. "Thank you, Aaron."

"Broken bones are no fun. Plus, I've been in the ER long enough today."

She slid in on her side, followed by him on his. "Good point." Halifax and Dartmouth sparkled in the winter air, even without the holiday decorations of the months before now. His car didn't seem affected by the roads as he drove them home.

Mandy wanted to chat, but being first cold, then hot, and having a full stomach left her drowsy. She wanted to rest on his shoulder as he parked in their complex. Shaking herself awake, she followed him up to their doors and leaned against him while searching for her keys.

He pulled her into his arms.

"Mandy? Is this where we say goodnight?"

His lips touched hers, and she trembled at the contact. They'd kissed before, but not like this. As if wanting to absorb her, Aaron held her closer, deepening their kiss. The rush of pleasure swept away her protests, and she melted into him. Their entryways seemed a lot less cold with his body heat searing hers. His lips left her mouth to nibble their way down her neck, giving her shivers. An unlocked door and shove inside, and they'd be able to give into this need.

He stopped kissing long enough to ask, "Your place or mine?"

"Mine is good." She turned around and began digging in her purse for the keys. He moved the hair aside and started kissing her neck. When he wrapped his arms around her waist, linking fingers over her stomach, she paused.

"Your skin is so warm and soft," he murmured. "I wonder if everywhere else on you is as sexy."

"Oh." Her hand shook as she unlocked the door. "I hope so."

He followed her in, turning the lock for her and shrugging off his coat. "More?"

She nodded, and he stepped forward, taking her lips in a passionate kiss again. He pushed her coat from her shoulders, letting it fall to the floor. Mandy moaned as he pulled her body against his.

Aaron's lips left hers to nip his way down her neck. "You feel like a rose petal. Maybe a marshmallow, so sweet and soft."

"I've never kissed a marshmallow," she gasped when his hands slid under her shirt.

"Think about how they feel against your lips before you bite them. That's how you are," he breathed against her skin.

She shivered. "I want to know how you taste. Can I?"

"Oh God, yes. Anything you want, anything." His hands slid from her and began undoing his pants.

"Um, Aaron?" His erection impressed the rational part of her mind. Very nice. The emotional side of her worked hard to not freak out. Almost as hard as he was. "I, um, that's really, just wow."

He unzipped and pushed his pants down. "The bedroom? That'd be more comfortable, and I could return the favor. Which would be a favor to me, really."

"Me, too, but I was thinking more of kissing your neck."

"Oh." He looked down at his pants bunched at his feet. "My eagerness is showing, isn't it?"

"A lot. In fact, I really like your, um,

eagerness."

"Good. The bedroom? Or the sofa is good. I've never done it in a kitchen, either."

All of those places left her knees weak. "I don't know. Sounds fun." She wanted Aaron, had a box of condoms that should have his name on it. Their sleeping together felt perfect and scary at the same time. What if she was bad in bed, if she'd been the real reason Geo couldn't stay faithful? Mandy knew better that his philandering had been his problem, but still. The nagging insecurity about how somehow she was to blame wouldn't go away completely. His thumb grazed the fabric in circles over her nipple, sending lust and fear through her at the same time. She glanced at his erection before looking back up into his eyes. "I want you so much, but I'm also terrified. I'm not sure I'm ready."

He put a hand to his mouth before saying, "I'm not going to laugh and won't say I'm not that big for you to be so scared before dragging you to the bedroom."

She laughed, tension easing from her chest. "It's ok if you laugh."

"No," he said while pulling his pants back up and fastening them. "I'm going to hang out here for a little while so you're not scared and just talk." He hugged her. "Is that okay?"

Betrayal

Melting into him, she nodded. "It's perfect. Thank you." Mandy rested her head on his shoulder until the panicky feeling eased. He patted her back as if she were a baby. Soon, she felt ready to tell him, "It's cliché, but true. It's not you, it's me." She let him lead her to the sofa, sitting when he did. "There's no real reason for me to be afraid. In fact, I think I'm an idiot for even thinking no. But, if we have sex, you find out why Geo ran around on me, and that he had a good reason for doing so? I'm not ready to hear why I suck in bed. And not suck in a good way, either."

He had chuckled a little before his face grew serious. "I'm sure you do, but only in the best way possible." Aaron lifted her chin, brushing his lips against hers. "Your mind says one thing, but your heart is saying another, isn't it?" She nodded, and he kissed her forehead. "Then we'll wait until all of you agrees. When that happens, I'll be happy to prove to you how great you are in bed."

"You don't know that," she managed to say before he kissed her lips, raking his tongue across the front of her teeth. She groaned, the invasion a tease of what could have been. When he deepened their kiss, Mandy buried her fingers in his hair. He pulled her over to straddle him. She hummed a little moan, feeling his desire for her hadn't faded. Why was she saying no, again? A sliver of fear sickened her stomach. Oh, right. She'd be awful, and he'd know why.

He broke off their kiss first. ""You're going to be amazing no matter where we have sex. It's tough remembering no means no when you're touching me like this."

She grinned and ran her other hand through his hair, close to his scalp. "You mean like—" A ridge on his scalp, one she'd only found while cutting a car wreck victim's hair, lay under her fingertips. "Dear God, Aaron. What happened to you?" She rose up on her knees, parting his hair to take a better look. The healing gash looked better than it had felt.

"It's from when Brad tried to kill me. I hit rocks all the way down." He stared into her cleavage. "Now is a bad time to ask if I can unbutton your shirt, isn't it?"

Seated back on her heels, she grinned. He couldn't be in too much pain, considering his libido right now. Plus, he'd been healing a little more every day she'd known him. Mandy smoothed his hair back into place. "Yeah, a little. I assume you're ok, no brain damage?"

He shrugged. "I had a concussion,

but no fracture or bleeding in the cranium."

"Oo, that doctor talk is so sexy," she said, leaning forward to kiss him.

His lips against hers, he grinned and said, "In that case, subdural hematoma, pulmonary embolism, and gastrointestinal distress."

She laughed. "If you're trying to make me feel sexy and desirable, it's working."

"Good. And speaking of job and work, four am is going to be way too early."

"I should get up." She slid her feet to the floor.

"Me too." He let her pull him upright. "Good night, and see you tomorrow?"

Mandy followed him on his way out as he grabbed his coat. "I'd like that." He kissed her once more before unlocking the door and leaving. She turned the deadbolt, resting her forehead against the solid wood door. Next time things turned sexy, she'd be ready with matching underwear and a copy of "How To Be A Good Lover" memorized.

Aaron looked up from the ancient magazine at the couple engaged in a little too much public affection right in front of him. The guy seemed to be a mechanic here, while the gal? She was a looker, for sure. He didn't care much for the type but had to acknowledge her appeal. If he were more into bombshell blondes and less into beautiful brunettes, he might be staring at the two.

"I'll let you pay me later, sugar. Trust me. I want to owe you a little something," the employee said, putting her at arm's distance.

The sexy woman cooed and reached for his belt buckle, "Or maybe not so little."

Their conversation left him a little queasy. He'd gone to Mandy's brother for an oil change today to find a peep show in the waiting room. He glanced back down at the magazine, wanting to focus on anything but other people around him.

A young man came in from the garage area like a blizzard. He stopped in mid-stride before going to his desk behind the open wall. "Swear to God, Geo, you two knock off the newlywed stuff, or I'm finding a new transmission guy ASAP."

Geo and his wife had already resumed their cuddling with him breaking off a kiss to say, "Come on, man. If I hadn't found her first, you'd be all over this luscious lollipop, too."

"Really? Cool it down or that's it. Final warning." He addressed Aaron. "Dr. Nicholson? Your car is ready. Everything is fine, and it's in great shape for the miles it has."

Realizing his mouth was hanging open, he closed it and stood. He could process this whole Marty keeping a skid like Geo on as an employee later. Never mind how Mandy must feel about it. In his mind, her brother just dropped a couple of notches on the decent guy meter. He went to the window. "Thanks. I ought to get a new one, but there's no reason."

"I agree. The new belt went on just fine. The old one was shredding and made the noise you heard. I checked out the systems, including that check engine light. If you're staying here, you might consider changing over your plates pretty soon. It's been a while." He slid a clipboard with the invoice on it over the counter top.

"Sure. That's my next stop."

"Do you still have that oil change card? I'll give you an extra hole punch since you're a family friend."

"Sure do." He fished out both, handing them to Marty. "I appreciate your looking at my car on short notice."

He took the signed invoice and cards. "No problem. I appreciate you looking after my sister."

"You know Mandy?"

Aaron didn't want to give Geo the

time of day but nodded while Marty ran his charge through. "Yes, we're neighbours."

"That's cool." He and the woman scooted closer to him. "She's doing, all right? We haven't talked since before the divorce."

He stopped just short of snapping a rude comment. The sour grapes expression on Marty's face amused Aaron and he grinned before turning to Geo. "Actually, I saw her last night, and she's doing great. We went to Craig Walker's wake, poor guy, and then out to dinner." He grinned at Marty and signed the receipt given him. "Her shop is my next stop. She said last night she wanted another reason to run her fingers through my hair. I can't tell her no on anything."

"Ha!" said the blonde clinging to Geo. "Mans is moving up in the world, dating a doctor."

He shrugged, and then put his billfold into its pocket. "I don't know if we're dating. I'd like to say we're dating, engaged, and all, but Mandy's enjoying her freedom." A mean part of him enjoyed the looks on everyone's faces. He wanted to lay it on a little thicker, just to needle Geo as much as he deserved. "I'm glad we're friends, but I want more, of course. Who wouldn't?" He looked down as if busted up about her and added, "Last night at Chez

Betrayal

Lobster she said she wanted to keep her options open. This one-sided love affair is breaking my heart."

"Aw, buddy." Marty stood up from his office chair. "You're a decent guy. I'm sure she'll come around."

"I hope so. Aaron worked to keep from grinning at the mulish expression on the woman's face and the stunned look on Geo's. "Catch ya later. I'm going to try winning over Mandy yet again."

"Good luck, buddy," Marty called out as the shop door jingled shut.

He just barely heard him say something about that guy having it bad and bit his lip to keep from laughing. He felt a little evil as he got his car and headed to Mandy's salon. Aaron parked, reading on the store front that they allowed walk-ins. He parked and went in before having the chance to change his mind. He saw Neil first and grinned.

Sure enough, the other man's face lit up like a sunrise. "Doctor Hottie! You're here to check on me." Neil held up his foot. "See? All better, thanks to your expert care."

"Is this the guy?" asked one of the stylists.

"It is! Isn't he a dreamboat?" Neil came over and gave him a hug. "He might be good enough for our boss lady."

Aaron laughed at the ribbing. "Might, huh? I accept that challenge."

"Good. She's worth it." He called over his shoulder, "Ms. Hays? You have a visitor!"

He didn't want to interrupt her work. "It's okay if she's busy. I'm just here for a trim."

Neil tilted his head while examining Aaron's hair. "Here for a shearing, looks like. I know some yarn spinners that'd love to get their hands on this wool."

"Come on, Neil, let the guy breathe."

He looked over at Mandy, and his breath caught. Her hair hung in waves around her shoulders. One side tucked behind her ear, a pencil keeping the mass in place. He'd seen the shirt and jeans on her before, but not the stylist's jacket. He couldn't help but grin at how cute, beautiful, and professional she was. "I was told my hair needed help."

"You could use some work, sure." She smiled and went to the computer. "Neil, when is your next client?"

"Not until after lunch. Do you want me to take him?"

In between tapping out instructions on the keyboard, she replied, "Sure. Whatever he wants and be careful, he has a tender spot on his scalp."

Betrayal

"Will do." Neil patted the back of his barber chair. "Have a seat and tell me what's going on."

"All right." He settled in, letting Neil wrap him in the apron. "I've been out running errands. Getting my car looked at…."

Mandy put her hands on her hips. "I have a few things to finish up in the office, so you'll excuse me?"

Neil waved her off, asking, "Anything seriously wrong?"

Aaron frowned, not ready to see her go. "Nothing bad. One of the belts was frayed and made a noise like an engine was dying. I brought it in and problem solved. It's edging up on two hundred thousand kilometers, and I want to keep it running for a while longer."

"Oh gosh, I'd have traded that baby in a hundred thousand ago." Neil began running his hands through Aaron's hair. "That hideous little Geo wasn't there, was he? Why Marts keeps him on, I'll never know. He's such a jerk."

He agreed but wanted to be the better person. Trashing the guy would be too easy and might make Mandy seem foolish for marrying him. Aaron grinned. "He seemed ok. A bit full of himself, but after seeing him, it's no wonder. He's an okay looking guy, surfer dude type."

"Very interesting. Did you talk to him? Does he know you love our boss lady?"

Aaron glanced in the mirror and didn't see Mandy. He stopped just short of saying love was a little strong. He did, but saying it out loud to her employees might be a little too real. "We chatted. I just told the truth about how lucky I am to be her friend. I also mentioned wanting more from her because who wouldn't?"

Neil put down the scissors and gave Aaron a hand mirror. "Ms. Mandy was right. You do have a scar, so I took it easy. Trimmed more off the sides, as you can see. Your neck is already pretty clean, but I can shave it if you like."

He ran his hand through much shorter hair, pausing to feel his scalp and how it had healed. The memory of the accident hurt worse than the actual injury did now. "Looks great. How much do I owe you?

The stylist laughed and gave him a large hand mirror. "First time is free."

The longer he looked, the more Aaron liked his cut. Neil had to be wrong, and he asked, "Are you sure?"

"Absolutely." He patted Aaron on the shoulder and winked. "Next time I'll charge you double."

"Gee, thanks," he retorted, giving back the hand mirror.

"My pleasure. Now go say goodbye to the boss before you go. She's been in a pissy mood this morning and needs cheering up."

Mandy's voice came through the open doorway. "I heard that!"

"You were supposed to, darling. I love you!" Neil grabbed a broom and began sweeping the floor, not stopping at his own station.

"Love you, too."

Aaron liked hearing her voice say those words, probably a lot more than he should. So much unfinished business waited for him in Vancouver. All of it personal, and all of it unwanted. He gave a final check of his hair in the mirror before heading to her office. He peeked inside, seeing her typing. Second guessing himself, he backed away, intending on getting out of there before interrupting her.

"So? Stop loitering around out there and let me see what he did for you."

Aaron went to Mandy's door and stepped in. "I like it. Are we still on for the funeral tomorrow?"

"Neil does good work." She stood and went to the front of her desk. After crossing her arms, she looked him up and down with a grin. "You look much more polished and professional and tomorrow? Yes. I need to pay my respects and going gives me a chance to see Sabrina. I miss her and want to see how she's holding up."

"Thank you." He quelled the urge to fish for more compliments. "I suppose closing the door for a kiss is out of the question."

She went to him, her voice soft. "Yeah, well, I might give you a peck on the cheek. Otherwise, a closed door is a huge sign of what we're doing in here."

Her perfume did things to him, pulse-pounding things. Aaron paused, unsure about saying anything more. He did want more of the kisses from last night and admitted, "Whatever you want to give me is fine. I do like appreciation."

"So do I." She kissed him lightly on his lips. "Sorry, I couldn't resist." She went back to her chair and sat with a sigh. "We're on for tomorrow, then. I'd suggest finding what you wore last night. You looked really good in it."

"Thanks. You looked really good last night, too." He fidgeted. His cheeks were hot, and his lips still tingled from her touch. "Are you stopping by before then?"

"How about coming over for coffee

tomorrow morning before we go? I'm off in the morning but won't have time for lunch after. I have a full afternoon."

"Sounds good. See you then." Aaron gave her one last smile before leaving. He waved to Neil, the stylist not stopping his story, just waving back.

Once in his car and headed toward the nearest motor vehicle registry, his day stretched out in front of him. Long and empty of fun. He shifted in his seat. Maybe a day off from everyone was what he needed. A full day of nothing but thinking. His stomach rumbled. And maybe grocery shopping.

Two hours and a kitchen full of snacks later, Aaron decided thinking was overrated. He slumped on his sofa with an arm over his eyes. A wise man would have brought his gaming system on the cross country trek with him. A wiser man would have a gym membership at a place a few blocks away. He checked the time. Too early for the evening, too late for the afternoon. Perfect for a nap.

He settled in on the couch, using the armrest as a pillow. His phone buzzed with an email notification, reminding him to turn down the volume. He bent his knee, and it ached, reminding him he'd not heard from Brad in a while. That was ok. Aaron took a deep breath, testing his lung capacity. After his brother had shoved him off of a rocky cliff, he considered Brad as a brother in name only. People who loved you didn't hope your body washed out with the tide.

The next morning, he knocked on her door, hoping she was ready to go and had a lint roller for his suit. The peephole darkened, so Aaron knew she'd seen him.
She opened up, saying, "Good morning and get in." Mandy stepped aside and shut the door as soon as he was inside. "Wow, you look amazing."
"Thanks," he said as she lifted her face. Aaron e kissed her, liking how doing so was now a new habit between them. She wore a pink robe that had seen better days. The colour gave her skin a warm glow.
"Come on in. A freezing day for a funeral, right? I'm not wearing a dress or even skirt."
"Won't that be cold?"
"Ha. So funny," she deadpanned.
"I'm brilliant that way. Do you have your coffee yet?"
"No, I'm on a tear this morning. Overslept and forgot to fill the maker last night."
"Ah, okay, so go finish getting dressed and I'll bring coffee when it's

ready," he said and went to her kitchen. Soon, the machine made horrible gurgling sounds. If he got her a Valentine's Day gift of a better coffee maker, would she take it as a sign he liked a better brewer? Or as a serious relationship gift? After a particularly obnoxious whine from the machine, he decided he didn't care. She needed something better than this.

She came back into the kitchen, in dark pants, a white shirt, and a red wool jacket. Her hair in rollers and her face bare, she said, "Don't look."

He grinned. "Too late. That housewife look is cute on you. From the neck up, anyway. You're rocking that young professional look otherwise."

"Gee, thanks. I wouldn't care what I look like so much but want to present a good image." She went past him to get a glass of water.

"At a funeral?"

"I know." She took a drink. "Morbid, but if I don't look good, people don't trust me to make them look good. And I want to be there for Sabrina and want to learn more about what happened to her and Craig."

"Remind me about how it's any of our business and how you can be her and Debbi's friend, too. Don't people pick sides in this sort of thing?" He retrieved two of her coffee cups, giving her a single splash of milk and a single spoonful of sugar.

"God, tell me about it." She sighed and took her cup. "I've been Craig and Sabrina's friend for forever. Then when Debbi happened, how could I be rude to her? It'd hurt Craig if I were and besides, Debbi's a nice person. Sabrina hates her, which I understand even if I couldn't hate her, too."

He shook his head and leaned against the counter. "Understandable, but doesn't answer why we don't let the police handle this."

"Mrs. Walker made me think about who had a motive." She put a hand on her hot rollers to check them. "Sure, I've texted my friend on the force about it, but he's busy with a lot of other cases. I want to know what happened to Craig, not just wander off and forget about it."

He took a sip. Her explaining how she felt loyal to all three people explained a little of why Marty kept Geo on. A little. He still preferred her brother kicking the guy to the curb for hurting Mandy. "I understand and don't blame you. In fact, you have me wanting to know what happened to him."

"Thanks." She poured more coffee into her cup. "I've meant to talk to you about yesterday. I had heard what you said to Neil about Geo and his wife. Marty called me last night. Did you mean it? She's not all that appealing to you? Because I've seen her and she's stunning."

That little sad and mulish expression on her face stirred his sympathies. She didn't need to doubt herself like this. They'd had breakfasts together, spend movie nights on her sofa, and now, even in curlers and no makeup, she had a natural beauty and charm he found irresistible. Aaron smiled. "I meant every word. You're right, she is amazing looking. I'll give her that. Neil was right, too. She's got that trashy sexy style that sells magazine covers."

She stared into her coffee cup. "Ah. Thank you for being honest."

"I don't know if you've noticed, but she's already showing sun damage. You'd have to look hard for the signs, but they're there."

"Not surprising since her and Geo met at my shop. She used to be a tanning customer when I still had the beds." She made a follow me motion and left the kitchen. "I'm a bad person for being glad about her skin, I'm sure."

He filled his cup before trailing after her. "I can see why you would be, but there's no need. Geo's new wife, like Debbi I suspect, probably doesn't look good soaking wet."

"Oh gosh, Aaron, who would?" She smoothed foundation over her skin. "Ok, men usually do, and women on a bikini photo shoot. But they're paid to look good, and there are teams of people standing by to make sure they do."

"You look good soaking wet. You've looked good every time I've seen you."

She grinned. "Really? I mean, I think you find me attractive, sure, but even as much as you do Geo's wife?"

"As much? No." Before she could misunderstand him, he hurried to add, "I'd told Neil the truth. You are absolutely beautiful and have been since the first moment I saw you."

Mandy paused in running her fingers through her curls. "Then we're even, because when we met, I was happy to have such a hunky neighbour." Their gazes met in the mirror, and she grinned. "Little did I know he'd be so easy to please. Maybe I can dazzle him with my gorgeousness in bed and not worry about anything else."

Her smile did funny things to his heart and totally shut down his mind. The mention of bed left him wanting more. "Does this mean we can have a late lunch early dinner today? I'm working nights the rest of the week." Finished with her face, he

Betrayal

watched as she put on earrings. "Please?"

"I'd love to. The first night you're off, we could have a sleepover."

He stared into his empty coffee cup instead of cheering or saying now was good for him and dragging her to her bedroom. "Good, I can't wait."

Aaron followed Mandy into the church. She stopped and talked with various people. He'd seen some of them in the hospital or around town but didn't really know anyone in particular. When Mrs. Walker nodded at him from across the room, he returned her somber greeting. Debbi leaned against Ken like he was a supporting post. He felt Mandy's hand hold his.

"There's Sabrina and Shari, their daughter. Let's go give our condolences before the funeral starts." She led him to the pair. "I'm so sorry about Craig."

He wondered about Sabrina's blood iron, her skin was so pale. Their daughter seemed the same, so maybe they were fine, just had a fair skin tone. When Mandy introduced them, he said, "Pleased to meet you, and my condolences."

"Thank you, Dr. Nicholson." She turned to Mandy. "I suppose Mom has recruited you to help clear my name?" At her nod, Sabrina continued, "She's been circling the wagons on this, determined to pin everything on Debbi."

"What do you think happened?" asked Mandy.

She gave a hard stare at Debbi, and when Aaron turned as well, he saw the younger woman fall into Ken's arms. He had to admit, she played the grieving widow to perfection. Sabrina sighed, catching his attention.

"I think if he were murdered, she did it."

Mandy didn't sound convinced to Aaron as she said, "He was pretty cut up from what the newspaper said."

Sabrina lifted her chin, looking down her nose at Mandy. "The article didn't tell you everything. Craig and I had been talking about our future together. He was tired of her running through his money and said the whole thing had been a mistake he wanted to fix."

Chapter 4

The preacher's words sounded faint in the thin winter air. Mandy shivered at the gravesite. Or rather, at the back of the crowd close to the grave. The warmth of Aaron's car faded fast in the biting wind. When she shivered, he put his arm around her, pulling her closer. She snuggled into him and lifted her chin to whisper into Aaron's ear. "My parents are here somewhere. So is Marty. Would you want to go out to lunch with us?" As soon as she'd uttered the words, his muscles stiffened against her.

He gave her a squeeze. "Parents? I don't know if I'm ready for curfews, broccoli, and being sent to my room."

She smiled, relaxing a little in his arms. "No guarantees."

This was her first funeral since her childhood. She wanted to ask Aaron how long the graveside services lasted but didn't dare. He probably had enough bad memories at the front of his mind today. She kept quiet, not wanting to add to any sadness he might be feeling.

Someone up front began singing to prerecorded music. He sighed and pulled her closer. "We're almost done."

"Good." When the last notes

sounded, the people up front began talking with the immediate family members. "I don't suppose we could sneak out?"

"Not where we're parked. We'd have to sit for a while." He glanced at her. "No, I don't have enough fuel in the tank for as long as the wait would take."

"Nuts." She began searching the crowd for her parents. "Thanks for keeping me somewhat warm."

"My pleasure. You kept me warm, too."

"Well, now you can do up your coat." She patted his arm while catching sight of her father. "You're such a sweetheart. Come on. Let me show you off to my parents." Mandy led him through the crowd.

Her mom saw her first, saying, "Sweetie! It's good to see you." She hugged her daughter. "Is this your friend?"

"Yes, it's Aaron."

"I figured so but didn't want to assume." Karen held out a hand, which Aaron shook. She added, "Very pleased to meet you."

"Let me do this properly, Mom," said Mandy. "Mom and Dad, this is Dr. Aaron Nicholson." She paused to let people pass by. "Aaron, this is Karen and Shawn. We're all Hays. I took back my name."

Betrayal

The men shook hands as Shawn said, "It's a pleasure to meet you, son."

"Likewise, sir, ma'am."

"So, is Marty around?"

"He went to the service, but skipped out graveside."

She smirked at his escape. "He's a smart guy."

"Mandy! Really."

"Sorry, mom."

After scowling at her daughter, Karen turned to Aaron. "So, are you going to lunch with us?"

"Sure," he said, taking Mandy's hand. "I'd love to hear all those embarrassing stories about her childhood."

She almost stopped in her tracks. "This might not be the best idea after all."

Karen tapped her shoulder. "Oh come on. You were an angel. It's Marty that was the mess."

Shawn nodded. "He was until we figured out Mandy always coaxed him into doing her dirty work."

"What? No, not me." Mandy slowed, her attention caught by a couple of plainclothes police. She knew them. The female cop came into her salon once in a while and always got the law enforcement discount. They took a couple of steps toward Sabrina where she waited with her daughter and former mother in law.

Karen whispered, "This doesn't look good."

The men nodded, all four of them looking and trying to be discreet about doing so. She glanced at her parents and Aaron. None of them said anything, trying to hear from where they were. Her mother gasped when Sabrina was led to an unmarked sedan.

Mandy didn't know whether to go help with Mrs. Walker and Shari, or just stay out of the way. "It has to be significant for them to bring her in, doesn't it?"

"Yes," said Aaron. "They have to have substantial evidence of the crime and think she's a flight risk."

"Oh no." Karen leaned against her husband.

Shawn asked, "How can you be sure when we're this far away?"

Aaron shifted from one foot to the other. "It's a long story."

Mandy suspected a lot more behind those few words. "Tell me later?"

He squeezed her hand. "Yes."

They waited as the plain car drove away with Sabrina inside. Mandy watched the remaining Walkers, with Shari crying as her grandmother held her. Ken and Debbi stood behind them, with her staring after the disappearing vehicle. Even from where she

Betrayal

stood, Mandy could see the satisfied gleam in Debbi's eyes.

She muttered out loud. "I have a feeling this is all we're going to talk about at the salon this afternoon."

Karen nodded, and Shawn said, "Probably for the rest of the week."

As they slowly made their way down the line of cars, Mandy let go of Aaron and took the chance to text her brother about lunch. "Marty wants to know where we're going."

Karen answered first. "How about Timmie's on Wyse? It's close to where you kids work."

"Sure. It doesn't matter to Aaron, he's off today, but this will be perfect for Mart and me." After texting a reply and getting into a conversation about the funeral, Mandy glanced up from her phone to see only Aaron next to his vehicle. "Oh, where'd everyone go?"

"Their car is on ahead."

"Ah." She went over and slid into the passenger seat. Her phone buzzed with a text from Neil. He represented all her other stylists, he wrote, to ask if what they'd heard about Sabrina was true and did she get photos. Mandy promised to tell him more after she returned to work. His reply made her laugh. "Neil wants me to say hi from him to Dr. Hottie. Sheesh. That guy."

Aaron laughed. "Itis good to be loved."

"I guess." Another text came in this time from Sabrina.

In holding area, waiting to be questioned. Mom said you'd help, I didn't kill C

Mandy frowned, hoping Sabrina called her lawyer before texting her. She replied *I'll do what I can. I'll find out who did.*

Aaron eased to a stop at a red light and asked, "What's going on? You look serious."

"Sabrina texted me."

"She can do that?"

"Yeah, they must not have arrested her just yet." Reading the *'k* Sabrina sent in reply, Mandy added, "She thinks I can help clear her name, but then, Mrs. Walker was the one telling her. That must be why she thinks I have these murder solving super powers."

He pulled into Timmie's parking lot. "Did she say anything else?"

"Just that she didn't kill him."

He tapped the steering wheel before getting out. "Wonder what evidence the police have against her."

"I have no idea, but I do have a

Betrayal

friend on the force."

Holding the restaurant door open for her, he said, "I'm not surprised. You know everybody."

"Between my salon, Marty's shop, mom's office, and dad's business, we've met everyone." She waved to her parents and said to Marty, "You didn't order for us?"

"I thought about it, but liver and gizzards aren't on the menu." He gave Mandy a half hug.

Shawn offered, "We can order for you ladies while you find us a table."

Mandy replied, giving Aaron's arm a squeeze, "I'm fine with whatever, okay?"

"Sure. Your usual with a single single?"

"Yep, thanks." She went to the booth Karen had found for them and sat.

Her mother leaned in, saying, "He's very handsome. Not in that pretty boy way Geo had, either. I like him. He isn't like most of the other doctors I know. Your Aaron is a sweetheart."

"I think so, too." She took off her coat at the same time as her mom. "It's kind of scary how right this feels between us. One of those too good to be true things."

Karen patted her hand. "If he's as nice as he seems to be, I like him. Your father's dying to do his taxes."

She laughed. "Oh gosh, no. Not unless he offers, first."

"I've already warned Shawn to wait. Plus, I asked around the office about Aaron and heard nothing but good. Keeps to himself, but not in a snooty way."

Mandy glanced over her shoulder to see the men leave the food pick up station. "We may have to talk more about him later." She kept watching them, catching Aaron's eye as he chatted with her father. She gave him a smile and turned to her mom. "So, has anyone said much about Craig's murder? How is Dad holding up, really?"

"Gosh, nothing I can tell you about Craig's death. Our office had nothing to do with him. Your father is as well as can be expected. It's a horrible thing."

"It is, and I'm worried for Sabrina."

The men arrived with the food, and everyone attacked. Mandy wondered what power funerals had over hunger. Everything tasted better than usual, something she chalked up to the joy of being alive.

Aaron was the first to say anything. "Mr. Hays was telling me he's a tax accountant."

Mandy laughed, asking, "Let me guess, he offered to do your taxes?"

Betrayal

"How'd you know?"

"I get a lot of my traits from him."

Aaron smiled at her. "When I'm ready to share, I'll let you, Mr. Walker."

"What? No. Mandy, I don't need to know anything. I just like the challenge."

Karen nudged her husband. "A self-employed doctor with employees and deductions, that'd be a challenge. I'm sure our Aaron here would have a standard T4 just like any other employee."

"Probably," Shawn agreed. "Still, do you have dependents or itemized deductions?"

Mandy gasped at the personal question. "Dad! Don't answer that, Aaron."

He shrugged. "I don't mind. No, to dependents, and no to itemized deductions. At least, not this year. I'm in the Emergency Department at Dartmouth General, easy to figure."

"You have plans for next year?"

Karen made a waving motion to her husband in a "let it go" way. Aaron grinned at both of them. "Sure. Eventually, I'll want to own a home of my own. There's never a rush but at the same time, I don't want to hit eighty and wonder where the time went."

Mandy took his arm and squeezed. He didn't deserve this interrogation on his future considering their casual friendship.

"I'm terribly sorry, Aaron. Now you see where I get my curiosity and planning for others. It's genetic, and you're under no obligation to respond to anything these two say."

He grinned, putting his hand over hers in reassurance. "It's fine. I'd forgotten how having parents to fuss over me feels. I like it."

Shawn and Karen had exchanged a look before her father said, "Mandy told us a little about your family. We're very sorry for your loss."

"Thank you."

They all fell silent, and Mandy didn't know how to pick the conversation up out of the gloom. No wonder he never mentioned his parents. She could guess why he avoided the subject of his brother altogether.

Shawn broke the ice first. "Mans, have you talked with Evan about what you could do for Sabrina?"

"Not talk as much as text. In fact, he owes me a reply." She brought out her phone and smiled at Aaron. "Evan is a friend of mine and an officer in Dartmouth." She texted him a quick *you there?* "We went to school together." Her phone buzzed.

Hey, good looking! Im here

Mandy glanced up at Aaron. Her face grew hot when their eyes met. She

Betrayal

texted, *Quick question, you've seen Sabrina Walker?*

Ye.p She's here. How r u?

She smiled at the good manners prompt. They'd not talked in person for forever. She had just assumed everything was status quo with him. *Good. You, too?*

Yeah. Hey, dinner tonight? We can catch up and talk about the Walkers.

Mandy shifted in her chair at how much like a date this felt. "He wants to see me this evening. I don't know if I should go."

"I don't know why not, honey," Karen said. "You two always got along when you dated."

Aaron cleared his throat. "They dated?"

Shawn crinkled up his sandwich paper and napkins. "All through high school, until he went to university, she went to college. I'd been rooting for Evan all along, even after Geo showed up."

Aaron said, "Tonight? I suppose you should if it'll help Mrs. Walker and Sabrina."

Some part of her had wanted him to protest, to be a little more possessive. She focused on her phone and ignored how schizophrenic this whole "love him, love him not" thing seemed. "Yeah, I'll let him know."

Her mom jumped in, explaining about whirlwind romances, her wedding to Geo, everyone's surprise to find out the guy was more than friendly. Mandy gritted her teeth and texted a reply to Evan about linking up after she closed shop. *Sure. Dinner is good. Does S have a lawyer?*

Great! Yeah, public defender.

"Damn," Mandy whispered.

Karen asked, "What is it, sweetheart?"

She glanced up from the little screen to see all three people staring at her. "Sabrina has a public defender. I think it's because the divorce left her broke."

Aaron shook his head. "I never think to search if life insurance companies give payouts to suspected murderers."

"If she did it, then no. No money and none to Shari until she is eighteen," Shawn said.

Karen began gathering everyone's trash. "Honey, it's getting late, and the kids need to go."

"Of course." He grinned at Mandy and Aaron. "She knows me too well. I could give a lecture on the financial aspects of an accidental or intentional death."

She followed Aaron out of the booth. "Don't knock it, Dad. Your lectures come to

Betrayal

mind every day at work."

"Good?" Shawn asked with a wink.

"Very." She hugged her dad first, then her mom, while Aaron shook their hands. "I'll call later if Evan has anything."

Once in his car, Mandy glanced over at Aaron. He'd been quiet for the past few blocks, and they only had a mile or so to go before getting back home. It hit her. "I told Evan yes to going out tonight when we already had plans." She retrieved her phone. "I'm so sorry. Let me change it to tomorrow night or any other but tonight and the next evening you're off work."

"No, I'm fine with it. You need to help the Walkers." He glanced at her while at a red light. "You don't seem to be okay, though. Having second thoughts?"

"A little." She struggled for a moment, wanting to tell him why but without sounding vain. Giving up, she said, "Evan tends to be a little too crazy about me. I've avoided him after the divorce because I'm not ready for a relationship, and he always is."

He eased into his parking space. "Maybe things have changed, and he's cooled off. Your chatting with him during dinner doesn't bother me and might help Sabrina's case."

That naggy little feeling of wanting

him to be more possessive tugged at her. She tried to keep the irritation out of her voice when she asked, "You don't seem to mind me going out on a date tonight."

He stared at her, narrowing his eyes as if trying to read her mind. "Wait. This isn't a date with you two, is it? I know we didn't talk about being exclusive, but he had his chance. This is mine."

She put her hand on the door handle and took a deep breath, enjoying his cologne. "You're right. It's not a date, it's a fact-finding mission."

He leaned over and kissed her. "That's better. Have a good time with your friend, and if you learn anything important, text me. I have work early tomorrow."

Knowing he'd be at work long before sunup, she said, "I'll wait until breakfast. You need your sleep." She got out of the car, adding, "Thanks for lunch and putting up with the folks. I owe you big time."

"They're great people, thanks for inviting me. Go before you freeze to death. I have errands to run, and you have Neil to corral."

"You're right. Later." His tires crunched on the sleet behind her as she unlocked her car. She started the vehicle giving it a few minutes to warm up.

Betrayal

Glancing at herself in the rearview mirror, her face was flushed. She grinned. He'd kissed her more in the past week than Geo had in a month. Fear and desire mixed in her heart. She dreaded being bad at sex with him, doing whatever she'd done to turn off Geo, but even one night with Aaron would be worth anything else that happened later.

She leaned her head against the steering wheel. He'd felt so good in her arms and his apparent desire for her when he'd dropped his pants? She chuckled. He'd been so cute and hopeful. Mandy looked ahead and put the car in reverse. Tonight after dinner, she'd research how to be amazing in bed so he wouldn't be disappointed.

Mandy hurried into her office, still cold from the drive. Everyone seemed busy, from what she saw on her way in. She peeked out and listened for a moment. Sure enough, the funeral and subsequent arrest were all anyone talked about. She guessed they'd give her two minutes before asking what she saw.

"So? Were you there?" asked Angela.

Not even a minute? She hid a smile, replying, "Yes. Let me hang up my coat and check messages. I'll come in and tell you what I know." Mollified, the stylist hurried back to her booth. Mandy had tried to resist gossip before this and had no luck. Her crew, while excellent, worked hard to get the facts from her.

She stepped out into the main area, looking for walk-ins. A few sat, so she double checked the appointment app on the computer. "Marian? Are you ready?"

"Yes." The girl hopped up and hurried to the chair.

"What can I do for you today?" She draped the apron over and around her client.

"I want something different, but am afraid of getting a disaster."

"Hmm." Mandy tested a strand of hair from the back, then front. "You have a lot of natural body, but have straightened it all out. Would you want those fresh new beachy waves? It's a little early for summer, but you might find the style faster in the mornings."

"Would it be a drastic change? Or how about pulling it back for sports?"

She ran her fingers through the client's hair. "I can leave enough for a ponytail, sure, and the only huge change would be the texture."

"Let's do it."

Mandy led her to the sinks, laying a towel down for her neck and warming up the water to a comfortable temperature. She began washing and glanced over at all the others in the salon. No one talked, very odd for her crew. She rinsed and worked in a healthy amount of deep conditioner through the hair. Another rinse and she wrapped the towel around her client's head. "Last chance to reconsider your cut."

"I'm good,"

Barb spoke first. "Did you hear about Sabrina Walker? One of Neil's regulars came in right after and told us everything."

She might have known her crew had heard the news. Most likely, she'd learn more here than at dinner tonight. "Ah, so I probably don't know any more than you all."

Everyone tsk-tsked and Mandy added, "However it shakes out, I promised Mrs. Walker I'd help Sabrina. I thought it was me and how special I was to be asked until I'd heard her talk to several others about helping her clear her former daughter-in-law." She measured the cuts, double checking their length.

"I'm sure they all agreed. Who could refuse such a sweet lady, anyway?" Barb walked her client to the front.

Neil grinned at Mandy as he removed his own client's apron. "I think the important thing is who's minding the store while you're out running around gathering evidence? Won't Dr. Hottie be lonely without you?"

Her client cut a glance at Neil. "A lonely doctor, huh?"

Mandy shook her head. "No, you're what, in grade eleven? Far too young for him." She grinned at Marian's pout and gave her a large hand mirror. "I'll check and see if he has a brother that's his equal, okay?"

Neil nodded. "Take her up on it, sweetie. Her doctor is a great guy."

"I like it," said Marian. "Both my hair and the younger brother."

"Good girl and thank you." Mandy removed the apron, careful to keep her client's clothes hair free. She led the girl to the register and settled up. Once the door closed behind her, she asked, "So are we caught up for now? I have the payroll to do."

Everyone talked at once, shooing her back into the office for counting out their money. Mandy laughed and spent the rest of the afternoon hunched over her computer. By the time she looked up, it was dark outside. Still, she could cross off both finances and next week's schedule on the must do list. Her phone buzzed on the wood desk.

How bout midlevel restaurant for dinner? Meet u there?

Betrayal

Nice place. She smiled, ignoring the jumping carp feeling in her stomach. *Sure. @ 8?*

Gr8! See what I did? Gr eight is great.

Some things hadn't changed since school. His lame humor, for one. *Yeah, ha ha, hilarious.*

By 7:45, Mandy arrived on Midlevel's threshold. Even outside, the food smelled amazing. She wiped a palm on her pants before grabbing the door handle to the place. This will be fun, she told her nerves. She liked Evan. He liked her. They'd have a very good time, and she wouldn't feel weird about Aaron.

The host looked up from the podium. "Ma'am?"

"Yes, I'm here to meet someone named Evan. Is he here, yet?"

He scanned the chart. "Um, yes. Right, this way."

She followed the guy to where Evan sat waiting for her. He stood, his appearance taking her a little aback. He'd grown up in a good way. Tall, fair-haired, and his physique had filled out nicely. His eyes were the same light blue. Evan was a nice slice of masculinity. He wasn't wearing a uniform, and now, Mandy almost wished he was.

"Wow, Mandy, you look great!" He went up to her, bypassing a handshake for a hug. "Thanks for meeting me here."

"No, I should be thanking you." She let him hold her a little, surprised at how solid he felt. A little dazed by his strength, Mandy added, "I'm sure you have better things to do."

He let go of her to pull out her chair. "Trust me. I have nothing better to do than to take a beautiful woman to dinner."

His consideration surprised and pleased her as she settled into her seat. "Oh, ha! Tonight will be more like hanging out and letting me ask questions about Craig's death."

"About that." Evan sat and gave her an intense look. "I do have limits on what I can say, even to you."

She knew that expression too well and laughed. "I'll try not to grill you too much."

"That reminds me." He held up a menu. "I recommend the grilled haddock."

"All right." She glanced over the listing and couldn't find anything better. As soon as they placed their orders, she smiled at Evan. "Tell me what you've been up to lately. You've obviously hit the gym a few times since I last saw you."

He laughed. "Yeah, a couple. I have

to keep in shape running down jaywalkers." Evan leaned back. "I'd spent some time in Toronto working on big city cases but came back when mom got sick."

"I'd heard. Is she getting better?"

"She is, thanks for asking. She's improving all the time."

Mandy wondered if family was the only reason he stayed in town. He had to be somewhat interested in the Maritimes for him to be working here. "Will you go back to the big city, or is Halifax exciting enough for you?"

Evan grinned. "It just got a lot more exciting when I found out about you and Geo."

"Ah, yeah, that was particularly humiliating." She smiled at the waiter when he set down their drinks.

As soon as the server went out of earshot, Evan said, "I'm sorry. You deserve a guy who knows what a treasure you are."

"Doesn't everyone need a person like that?"

"Sure. I know of one man in particular who's somewhat decent and thinks you're incredible."

"Only one?"

He paused as the waiter placed their salads and appetizers. "You're not here because I'm irresistible. You're here to find out more about Sabrina's arrest, right?"

She put a napkin on her lap, toying with her fork. Mandy debated on how much to tell him. Especially since this grown up, Evan appealed a lot more now than he had in high school. "That was my main reason at first."

"Something changed?"

She shrugged. "More like my motives expanded."

"Motives? Speaking my language, gorgeous."

She laughed. "Ok, I'll ignore my urge to protest that. Anyway, I didn't realize how good it'd be to see you. It looks like you're doing well, and I have to admit, you've matured really well."

"So have you. I've seen you around town a few times, but you seemed too busy to stop and talk."

"Oh, I'm sorry I didn't notice you."

He waved her off. "Don't be. You had major upheaval in your life. I've talked to Marty a few times."

Of course, her brother would tell Evan everything. Why not? She shook her head, not happy with Marty. "That little shit."

He choked on his salad. "Miss Sweetness saying what?" He held up a hand before she could protest. "I'm kidding.

We're adults here. So, let's get the Walker case out of the way before our order gets here."

She nodded and tried to be calm. While Evan could be as forthright as Aaron, which was not enough for her curiosity, he'd be able to tell her a different angle. Both men's point of view would give her a much better picture of why Craig had died.

"Let's see, what can I tell you that's not a breach of policy? You know he was cut up, but not with what. Since Sabrina's been arrested, I can admit to the department finding clues at her home, thanks to a tip."

She put down her salad fork and pushed away the empty plate. "Anonymous?"

"Yeah, it was supposed to be. I'm not sure I can admit to knowing who it is." Evan mirrored her actions.

He had to tell her. She leaned forward, murmuring in case anyone eavesdropped, "You know despite the caller being anonymous?"

"One of the guys recognized the voice from someone we'd brought in for questioning."

Mandy almost cackled with glee, knowing the suspect list just got smaller. "Chances are, the person who called in the tip could have planted the evidence."

"Not likely." He waited while the server placed their meals. "We're good, thank you." As soon as they were somewhat alone again, Evan continued, "This isn't public knowledge, but Sabrina had one of those tiny garden hoes in her shed, all bent up and rusty. The detectives used luminal and found blood. She verified it was hers, and we only found her prints. No planted evidence."

"Oh no." She stared at her food. Is Sabrina in real trouble?"

"Yeah, and I hope this doesn't upset your stomach, but the hoe was almost a perfect fit for the murder weapon."

"Almost? But it isn't?"

"Nice try." He began cutting up his steak. "I don't blame you for asking. There's a lot more detail I could go into but won't. Let's just say, thanks to the conditions we found him in and the information from the second Mrs. Walker, Sabrina is our only suspect."

She already dreaded telling Craig's mother that her former favourite daughter-in-law was the culprit. "So there's no one else even close to being the murder?"

"I've hit and plowed through my limit of what I can tell you." He put down his fork, staring her in the eyes as if ordering her. "I'm hoping this stays out of your salon

Betrayal

entirely."

"It doesn't even get near there." She had missed his intense expression and those baby blues still charmed her. Leaning back, she smiled at his hair dark at the roots, growing out the summer sun bleach. He'd be a dark blond by April and a light blond by September. It was a small detail, but Mandy liked knowing that about him. "Why did we break up, again?"

"I was an idiot and wanted to keep my options open while at the academy."

She laughed at his shamed face. He'd always been honest with her and after Geo? Honesty was her favourite policy. "That was probably for the best, all those cute girls in uniform."

"They were nice, but now? I wouldn't mind reliving the past and being a part of your future."

"Oh?" She took a long drink of water before responding. "Well, I'm a little bit new to dating."

"How long were you and Geo married?"

"Five years." Mandy refrained from adding the months and days to the count. "Or not that long if you take into account all the time he spent with other women."

Evan frowned. "I've seen him in the garage. Nice looking guy."

"Yeah, lots of people think so." She pushed away her plate and placed the napkin on the table.

He shrugged. "Giving one of us common guys a chance might work out better for you."

She laughed, not giving into the urge to argue his looks with him. "Fishing for compliments?"

"Hey, whatever gets your attention." He leaned forward, pushing back his plate and putting his hands on the table. "Being serious for a moment, I need to confess something. I didn't expect to miss you so much. Not until I saw you again. You were my first love and I believe we should try a relationship. Find out if it works now that we're mature."

Dinner didn't sit well in her stomach at his declaration. They'd been distant friends since the breakup. And now? A lot of time had passed, too much for them to pick up where they left off. She motioned for their server, and when he came over, Mandy said, "Separate checks, please."

"Is that my answer?"

His sad expression hurt her heart but didn't change her mind. "It's a maybe. We're here because I want to help Sabrina." When the waiter returned, she signed the receipt and retrieved her credit card. "It's been a long time, Evan, and I'm fresh out of a bad marriage. Any relationship we renew is a happy accident."

He stood, going over to help her with her chair. "Fair enough. Can I text you sometime? Maybe ask you out?"

She walked out of the restaurant with him and squeezed his arm. "Haven't you already? I can't guarantee my schedule will be clear."

"Of course not. You're gorgeous, smart, charming, wait, are you seeing someone already?"

She bit her lip, not sure how much he wanted to hear. "A little. Okay, yes. I'm seeing someone. I like him, but have no idea where the future is for us."

"That's fine." He held the restaurant door open for her. "No ring means I have a chance. So expect me to ask you to the movies or something this Saturday."

She clicked the unlock button on her keychain, liking how he walked her to her car. "Should I wait until you text me then?"

"No. You should plan on me picking you up on Saturday." Evan pulled her into his arms. "I'll text you what time I'm off work before then."

She laughed at his nerve then froze as he moved in for a kiss. Their lips met, and he groaned, hugging her closer. He radiated warmth, and she shivered. He held her close against him, his body hard against hers. Her mind compared his every touch against how Aaron had felt when doing the same to her.

Evan pulled back. "I'm sorry. You're freezing, and I'm thinking about how good you feel."

"It's fine. I'm glad you're so warm."

"Saturday, then?"

Her mind froze, unable to remember when she'd promised Aaron their sleepover. He'd never said, and she couldn't remember how the schedule went at the hospital. "Saturday," she squeaked. "Saturday is good."

Chapter 5

Aaron opened his eyes at the annoying noise. His head ached from more than usual beers he'd needed to sleep last night. He grabbed his phone, hoping for a text from Mandy. No such luck, just an alarm.

He had crashed early last night and didn't hear her come home. Still, she might have been quiet. He'd have to get up to look for her car. After considering getting out of bed for a moment, he knew he couldn't. If she walked up while he stepped out in his pajamas, she'd know he had been hopping from one foot to the other, waiting.

Imagining her reaction to him peeking out for her had him pause. If Mandy caught him checking up on her, would that be the worst thing to ever happen? He turned on the shower on his way to the coffee maker. She knew he cared for her. He undressed and hurried under the hot spray. Melting in the warmth, his fretting over her possibly spending the night with that guy nagged at him like a mosquito in summer. A hungry one, too.

Toweled off and in clean clothes, he double checked his texts while a couple of frozen waffles heated in the toaster. Jackpot!

One from Mandy waited for him.

Hi! Evan says Sabrina is stubborn, thinks Debbi killed Craig with Ken's help. E also says S is crazy. I don't know what to think.

His waffles popped up just as he was starting a reply. He could talk easier while eating than text, so Aaron hit the back button. Once his plate was ready, he called her.

"Good morning and you got my text?"

"Yep, and I agree on not knowing what to think."

"I want to believe this was an accident more and more. Plus, neither wife nor ex had a good motive for killing him. Even Sabrina loved him. She's not the 'if I can't no one can have him' type."

"I totally agree and asked Evan what the evidence said. All he could tell me was no one stood out as a likely suspect."

"So he's back to square one?"

"Pretty much. Sabrina wanted him to recheck the boat, there had to be blood evidence they'd missed. Evan told me there wasn't anything on or under deck they didn't know about. Still, I'm dying to have lunch at the marina and 'accidently' look around.

He nodded. "Maybe peek under

those cushions we sat on, or check the mattress for blood. No one gets cut up like that and just falls overboard without a trace until they hit the shore. We could meet there in a couple of hours. I'm eating breakfast now, but can be hungry by then."

"I can't. Edie called in sick at the last minute, and I'm booked until closing."

"In time for dinner?"

"They don't serve it, and since Debbi goes there, Sabrina doesn't anymore. It's kind of the place to be seen and the lobster rolls are amazing."

He paused the waffle laden fork. "Really? I might go for lunch and stay to check out the boat."

"I had you at the lobster roll, didn't I?"

"Of course. Do you want me to drop one off at your salon for you, too?"

"It hurts to say this, but no. We have a takeaway order called in already. Oh, there's my next customer. Next time for sure?"

"You bet. I'll text if I find out anything."

"Thanks, I appreciate that. Bye."

"Bye." He smiled while tapping his phone. Hearing her voice had brightened his whole day. Aaron seriously doubted he'd learn anything on the boat, even if he could get on board. Still, lobster rolls. That was reason enough to hang out at the yacht club. Before he could clean up, his phone buzzed with a text.

Wear what you would to work & use dad's name to get in. He has a membership.

His eyebrows rose at the information. Shawn Hays must have thought the cost was worth it to his business. Aaron resumed is cleanup and headed out to his car. Access to a beautiful place on the marina was one small reason among many larger ones as to why he enjoyed having Mandy in his life.

He found a place to park at the club. As he'd expected, the wind from the Atlantic chilled him to the bones. Yet, the temperature seemed warmer than the Pacific gales he'd experienced all his life. Aaron grinned at how thin his blood had become in the more temperate Maritimes. He went inside, giving the hostess Shawn's name as Mandy had suggested. Soon, he was settled in with an order placed and a warm mocha in front of him.

Just past the marina, the harbor still bustled with activity. He shuddered and wondered at how long Craig had floated in that hidden cove before being discovered. As if on cue, his food arrived. "Thank you."

The waiter refilled his half-empty

Betrayal

water glass. "Let me know if you need anything else, sir."

"You bet. Thanks." He bit into the sandwich and had to agree with Mandy. The fresh butter-soaked lobster melted on his tongue. He set down the roll and realized this was the beginning of a hard new addiction. In theory, he wasn't hungry, yet wanted to order a freezer full of the sandwiches for later. And not share with Mandy.

Sunlight glinted off of the white boats and water. Still, he must have caught Mandy's curiosity like the common cold because he watched to see for anything suspicious. The gashes on Craig's body wouldn't leave Aaron alone. He'd seen how deep they cut into the man's flesh when EMTs brought him in. He shuddered and put down the roll for a moment. He took a sip of water, a couple catching his eye. As they approached the club from the walkway, he realized they were Ken and Debbi. He continued to eat and watched to see if they left or came in for lunch, too.

They stopped, huddled together and both leaning against the rails. He didn't blame them, considering the cold. They stood too far away for him to read their lips. From where he sat, Aaron could at least see their body language. The actions, if he didn't know their relationship already, said they were good friends.

The couple stared out at the harbor, Aaron assumed. Ken held her, with Debbi's head resting on his shoulder. She'd look up at him every so often. They'd talk before she'd settle in against him again. After another couple of minutes, they walked away, hand in hand.

He sipped the lukewarm coffee. If a romance blossomed now between the widow and her husband's business partner, fine. He drained the last bit in his cup, enjoying the whipped cream. He motioned to his waiter and stood, stretching his left leg to warm it up for walking back to his car.

"Your check, sir?"

"Yes, please, and add another lobster roll to it."

"Very well, sir. Give me ten minutes."

As the waiter left to fill the order, Aaron sat. The place had become crowded since he had arrived. Every window table had customers. Worse, those people would see him go out to the Walker's boat and if anything happened? Witnesses could place him there. He'd rather text Mandy about Ken and Debbi and wanted to suggest Evan spray under the cushions and mattress with Luminol.

Betrayal

He checked the time and had long enough to swing by the hospital to check Craig's records before signing into work. If the medical examiner was there, Aaron could ask for theories on what had cut up the body. Was it Sabrina with a kitchen knife, Debbie with a meat cleaver, or Ken with an ax? Or even someone in a random attack? Autopsy records would list what Craig had in his pockets or more revealing, what he didn't have on him at the time of death.

He glanced up to see his server with a white paper bag and his check. "Here you are and keep the change," he said, giving the man a fifty.

"Thank you, and have a nice afternoon."

"Will do." A while later, he parked in the hospital's front lot, using the main door to enter. Coming in through ER might get him snagged to work. Aaron grinned and nodded in greeting to the information desk lady as he passed by her. She had that "You look familiar, but I don't know you" gleam in her eye. He took the elevator down to the basement, soon finding the medical examiner's office.

The office light was on and the door ajar, so he gave a light knock. "Hey, Dr. Stephens?"

"Yes?" The older man stood. "May I

help you?"

"We've not met formally, just in the ER. I'm Dr. Aaron Nicholson." He and Dr. Stephens shook hands.

"Ah, yes. I thought I knew you from somewhere. Alive, too."

Aaron already liked this guy's sense of humor and reciprocated. "Thanks, that's my preference."

Dr. Stephen's silver hair glinted under the florescent lighting as he went back to his desk. "But you didn't come down here to shoot the breeze. Hope it wasn't to hang out with the cadavers."

He chuckled. "No, not this time. I'm actually here because a friend of mine can't let go of something in the Craig Walker case."

"Oh? Who is this person and why do they care?"

He refused to squirm under the older man's piercing gaze. This wasn't university and not a pop quiz. "She's just a friend of both the victim and me. And a friend of the victim's entire family, past and present. All of us." So much for playing it cool.

"I see." He drummed his fingers on the desk before motioning to Aaron to take a seat opposite him. "What does she think you're going to tell her? Most of what we do is confidential."

"That's precisely the problem." He pulled out a chair, the bottom of the legs squeaking against the floor. "She's asking questions that I can't answer for her."

Stephens nodded. "Good thing you don't."

"But they do get me to thinking about how Walker died."

"Or what killed him."

Aaron leaned forward, easing the stiffness in his leg. "Exactly. Someone's been arrested for the crime and my friend isn't convinced the former Mrs. Walker is guilty. What if you know the detainee couldn't have done the crime?"

"There's no possibility?" At Aaron's nod, Stephens continued, "Then, I tell the detectives handling the case as soon as I can. I have an obligation to get justice or closure for the victim."

"I might find out more tonight on what the authorities suspect happened."

"Ah, but what they suspect or believe doesn't matter. The facts are the facts. The only reason I'm telling you is because you saw it all for yourself when he arrived."

He recalled, "Mr. Walker was bludgeoned around the head and shoulders, with several evenly spaced lacerations down his left arm and back."

Stephens stood. "Come with me to the cafeteria and I'll let you buy me a drink."

"Sure, be glad to and I appreciate your candor." Aaron followed him out to the hallway, waiting as the older man locked the office. "Do you know if the head trauma or the slices killed him?"

"You're forgetting drowning, but no, before you ask, drowning didn't." He held open the stairway door. "It's almost as if two people attacked him, someone with a lead pipe and the other with a meat cleaver."

Aaron ignored his tendons protesting as he walked. "Two killers? Walker was supposed to be alone on the boat."

"Then that rules out my second theory, him hitting his head a few times and falling into a giant paper shredder." They entered the cafeteria. "Since there are no schools of sharp objects roaming free in the Atlantic, I'd say the victim has two very determined enemies."

Chapter 6

Mandy turned the key in her front door's lock. Today could not be over soon enough. Her feet hurt. Her stomach ached from a very early lunch and no snack in between. A glass of wine sounded perfect right now. Aaron's door opening caught her attention, and she turned to see him.

"Hey! Hello! I'll just go and get some vegetables I found yesterday." He left his apartment open and disappeared inside.

She followed him in, asking, "What are you doing home, handsome?"

He stopped at that, turned, and pulled her into his arms. "Dinner break, beautiful. A couple of interns are covering for me, and I'm taking advantage before we lose them to Cape Breton at the end of the week."

"What happens then?" She leaned back a little to look up into his eyes.

"Then Dr. Shaw and I trade off until we get another doctor to share the fun."

"Ah, so you're not off for very long?" she asked. When he shook his head, she gave him another hug before pulling away and said, "Grab some veggies while I get into sweats. Let yourself in if I'm not ready before you are."

"Great."

Once inside with her bedroom door shut, she began shedding clothes, not taking her time to put anything away. She smelled food cooking and grinned at her reflection in the mirror. It wasn't a lobster roll but made her hungry anyway. Her stomach growled an agreement.

He stirred onions simmering in a pan of her garlic infused olive oil. "I had a very productive day today. Lots to tell."

"Oh?" She took a bottle of wine from the fridge and opened it. "Want some? Oh, wait. You can't."

"Nope, but go ahead." He waited while she poured a glass. "A lot has happened since we last talked."

Mandy settled into the kitchen chair. "Tell me all about it while you cook."

Aaron laughed. "Sure. First thing I have to ask is if you're all right."

She waved off his concern. "I'm fine. Just a stressful day. It's actually nice you're taking over in here."

"My pleasure." He added fresh asparagus spears to the pan, stirred to coat them, and turned to her. "I'm not sure where to start. At what the ME told me, or about seeing Ken consoling the grieving widow."

She stopped toying with her wine glass and sat up straighter. The guy had serious news. "Oh wow. Tell me about Ken and Debbie first."

"I did as you suggested, of course, and had the lobster roll." He pointed to a bag next to the stove. "We're splitting one with caramelized onions and asparagus."

Her mouth dropped before she grinned. "You're sharing your lunch with me?"

"Not quite. I had all my lunch, but ordered another for dinner." He began fixing himself a glass of ice water. "When I had the chance to come home and share, I took it. Thanks for letting me use your dad's name to get in. If I had a boat, I'd get a membership, too."

She made a mental note to do something just as special for him. "He just has the access, not the boat. He says getting one will be his retirement gift. But back to our dynamic duo. Were they acting romantic or just walking close together?"

"Walking at first. Both looked out over the harbor, toward the lighthouse on that one little island—"

"Georges Island," she offered. "It's where Geo got his name."

"Geo from George?" He paused before going back to stir the vegetables. "I didn't see anything overtly improper, but if I didn't know them, I'd suspect they were dating at least."

"Wow. That's really suspicious." She chewed on her lip for a moment before asking, "I'm not sure what to think."

He shrugged. "It makes me wonder if Sabrina is right, but doesn't prove anything. The two of them are good friends."

"You mentioned the medical examiner?" Mandy prodded, hoping he'd spill everything.

"Yeah, and I can't tell you much. He said how he suspected homicide, but thinks two people were involved."

"Two killers? Sabrina didn't do it, then." She poured the last bit of wine into her glass. "Or maybe Debbi had Ken help her."

Aaron nodded. "So, you're finishing the bottle, and you never do that. What's wrong?"

Mandy debated about being honest with him. Her clinging to him while begging him to stay in Halifax wouldn't work, so she hedged a little and deflected. "I'd hoped to hear more from you."

"Wow." He turned down the heat and sat opposite her. "You do know I can't tell you as much as I'd like to, right?"

She didn't say anything for a moment. "Sometimes I think Evan trusts me more than you do." Mandy crossed her arms and leaned back in the chair.

He narrowed his eyes. "What makes you think that?"

Uncomfortable with the eye contact, she looked away first and stared at the last bit of wine in her glass. "He told me all about the evidence they'd found at Sabrina's and why they think she killed Craig. And, he said all this last night while we were out."

Aaron nodded and went back to the stove. "And I didn't tell you anything I knew until just now?"

She didn't like his frown as he'd left the table. Nothing else about his body language said anger, but the disappointment showed in his eyes. "Something like that, yes."

"It's because I didn't learn anything until this afternoon. You were at work. I don't like to call when you're busy." Aaron set her plate of food in front of her and sat without his. "Is that all, or are there other issues between us I need to resolve?"

She glanced at him. His question amazed her. If he were her ex, he'd have already run like a scurvy dog. Mandy shook her head. "No. No other." She picked up her half of the roll and lifted it a bit. "Are you going to eat, too?"

He stood and retrieved his own food, saying over his shoulder, "I am. After you're done telling me what's bothering you."

"Nothing really." She laughed at his raised eyebrow and speared an asparagus. "All right. I'm worried about our sleepover. I know it's no big deal, that we're just good friends, but I'm concerned about afterward."

Aaron sat with his plate. "My plans are for us to be friends then, too."

"Yeah." She pushed the food around, not hungry now. "You should know, I'm not a good candidate for friends with benefits. I get too attached and am going to want more. What happens when you move back to Vancouver, and I'm in love with you? I can't leave my business and family."

"That's a great question, and I wish I had an equal answer." He fidgeted in his chair before poking at a bite of lobster. "I have too much going on at home to start something here with you. I can't promise anything."

She pushed her plate away. The few bites she'd had were excellent, but now? "Aaron. I've known all along you hadn't planned on staying here, but when you extended your lease to six months at a time? And then planning a sleepover?" Mandy couldn't look him in the eyes. "I'd begun to believe in something between us, eventually."

He scooted the chair back and took

her plate. "I still do want to move back home and know that's a huge problem." Aaron put her dinner into a couple of plastic containers for later. After placing tomorrow's lunch in the fridge, he went back and sat down in front of her. "As long as we're being honest, I'll admit I woke up this morning thinking about you and your dinner date last night."

She got up and grabbed his empty glass. "Just dinner."

"Yeah, but I don't know what to do about this Evan guy. It pisses me off every time you say his name."

"Should I call him something else? Like Fred or Barney?" She grinned at his laugh and refilled his water.

"How about Gone? Absent, Moved, Not Here all work for me as new names for him." He took the glass. "Thanks. Seriously, I know I ran away from a mess in Vancouver, but I like it here, really like you, and wouldn't mind living here permanently." He reached out and caressed her arm when she walked past him on her way to the fridge. "But until everything's settled back home, I can't promise anything."

She retrieved a bottle of cheaper wine and a bottle of sparkling water. As she returned, Mandy ruffled his hair. "You're a dog in the manger, like Aesop's Fables."

"The one where the dog didn't want anyone to touch his hay, and he didn't want the hay for himself?"

She nodded, liking his smile and how he helped her pull the stubborn cork out of the bottle. "Yes, exactly. You're the dog, and I'm the hay."

"That's crazy. Evan can want you. That's not a problem." Aaron crossed his arms. "I just don't want him to have you."

Mandy grinned at him while pouring a glass of half wine and half sparkling water. "Not your call at this point, sweetheart."

"I don't like how right you are. We're running out of my dinner time, so let's move on." He set his fork down on the empty plate and got up, putting all the dishes in the sink. "Did Evan mention anything else about the suspect's weapon?"

She stood to help wash, unsteady thanks to sore feet from a heavy work day and good wine. "I can't say because he couldn't tell me."

"Sure. They have to keep some facts back to confirm any confession."

"Right, it seems they found evidence at Sabrina's, you know, and that evidence has blood on it. They're running tests to see if the DNA matches Craig's, but it's a sure bet."

Betrayal

He paused for a moment before handing her a rinsed plate. "What did he say had the blood on it?"

"All I can tell you is he knows what weapon it was, and that's all you get."

Aaron chuckled and shook his head. "Unless Sabrina ran him over with a field plow, I don't think anything she has on hand could do what the killer did to him."

She almost laughed at this tidbit of information. Mandy acted unconcerned as she put a second dish in the dishwasher. "Are the wounds pretty bad, then?"

"Very." He held up a soapy finger, pointing it at her. "This goes nowhere." She nodded, and he continued, "The medical examiner probably told the police already, and I shouldn't admit anything to you. But, I'm starting to believe Sabrina couldn't have murdered her ex-husband. The cuts on his body were too deep and sharp for anything from a household to cause."

She wondered if a garden hoe counted as a household item and guessed yes. "Hmm. So how do we prove Sabrina's innocence and someone else's guilt?"

"Wait for the blood tests to come back. Unless the evidence is old and, Craig has scars from a prior altercation with a rake—"

"Or something similar to but not

quite it?"

"Exactly. I had expected the tests to come back as not his blood." Aaron shrugged. "They'll have to let her go."

"I'd hoped we'd solve something tonight, but now all I want to do is snoop around on those two."

"You and me both." He watched as she dried and put away her dishes. "Do you think your cop friend will tell you anything more if Debbi is brought in?"

"I'm not sure, but can ask when I see him again."

He went to the table with a rag, wiping it down. "A Saturday night is pretty serious in the dating world, isn't it? Not like a Friday or Sunday."

Mandy followed, pushing in the chairs. She tried to not smile at how hung up he seemed about her seeing Evan. "Yeah, usually, even if Sundays and Mondays are more my weekends."

She followed him out into the living room and hugged him. His smell held her as much as his arms and the warm spicy scent seduced her. Enveloped in his warmth and strength, she struggled to keep the urge to go further than casual. "You're really a great guy."

"Says the brilliant and beautiful gal." He gave an extra squeeze before letting her go and getting his coat. "See you later but not tomorrow night, even if I get another dinner break?"

She laughed at his frown. "You're going to be bitter about that for a while, aren't you?"

"Absolutely," he teased with a wink before pulling her into his arms. "No, I'm okay with you hanging out with him. You're friends."

"We are. And I consider you and me as more than friends."

"Good." He held her closer. "I have time for a few smooches before needing to go."

"Let's get started then." Mandy leaned forward and kissed him. She smiled when he groaned. His lips against hers felt so perfect it scared her.

He broke away to rest his cheek against hers. "I don't want to be late."

"You don't." She took a step back. "Will you get a chance tomorrow for—" Mandy began.

"Yes, but no. You won't be here." He gave her another quick kiss. "I need to go get my coat and don't worry. We'll work something out tomorrow or even Sunday."

"All right. See you soon." As soon as the door closed behind him, she locked it and sank down on her sofa. If her phone weren't in her purse, the alarm unset, Mandy would pass out where she sat. "Ugh," she said, standing back up. Fear, rebound, or anything else didn't matter. She'd marry the next guy who massaged her feet, no questions asked.

The next evening, Aaron paused at Mandy's door. After yesterday's discussion about their relationship, she had been on his mind all night and day. He'd spent a sleepless morning mulling over returning to Vancouver versus staying in Halifax. Her car was parked downstairs, probably because Evan had picked her up so he decided against seeing if she had time for a quick visit.

He opened up his place which now seemed sad without her. Aaron shook off the lonely feeling. He'd always been fine before now. Girlfriends and even friends came and went. He'd be fine.

In the middle of making hot chocolate, a knock on his door startled him. Mandy usually tapped a lot lighter than this. He went to the peephole first and saw someone at her door, not his. Tall, blond, and when he turned his head to look down at the parking lot, he had a decent profile.

Aaron had to admit he was okay for a guy. Not liking the feeling he was spying,

Betrayal

he backed away in time to hear her greet her date. He couldn't hear words, just the tones. The guy even sounded attractive. Aaron hated him. He ignored the feeling. Evan and Mandy were just friends. Only a jerk wouldn't want to see her happy when he wasn't around, right?

This cop even looked like her ex-husband. Clearly, she had a preference for blondes. Didn't matter to him. If this Evan were dark haired, he'd still dislike him. Aaron went to the microwave to warm his cold drink. He waited for the countdown to zero. The real possibility of the cop spending the night with her had him gritting his teeth. Why wouldn't the guy, if Mandy were interested? She was a beautiful, sexy woman and Evan might be ready for a relationship, something he couldn't guarantee at the moment.

"Damn it all to hell." A wise man would have hidden out in the cafeteria with an e-book to avoid seeing another man take the walk of shame from Mandy's house in the morning. "I'm an idiot." Disgusted with his emotions, Aaron made a hot tea, grabbed a small package of cookies, and swiped on his phone.

Right in the middle of his go-to book for cheering himself up, a call came in from his brother. He let it ring a few times and picked up before voicemail could. "Hey, Brad. What's up?"

"Nothing much, just wondering how you are."

If he'd gotten take out Chinese food at lunch, the fortune cookie would have said, "Your day is hosed. So is your night." He did not want to say anything to the reprobate he had as a last remaining family member. For propriety's sake, Aaron replied, "I'm fine. You? Doing well, I bet."

"I'm ok. They kept me on at work, thanks to my lawyer."

When Brad paused for a while, Aaron didn't rush in to continue the conversation. He'd done that enough for a lifetime. After a "You there?" from his brother, he said, "Sure. I don't have a whole lot new going on, so, I'm letting you talk."

"Oh." The seconds stretched out until Brad said, "Didn't you move, or quit, or something?"

Aaron grimaced at the accusatory tone ringing through the words. "I did all the above. Figured it was time for a fresh start."

"You weren't here to pick me up when they released me from the center."

He coughed, wanting to give a smart-assed response. Aaron took in a calming breath. "No, I thought you might have someone else drive you home."

Betrayal

"I wanted to say sorry."

"I guessed that from the voice mails you left." He closed the e-book app, giving up on reading anymore "They all said you were sorry, too."

"You don't have to be a dick about it."

Aaron grinned. There it was. His brother's best side, and so soon? "Nice. You're still calling me up like we're buddies or something, so yeah, I do." The phone clicked off, and he laughed. Just as well. Two more sentences and the jackass would be asking for money. The phone rang again, and he laughed at the caller ID. "Feeling bad already? Sorry, but I'm not loaning you any money. You have a job."

"I also have legal bills. And you have plenty of money. Mom and dad would want you to help me."

"Are you fucked in the head?" Another click and he'd been hung up on again. This time served Aaron right, but still. Brad playing the dead parents card pissed him off every time. He sent his brother a text saying, "I'll be at work until 4 am tomorrow. Don't call," and turned on the airplane mode for his phone.

He had no more time to read, now, so finished up his tea and ate the last cookie. Once outside, Aaron eased down the stairs.

He went a step at a time, pausing in the middle. The sudden cold snap and being on his feet for hours at a time irritated his healing knee.

"Hey, you need help, buddy?"

Aaron glanced back to see a youngish guy walking down the stairs behind him. "Naw, I'm good. Thanks."

"Sure. Looks like you wrecked a hammy at the gym."

He glanced at the man, trying really hard to not like him. Evan seemed the kind of guy who'd be easy to be friends with. "Not the gym, more like a hiking accident." Aaron hugged the side railing. "You can go on. No need to wait for me."

"Ok. I don't mind breaking your fall when it happens."

"When? And here I was just now, thinking you were decent."

He laughed. "Fooled you, huh?" He loitered at the bottom. "When did your accident happen?"

"Thanksgiving Day," Aaron replied

"Running off the turkey?"

He grinned at the remark. "Something like that, yeah." He had a tough time admitting to anyone in Halifax but Mandy about Brad's shoving him off a cliff.

Last time he went to court, he testified about the impersonation mess, how

Betrayal

Brad had taken his ID and signed in as Aaron everywhere. And while he should practice saying, "My brother tried to kill me," out loud, just not now. He took the last step, looking the suspected Evan in the eyes, and tried to hate him.

"All right. I'll quit hovering." He tilted his head. "Mandy mentioned having a doctor for a neighbour."

Aaron grinned. Talked about him, did she? He liked that, a lot. "That would be me."

"Cool." He unlocked the car door with the key fob. "Probably catch ya later, then."

"Probably so. Take care." He unlocked his own vehicle, waving when Evan drove out first. Good looking, great guy, and Aaron already liked him despite himself. Mandy did, of course, or the guy wouldn't be wandering in and out of her place like it had a revolving door. Asshole.

Laura Stapleton

Chapter 7

Aaron walked into the ER a little less angry but still not thrilled about Mandy seeing Evan. He checked in, determined the matter to the back of his mind. He stared at his patient list and then beyond as a few of nurses came in for their shifts. Several of them were cute and single. He could always date someone else.

His cell phone vibrated again with a half dozen messages from Brad waited, distracting him, and Aaron didn't want to deal with anything right now. Not his brother, his lack of a love life, Mandy's former boyfriends reappearing. None of it.

"Dr. Nicholson, do you have a minute?"

He turned to see the medical examiner behind him. "Yes, and from this chart, it's exactly one."

Dr. Stephens laughed and said, "I understand. Let's find a quieter area."

Aaron followed the other doctor to an empty room. "I assume you found something vastly interesting?"

Stephens shut the door and went to his desk. "His tox screen came back clean. He had some alcohol and analgesics in his system."

"Not enough to kill him?" He took

the medical examiner's lead and half sat on the desk in a mirror image of the older man.

"No, not usually, and I don't think that's what did it to him." Stephens thought for a moment and added, "Walker was dead before he hit the water."

He frowned at the news and almost blurted out a "Duh," before catching himself. "I'm assuming the blood force trauma or slices killed him."

Stephens shrugged. "I thought so, too."

"But they didn't?" At the censoring look from him, Aaron chuckled. "Right, you can't say. Is there anything else you can tell me?"

"I called the cops this morning with the results. The first Mrs. Walker should be released, and the charges dropped sometime soon."

He sighed, thrilled for Sabrina's sake. "Thanks for telling me as much as you did."

"You're welcome. I appreciate your keeping quiet about it." He opened the door and ushered out Aaron first. "Besides, I knew they had the wrong suspect and figured you did, too."

"You did?"

"Sure. You were the first person here to see the body, how the wounds first appeared." He patted Aaron's back in a fatherly *we're done here* way. "Go from there and you'll get what happened. Catch you later."

"All right." He turned back to the emergency area. Later, when the patient flow slowed, he'd go over what he remembered about Walker's body. The living needed him more at the moment.

He grabbed a chart, amused as usual by how they still used paper here. There were worse things, and he liked the clipboard and paper. Soon enough, the hospital would be all digital. His phone buzzed again, irritating him. He grabbed it, checking the sender. Mandy? He didn't have time for a conversation but had to check anything from her.

"Evan gave me info, busy now?"

Aaron responded with a quick, *I am, but curious too*

Sabrina to be free soon.

Good! He grimaced at his next thought. He didn't have time for this but couldn't stop himself from adding, *Met Evan outside this evening. Great guy.*

He's awesome, went out and retrieved take out for us.

He chuckled. *Poor girl, dinner in with two guys two nights in a row?*

Yep. Doing something wrong. Need a

better class of boyfriends, lol!

His breath caught at her message. *Or I need to step up my game.*

Sorry, autocorrect, meant BOY friends.

Aaron frowned at what seemed to be a demotion in relationship status. He didn't need to let her know that in a text. Showing her the next night he had free appealed to him a lot more. He smiled and texted, *No worries. I'm good either way.*

Ok! Want an early dinner or late lunch before work tomorrow? I'll clear my schedule if you say yes.

He grinned, liking how much she wanted to see him. Sure, a Sunday date wasn't quite as serious as a Saturday one, but as she said, their weekends were not the norm. When hearing his name over the paging system, he typed back, *You bet, girl friend! Gotta run but want to talk.*

Great! See you when?

Two! Can't wait! He automatically hit send and instantly regretted doing so. It was too much. Shit. He put away his phone before adding anything else stupid. Aaron shook off the feeling by focusing on work. He'd either ignore or deal with the whole boy friend and girl friend issue tomorrow over dinner.

Betrayal

Mandy walked into her business a few minutes until ten in the morning. A client sat in her assistant manager's styling chair. She went over to them, a little surprised and pleased at how she'd started working before opening the salon. "Fiona, I'm taking off part of the afternoon and still plan on closing tonight."

The assistant manager gave her client a hand mirror. "Sure. I'll block off your time on the schedule if you want."

"It's fine. I'll do it in a few minutes," Mandy said.

Fiona smiled at the person in the chair. "What do you think?" She pulled the sides down a little, checking the length. "They look perfectly even."

"I love what you did."

She removed the apron, letting the chair down so the woman could leave. "Hope so. This style should be easier to wash and go in the morning."

The two went to the register while Mandy grabbed a broom and swept clippings. Everyone seemed quieter than usual, giving the shop a library feeling. Once the customer left, she said, "This silence is sort of creeping me out. Everything echoes too much."

"How about some music?" She took the broom and dustpan from her, setting them back in the small closet. "I'll turn on the radio after I put these away. Did you hear? Rumor is Sabrina didn't kill her ex after all."

"And everyone is speechless?"

"Yeah, mostly over who did do it." She paused and motioned for Mandy to follow her into the back area. "There is one other thing. I don't suppose you've Googled your doctor friend, did you?"

A cold lump settled in the pit of her stomach. So Aaron had more skeletons in his closet than being banged up by an asshole brother? She swallowed before answering. "I'd planned on it, but with everything going on, I kept putting it off until later."

"Before Neil tells you, just be warned," Fiona said, leaning in to lower her voice. "Dr. Nicholson was falsely accused of something his brother did. Then, they both had a huge fight on a mountain. Your doctor fell several stories and nearly died. Neil said they had to medivac him out of there."

She closed her open mouth. Apparently, Aaron had left out a lot of the story. She imagined him tumbling down the Rockies in British Columbia and shuddered. "Wow, how horrible."

Her assistant manager smirked. "Considering it's coming from Neil? I'd say water everything down if you want the truth. Or Google it for yourself."

Mandy leaned against the counter with a sigh. "I'll have to. The two stories don't match at all."

"Happy hunting, Boss. See you Tuesday."

"Sure thing, Fee." She waited until the back door closed with a solid click before sinking into her office chair. Aaron had needed a Medivac just a few months ago? He'd said very little about his past, or at least, not as much as she'd thought.

She settled in behind her computer and flipped on the monitor. Searching Aaron's name resulted in too many hits, so she added more search terms. Headlines with him and Brad also popped up, so she followed them.

A few news items caught her eye. "Brothers Fight in Whytehouse Park. Slow news day, or what?" After clicking the links, Mandy learned Neil had definitely exaggerated a few things. Or maybe the reporter had underreported a few. Either way, Aaron couldn't have been hurt all that bad. He was up, walking, working, and healing just fine.

She hit the back button and kept scrolling for more information. Obituaries popped up, and she learned his parents had died as he'd said, around ten years ago. He'd been younger than Mandy, and she wanted to cry for him. Poor guy. She couldn't begin to think of life without her mom and dad.

Blinking back tears, she went to the bottom of the page and found another interesting link. He'd won some sort of kayaking award, and scuba dived in his spare time? She propped up her chin with her right hand. He'd mentioned his kayak but not scuba gear. Mandy smiled, remembering how they'd met on Halloween. Well after the time cold weather set in and being the last week of January now, he'd have a lot longer before spring. Owning outdoor sports equipment too heavy for a guy with broken ribs to lift meant having a good reason to rent storage.

His brother, Brad piqued her curiosity. She lightly tapped the mouse button, frowning at the screen. A Google search turned up a few items before it went to sites having Brad and Nicholson listed separately. She clicked on Brad's social media link. The attractiveness of the guy surprised her. "Wow," she whispered. He had a charming smile, gorgeous blue eyes, brighter than Aaron's dark gray, and more of a boyishly cute face.

She read some of his public statuses and leaned back in her chair, already

Betrayal

disliking him. Geo was the same type of guy Brad appeared to be. Handsome on the outside, insecure and mean on the inside.

Scrolling on down, closer to the time they'd fought, Brad's social postings turned into more photos of him with his family. Had Aaron seen these? She stared at each one. The times went all over the place. One would be of them as adults, the next, when they were children. She smiled at the happy family. The boys looked a lot like their father and Aaron as almost a young man? She'd have crushed on him for sure. Mandy bet he'd been the cutest little baby. She scrolled down to see if Brad had included anything else.

Her desk phone rang, startling her. "Hello?"

"Mandy!" said Evan. You weren't answering your cell, so I'd hope to catch you at work."

"Oh. I have the volume too low, I guess." She rolled over to her purse and checked. After deleting the call log and turning up the ring tone, she said, "There. I've upped the volume and shall never miss a word from you again."

"Ha ha. The only word I'm thinking of is lunch. Have you eaten yet?"

"I can't. I have plans for an early dinner. We'll have to get together later sometime."

"That's cool. And hey, I need to mention, I met your neighbour this morning."

"Yeah? He's a great guy." She right mouse clicked and saved at his childhood photo on her desktop.

"Yeah, and I was going to tell you more at lunch about how we cleared Sabrina."

Damn! She really wanted to have a sit-down conversation with him. Mandy sighed. This would have to be enough. She went to shut her office door. "I have time for a quick chat, so tell me a little bit now?"

"Turns out it had been snake blood on the spade."

She liked being right about the blood. The extra effort served the entire department right for Evan not listening to her about Sabrina's innocence. "No one minds if you tell me the details?"

"Naw, she's not a suspect anymore. I can't tell you who is next on the list, though. Mainly because we don't have one."

"No idea, seriously?" She bunched up a scrap piece of paper in one hand and threw it at her wastepaper basket. "So Craig's murderer is still out there? What will you do? What can you do?"

"Go back to the scene of the crime.

See what we missed."

She glanced at her watch. She didn't have time. Her next client was due any minute but wanted to hear every little detail. Mandy fidgeted in her chair. Her staff knew to knock when they needed her. She refocused on Evan and his information. "You've been there yourself?"

"At the marina, yes, but I wasn't at the cove where he washed up. The day we found him, his boat was the first thing forensics examined. I was in the car investigation group at the yacht club while the others searched the Walker home for evidence."

Her heart ached for the way they'd found Craig. She imagined hundreds of police swarming all the sites. Maybe not hundreds, since the area's force had to be limited somewhat. He hadn't been dead that long, a week, maybe two. "How many days did it take to do all that?"

"One, because several of us were working at the same time. Sabrina let the team in at her home. We're going back over the boat for anything that makes sense based on the facts so far."

"The boat?" That triggered her memory, and she needed to mention, "You'll find mine and Aaron's prints there. We visited Debbi there a night or two after

Craig's death."

"That doc and you were out there with her? Let me make a note that your prints and shoe impressions will be there. She's not been eliminated as a suspect, yet. If she knows about Sabrina's release? Hell, she could be out of the country by now."

Dread went through her like an electric current. Debbi? Murder? Fugitive? And all because of what Mandy didn't say? "I'm sorry. I should have mentioned something earlier."

"Yeah, I'd have liked that." After a short pause, he continued, "I need to update some reports and review some evidence so we'll link up sometime later? When our schedules clear a little?"

"That'd be great." When he ended the call first, she put the phone down and buried her face in her hands. Mandy had wanted to help find Craig's killer, not make more work for Evan. Since he'd been interested in her and Aaron seeing Debbi at the boat, he might want to hear about Debbi and Ken being friendly at the pier.

She dialed Evan's number. "I'm sorry to bother you so soon, but there's more you need to know."

Chapter 8

Debbi walked into her salon office. "Mandy! You have to help me like you helped Sabrina! A detective called and said if I weren't at the station in an hour, they'd come to get me."

She closed her dropped jaw and stood up, going to her. "Oh no, Debbi, I'm so sorry, but it wasn't me. The police didn't have the evidence and couldn't hold her."

The woman hugged Mandy, saying, "I don't know what they have on me. I'm so scared I'm going to fry."

She tried not to smile at how someone was watching way too much television from the States. Mandy patted her back, wanting to ease the other woman's panic. "You're not going to fry. We don't have a death penalty here, remember?" She let go of Debbi. "Besides, you didn't do it, and they'll soon find that out when you talk to them again." She motioned for her to take a seat opposite. "Do you need anything to drink?"

Debbie picked at her ragged fingernails. "No, I just need to leave the country."

"That's the worst thing you could do." Everything she and Evan had discussed earlier compelled her to add, "Fleeing will tell the police you're guilty."

"You have to help." She first leaned forward and then scooted her chair to the desk. "I don't want to have my baby in jail."

"Of course, you don't." Mandy reached across to take her hand. "There's just one thing. I can't help you if you're not honest with me. Did you kill Craig? Intentionally or accidently doesn't matter to me, did you?"

She jerked her hand away. "How can you? No, no I didn't. I love loved him. He's the father of my child and I'd already planned on how we'd grow old together." She sniffled. "Him first, you know."

"I suspected." She got up to get her some tissues. The woman had black tears running down her face, so Mandy went to get some makeup remover from the storeroom. After returning, she said, "Here, take one. I'm assuming you told them everything? Every little detail?"

"Yes. Craig wanted to go fishing, I didn't." She began loading up a tissue with the remover. Once the liquid saturated the wipe, she began swabbing under her eyes. "The day was calm and clear, not too cold, either. I almost went, but stayed to shop for the nursery."

Mandy picked up a pen to write the

word *alone* on her desk calendar. It showed the prior year, and she really needed to update it. "So you weren't even there with him. You couldn't have hurt him, even if you wanted to."

"No," she said, choking on a sob.

She glanced up at her, remembering her audience. Her discussions with Aaron and Evan had been such a matter of fact. "You poor dear. Let me make you something to drink. Coffee? A sweet tea?"

"I'd like the tea, please."

"All right." Before she could stand, Mandy's cell phone buzzed, distracting her. She glanced at the screen, tapping the text app. "Aaron! I'd forgotten about our early dinner."

"I can go." Debbi stood also.

"No, you can't." She smiled at her to soften the words. "Stay here, unless you want to come with me to the break room." Mandy scooped up her phone to text him once the coffee or hot water brewed.

Debbi put her purse strap on her shoulder and played with the only frayed spot on the leather strip. "I don't mind following."

"Okay. We can talk more after I take care of something." She rinsed out the coffee pot and refilled it with cold water. Once the machine began work, she turned back to her cell phone. From the corner of her eye, Mandy saw her guest wander around the break area. She kept busy reading the employee bulletin board Neil had insisted they had. Satisfied Debbi was distracted, she turned to her cell phone and read Aaron's text.

You ok? Don't answer if you're on your way here and driving.

She bit her lip, not wanting to cancel on him at all. Still, Debbi needed her for support. *Debbi is here, and the police want her to come in.* She asked her guest, "Did you want anything to eat?"

"No, I'm good. This coffee is fine."

Do you need me there? Aaron responded.

Always, but in this case, some help would be good. Bring food for us but leave in the car until we're done with helping her?

Can do, be there in twenty at the latest.

Her stomach growled. *Thank you! Starving.*

LOL! Be there in fifteen

She added, *Come to the back, you'll see my car.*

'k

Mandy slid the phone in her pocket. "That was Aaron. I've asked him over to help us think of a solution for you." She took three cups from the cabinet. "He'll be here soon."

"How can he help us?" Debbi asked while whipping her eyes.

"He knows things we can't, due to privacy. He'll ask questions we'll have no way of imagining." She put two sugars in her cup, leaving the other two empty.

"I should be able to know everything. Craig was my husband." Her voice faltered on the word *husband*.

Mandy gave her a quick hug, nothing in her mind sounding comforting enough to say. "I agree, but…well, we can see when he gets here."

Debbi sank into one of the small chairs. "I have forty-five minutes to figure this out."

She toyed with how much to tell her friend. "You might have longer than that. One of the constables on your case is a friend of mine. I could call him if we run out of time and say you're on your way."

After a snort, she said, "Or, tell him to look at someone else because I didn't kill my husband."

Mandy detected some fear in Debbi's bravado. "If I could, I would." The machine gave one final gurgle. Mandy went to start their tea bags soaking, glad Aaron hadn't heard the rumble. He already wanted to give her a new coffee maker for the apartment. If he gave her one for here and one for home, she'd be in love. "Do you have a preference in flavors, Debbi?"

"Nothing herbal, please. Black Pekoe is fine, and I'll use one of these sugar packs."

She put a stirrer in with the bag, giving her the mug. Mandy started to ask about the baby when someone knocked at the back door. "That's Aaron. I'll be back in a minute." Opening the door, she smiled when seeing him. "It didn't take you long at all."

"The city is pretty quiet." He gave the door a once over. "Did you check through the peephole to make sure it was me? Your opening up to a burglar is going to worry me, now."

She patted his arm, drawing him into the shop. "Later. Right now, we have a little more than thirty minutes before Debbi turns herself in to the authorities for questioning." A quick check after locking the door and she led him to the break room.

"Damn."

"I know." She took a second to stop smiling about how he cared for her. Debbi might take her warm fuzzies as apathy for her circumstances. "Aaron, do you want tea or coffee?"

"Tea. Let me choose mine and you fix yours." He went to the sink and coffee maker. "Hot water is in here?" At her nod, he grinned. "You shop the second-hand stores, don't you?"

She gave him a heavy-lidded stare, knowing what he'd meant about her appliances. "I do. It's the best way of recycling." Mandy sat at the table where she'd placed her cup and smiled at Debbi. "You told me they'd already asked you questions, and I know they searched everywhere for clues."

"I also told you I didn't do it." She dunked the tea a few times, hard, before removing it. A folded napkin absorbed the drips when she put the bag on the table.

Aaron came over and took a seat in one of the chairs. "Debbi, if one of the cops tells you the prisons are full of innocent people, pop them in the mouth for me, would you?"

"That's not helpful," Mandy interjected.

He focused on his tea, not meeting her eyes. "Sorry."

"So, anyway." She gave him a glare before turning to the woman with them. "Is there any detail Aaron or I could investigate while they're talking to you? Something he might know, since he's a doctor and all?"

"The only thing possible is Craig had suffered a stroke. Ken thought so, too, at first because their headaches had become so similar. My husband even had an appointment scheduled with a neurologist Ken recommended."

Aaron snapped to attention. "Hold on, Mrs. Walker. You said he'd been having headaches? Like Ken's?"

"Yes. He'd always had tension headaches. Over the counter, stuff worked for them, but these latest ones never eased up on him." She took a sip of her tea, eyes distant. "All the medical stuff didn't matter once I found out how beat up as he was when they found him."

He frowned. "So the two men had been talking, Craig borrows Ken's medicine, and keeps it stashed on the boat?"

"We always let Ken kept a few there because the sunlight reflected off the waves gave him problems." She shrugged. "Everyone kept doses they might need in our little cabinet. Craig didn't like to come back to shore after he'd set up the reels."

Aaron thought for a moment. "I'd seen several prescription meds and a few over the counters in there when we first visited. Craig had hypertension, from what I saw prescribed to him, and taking the migraine meds might have caused a stroke."

Betrayal

Mandy glanced at Debbi, wondering if she was as pale as her client. "What's hypertension?"

As if she'd not spoken, Debbi whispered, "Ken's headache medicine? Are you sure?"

He took and squeezed the stricken woman's hand. "I'd need a blood test from him to be positive, but yes. I'm sure, but will talk to the medical examiner to see what he says."

Debbi shook her head. "No, you're wrong. Craig would never take someone else's medicines, ever."

Laura Stapleton

Betrayal

Chapter 9

Logically, Aaron knew shock led Debbi to tell him he was wrong. Emotionally was a different story. He ignored his irritation. "Not even if he were desperate and knew what Ken had left on board might help?"

She stared at her hands for a moment, tight-lipped. "Maybe. All right. He might have."

Instead of saying ah ha, Aaron told her, "It's completely understandable if he did. Migraines can be some of the worst pain a person experiences."

"So, it's not his fault if he did?"

The pleading in her eyes broke his heart. He smiled a little at her in support. "No. He shouldn't have if he did, but no one who's ever had a migraine would blame him."

Debbi stood and hugged Aaron. "Thank you. I appreciate the reassurance."

"You're welcome." In his arms, she seemed delicate, almost fragile. "And anytime, okay?"

"Sure. I'll remember that the next time I need a doctor." She gave him a watery smile and took another tissue before wiping her eyes. "I'm ready to talk to the police. It'll be the same thing again."

Mandy stood. "That's fine. It'll show you weren't lying either time."

"Thank you for helping. I know you've been Sabrina's friend all these years, and I'm glad you're mine, too."

She patted Debbi's back. "You're very welcome. Call if you need anything, okay?"

"I'll call and let you know if anything happens," Debbie added.

"Thanks."

As soon as she left the break area, Mandy said, "Now that she's taken care of, I need food."

Aaron grinned when Mandy's stomach growled. "It's in my car."

"We could eat in there for more privacy," she suggested. "I like your back seat."

Her idea thrilled him, and he glanced at the breakroom clock. "Damn. I can't." He kissed her forehead and took her hand to lead the way outside. "I'm out of time and need to go. How about I make it up to you later?" He unlocked his car, grabbing her dinner and drink.

"No, because it's on me to make it up to you." She took the bag he handed her and lifted it a little. "You were my hero bringing food and helping me with Debbi. I owe you big time, sweetheart."

"Okay, I'll let you." He pulled her in for a lingering kiss. "The first night we're both not working?"

"I so hope so."

Once he had a break in treating kids with strep throat and heart patients, he made his way downstairs to the medical examiner's office. He liked how the guy had an open door policy. Knocking on the threshold, Aaron asked, "Is now a good time to talk?"

Stephens waved at the chair across from him. "Sure. Have a seat. I have a feeling this is about the Walker case."

"You're psychic." Aaron sat, settling in and wondering how much the other man already knew. "The first wife was free to go yesterday. Now it's his second wife who's on the hook."

He leaned forward, putting his elbows on the desk. "Really? I sent a message yesterday that Mr. Walker showed signs of an aneurysm. He didn't need the beating to kill him. He was dead before he hit the water."

After a moment or two, Aaron closed his open jaw. "So no one killed him? And you didn't notice he'd had an aneurysm before now?"

Stephens gave him a sardonic smile. "The crushed skull and massive lacerations on the man's torso distracted me, sorry."

He grinned at his superior's sarcasm. "No, I'm sorry and don't blame you. Most would have stopped looking past the surface injuries."

"I would have, too, but some of the brain tissue looked off for a head injury but perfect for a cerebral hemorrhage."

"As if he shouldn't have used a friend's Naratriptan for the headaches?"

"That's one of the worst things he could have done. Do you have a hunch or information pointing to that drug specifically?" At Aaron's nod, Stephens swore under his breath before saying, "Very well, I'll check and see what lab screens for triptans. If you'll excuse me?"

"Sure." Aaron left the room, uncomfortable at the ME's foul mood. He wondered if Debbi had noticed any other symptoms besides Craig's headaches. He leaned against a wall and retrieved his cell phone to text Mandy. *Something important. Craig's death seems an accident.* His message chirp sounded almost immediately.

Really? How so?

Typing in Naratriptan, cerebral hemorrhage, and secondary symptoms were not appealing at the moment so he texted,

Betrayal

Long story. Talk?
At dinner with Evan right now. Join us? 2 birds 1 stone?

Aaron grinned, almost feeling her fidget just from reading her words. *Can't, but breakfast tomorrow?*

Sure. The usual?

He grinned, texting, *"Our Timmie's around 8 am?"*

Yep! C ya. Oh wait, Evan will be there too. He wants to talk with both of us.

Aaron groaned out loud. He wanted her to himself, not with what's his face loitering around. "No, no, and no," he said aloud while texting back, *sounds good, bye.*

He spent the rest of the work shift in a funk, not even minding when Dr. St. Clair asked him to stay a couple of hours late. It beat sitting at home, waiting for eight o'clock. When Aaron arrived at Timmie's, he ordered a double, single decaf. He'd debated ordering for Mandy, but didn't know what Evan would want, so passed. He settled into a large booth with his tablet after picking up his drink.

Emails from Brad about the next court date filled his email inbox, read but unanswered. He'd not cleaned out his messages in a while. Reading medical newsletters kept him busy until Mandy and

Evan came in together. They'd caught his attention when walking up to the door, and Aaron suppressed a growl at how good they looked as a couple. She waved when spotting him. He smiled back, really not liking Evan in his uniform. Even worse, every woman in the place perked up at the guy's entrance. Aaron closed apps on his table's desktop, bringing it when walking up to meet them.

Mandy hurried over to him. "No, stay there and keep our spot. I can order you something, no problem."

Evan leaned forward, asking her, "Aren't I taking you out this morning?"

She gave him a slight elbowing with a grin. "Dutch treat, buddy, remember?"

"I guess."

Damn it, Aaron did not want to like this guy. He seemed genuinely distressed at not being on a date with her. "I feel your pain. She doesn't let me take her out very easily, either."

"She was a lot more easy going before university," Evan said while following the other two to the booth.

Aaron snorted. "I regret I missed that part of her life."

Evan snickered, too, as Mandy frowned at both of them. "How about we get back on target and stop talking about me when I'm right here? Can we chat about medical and police stuff here? Or should we grab and go to one of our homes?"

Aaron and Evan had exchanged a guilty look before Aaron said, "I agree. Some of this stuff isn't for public consumption. We'll need a three-sided coin to flip."

"How about Mandy's, since you live there, too?" Evan offered.

She leaned against him, grinning. "Ha! I didn't know my sofa was that comfy."

He kissed her forehead. "It wasn't. I'm hoping to be promoted to the bed."

Mandy snickered. "Good luck, buddy."

Evan gave Aaron a grin. "She even wishes me luck. Nice."

He unclenched his fists so his fingernails would stop digging into his palm. The two had been friends a long time. He needed to remember that. They also needed a little space between them and he was the man to do it, so Aaron cleared his throat. "By the way, I'm Aaron Nicholson, her neighbour."

"Figured you were. I'm Evan Rogers, her high school boyfriend."

"Good to meet you."

"Same here." Evan reached out, and

they shook hands.

Aaron hated the firm, sure grip of the guy. He smiled at Mandy, "I'd ask your place or mine, but I suggest yours. My couch is too comfortable. I'd never get rid of Evan."

He smirked. "Funny guy."

"Thanks." Aaron didn't suggest she ride along. He wanted time in his own car to dwell on how to be casual about her relationships with other men. This whole jealousy thing left him feeling weird. He'd never been the possessive type until seeing Mandy standing a little too close to that guy. "Should we order here or drive through?"

She looked from one man to the other. "Here is fine, since we're almost in line, anyway."

"Sounds great." He turned to Evan. "Have you lived in the Halifax area all your life?"

"Most of it. I was in Toronto for a while at University for criminal justice."

Aaron glanced from the menu to the other man. "Is that a requirement for law enforcement?"

He shrugged. "No, but it helps grease the skids."

"Did that help you to bypass the academy?"

"I didn't check."

Betrayal

Mandy stepped back, putting her wallet back into her purse. "Your turn to order, guys."

He let Evan order first, a little impressed. Getting a university degree in addition to a certification or attending an academy was what he would have done as well. Aaron stepped up. "I'll have a ham and Swiss, and a single single."

"We'll catch you at home?" Mandy asked.

He smiled at her hand on his arm. "Sure. Meet you there."

With his food in hand, he eased into his car and started the engine. Hearing how Evan would be sent to the couch despite being a former boyfriend felt good to his jealousy. And they dated back in high school? No one ever got over their first love. All of a sudden, he hoped Mandy had gone out enough that this other guy was her tenth love. He wanted her romantic interest in Evan too dead to ever resurrect.

Aaron gritted his teeth as he eased to a stop for a red light. All this fretting about who she did and didn't like just pissed him the hell off. Good looking, wore a uniform, and a decent person? Evan irritated the shit out of him, and he hated even more how much he liked him. He'd expected a sour attitude or jealousy from the younger man, not an easy friendship. Jerk.

Mandy went up the stairs first, coffee in one hand and the handrails in the other. The last thing she wanted to do was stumble on the ice and fall back onto the guys. There'd be food and drink everywhere. She fished around for her keys during the last few steps. Soon, she hurried inside, letting the others close the door as she turned up the heat.

"Can we eat now? I'm starving," Evan said.

Aaron settled into his usual kitchen chair. "I say we can, 'cause I'm starving, too."

She grinned seeing how both of them had preferred seats. "Why not?" They tore into their fast food bags, each eating more than talking. About halfway through, she asked, "Hurry up, Aaron so you can tell us how Craig's death was an accident."

Evan's eyebrows rose. "Accident?"

He nodded. "Dr. Stephens said he had sent the message to the precinct. Walker was dead before he hit the water. Not from the beating, but from an aneurysm."

Mandy shook her head, her stomach protesting a little. "How is someone killed like that?"

Betrayal

"There are ways, but it's not the easiest or most reliable. Plus, people aren't murdered that way." He shrugged. "At least no one I've ever heard of has caused one in another person."

"So what's the working theory?" Evan began gathering up the trash to throw away. "Someone gave Craig an aneurysm, beat him up, cut him up, throw him overboard, and then left? Sounds like a lot of trouble."

"I agree. Coffee, Mandy?" Aaron got up and filled her coffee maker at her nod.

Mandy thought back to everything she'd discussed with both of them in separate conversations. The simplest answer kept coming to mind. Nothing in anything said before now explained the apparent reason Craig died. "Why are we ruling out him getting run over by a boat and propeller?" she asked.

Evan spoke first. "Because his boat was anchored in the open water, and we found his body in a quiet cove."

Aaron asked, "How quiet? No one for miles quiet, or no commercial fishing quiet?"

"No commercial fishing," he replied.

She looked at Aaron. "You don't think someone ran over him, either?"

"Actually, I do. A hull bashes his

head continues to do so as the vessel scrapes down him and the propeller leaves its marks. If I'd been better at physics, I'd be able to figure out how fast the boat was going when it hit him." He shrugged, getting up for the coffee. "Which doesn't matter, because of his brain bleeding out in his skull."

Mandy got up, too, to refill her Tim's cup with fresh brew. "Debbi needs to know that no one killed him."

Evan put a hand over his own cup in the universal, "No more," gesture. "She's out on her own recognizance."

"It looks right now like his death was an accident." Aaron went back to the kitchen, calling over his shoulder. "He took Ken's migraine meds, thinking they'd cure his own headaches. Which either wouldn't help or would cause a stroke."

His eyes narrowed. "Medicine prescribed to Ken? How did Craig get a hold of them?"

Mandy offered. "Debbi told us they kept backups of everyone's medicines on their boat. So Craig wouldn't have to cut short a fishing trip."

The younger man shook the ice in his soft drink and drank the water. "Hmm. What drug was it? My mom has migraines, and I'll swing by the pharmacy for her sometimes."

Betrayal

"Naratriptan. Here, I still have the photo on my phone." Aaron came back in to pull up the video taken of the pill bottle. They watched as he turned the bottle around, and heard Mandy ask him to find water for Debbi. He tapped *pause* when the clear part of the container showed the actual pills. "See? I thought these would match the label, but they don't. These are baby aspirin. The original medicine has a softened triangle shape, in or out of the blister pack."

"Blister pack?" she asked.

"Yeah, this brand is usually boxed and each pill encased in a little plastic cell of its own."

"Ah."

"Some pharmacies will fold the sheet of pills into a labeled bottle." He paused. "I don't know why. Huh. I'll have to ask our pharmacy department sometime because now I'm curious."

"Let me know, too." She tapped out a message on her phone.

A text from her hit the notifications on his screen, and he laughed. "Of course, I will, my curious little woman."

Evan ran a hand through his hair. "We took photos, too, but didn't take the drugs into evidence. The names and pharmacies were legit and with Craig's injuries? We focused on them."

Mandy asked, "Did Ken switch them out because his name is on the bottle? And why baby aspirin and nothing else ?"

"Lots of people take a baby aspirin a day for heart health, so I'm not surprised Craig would have them there." Aaron closed the photo app. "Now I want to know where Ken's meds went to. If someone put them in Craig's aspirin bottle and he took the triptan instead of the chewable aspirin? The taste would be awful and the results just as bad."

Chapter 10

Evan ticked the items off of his fingers. "So, the beating didn't kill him. The aneurysm or meds might have. We don't know who switched what, and now everyone's a suspect again?" He put his hands up in surrender. "That's it. I'm out."

"Can you quit like that?" asked Mandy.

He grinned. "I wish. Every time I think this is wrapped up, something changes."

She said, "Does this mean both Mrs. Walkers are suspects again?"

"Anyone with prints on the scene or on the bottle is suspect," Evan replied.

Aaron groaned, having had his Criminal Records Check done the day after moving here three months ago. Doing so was no big deal. Every Canadian doctor working with children or other vulnerable people went through the process as a precaution. But adding the background search to Brad's stealing his medical id and pretending to be him? He was done with fingerprints, police stations, and being investigated about anything. "My prints will be there and on the bottle."

Evan shrugged. "I know. They came

up when we ran them, and it doesn't matter. You're not a suspect at the moment, but don't skip town for good until the case is closer to settled."

His stomach soured, and Aaron regretted eating anything for dinner. Sure, he had nothing to worry about. He'd also thought that before the police hauled him in for a lineup last year. "I'll be here, or across the hall. You know where I live."

He didn't crack a smile. "Do you work tomorrow?"

"From four am to four pm."

Evan tapped in a message on his phone. "I have my own theories about how Craig went overboard, but can't prove anything. Let's just say I need a second opinion and who better to ask than a doctor? What's your number?"

Aaron got the feeling Evan didn't want to say anything in front of Mandy, so he said, "604-555-8978." He stifled a yawn. "I need to grab a nap, catch up on some sleep."

Mandy stood, patting his shoulder. "Of course. Do you want me to walk you to your door?"

He got to his feet, his knee objecting with a few sharp pains. Using the table for balance, he bent the protesting joint a few times. He hoped to get it limber enough to keep him from limping. "I'll manage. See you later?" When she nodded, he turned to the other guy. "Evan, good to meet you, and I look forward to that text."

"Hey, no problem. If Mandy likes you, you're all right." Evan stood and grabbed his coat, handing Aaron's to him. He hugged Mandy. "I'd better get to work. You'll be at the salon all day?"

"Sure, until closing."

Aaron put the coat over his arm and opened the door, catching a glimpse of Evan kissing her cheek from the corner of his eye. He frowned before catching himself and stepped outside. The two were friends, no big deal. He could unclench his jaw. Mandy was sleeping over tonight with him, not with Evan. The knowledge restored his good humor, and he smiled.

She stood in her doorway. "See you later, Ev. Good night, Aaron."

He faced away while unlocking his door and winked. "Night, Mandy. Later."

Once inside, he locked his door again so he wouldn't have to get up again. The mental image of Evan touching her pissed him the hell off. Aaron went to his bedroom, undressing and getting ready for bed. He didn't want to think anymore, didn't want to admit this possessiveness toward her.

Mandy twisted the deadbolt and heard Evan's boots tromping down the stairs. She wanted to lean against the door and slide down in embarrassment but stayed upright. That kiss was so unplanned, and she'd caught the look on Aaron's face. Surprise before that bored expression he wore when hiding his feelings. She sighed. At least it had been on the cheek.

They were both great guys, and Aaron knew she preferred him. Still, there'd been a flash of unhappiness in his eyes. She shook off the urge to feel bad for him. He'd find out how much she wanted him tonight during their sleepover. She grinned, glad to have time before work to shower and shave her legs.

She let herself into her salon. This early in the day, she kept the front locked until opening time. She turned on her computer and stared at the monitor while it powered up. She put a hand on the mouse and lightly tapped. It would be difficult to not pester either Evan or Aaron for information today. They'd compare notes about the medicines, come to some conclusion, and she'd have no idea until later tonight. If then. The welcome chime sounded from the back door, letting her know one of her crew was here.

Betrayal

"Good morning, Boss Lady!"

Her eyes dried almost too much to blink, she hollered back as he walked by, "Good morning, Neil."

Stretching, she heard more employees come in from the back. Mandy returned their greetings as she pulled up the day's schedule on the computer. When seeing Debbi among the first customers, she grinned. The new widow was assigned to Neil, and while she didn't want to switch clients with him, she did want to chat. She owed it to Aaron, Evan, and Craig to learn everything possible. The lock to the main door was slid open, and she stepped out of her office.

"Boss!" Neil waved her over. "Did you see who's in for her usual this morning? Do you think the police still suspect her?"

"Yes, I did see, and it's why I'm hanging out with you." The door jingled, and she saw in the mirror when Debbi walked in.

He nudged her. "Sure, pretend it's not my charm." Louder, he added, "Ms. Walker! Hello, come right up."

Mandy stepped aside to let her pass. "How are you, Debbi?"

"Good, considering." She settled into the chair with a sigh. "I suppose everyone knows how I was pulled in for questioning yesterday?"

"You poor dear. Let me wash that ugliness from your mind." He put an apron around her neck with a towel at the back. "Let's go, sweetie. I'll use my extra moisturizing conditioner."

The two left, and she settled in the next booth. The water would drown out any conversation between them. Better to just wait. By the time they came back, all the other stylist had chatted and worked with their clients. Mandy smiled at her as Debbi sat down. "Feel better?"

"Yes. That scalp massage was just what I needed."

Neil grabbed his scissors and comb. "Those neck muscles? I've known piano strings less tense."

Debbi said, "I have a favor to ask."

"Sure, what can I do?" Mandy couldn't imagine losing a husband to death. An image of Geo and his new wife flashed in her mind. Okay, maybe losing one she'd wanted to keep. Anyway, poor Debbi to be pregnant and alone.

"If I send in Ken, could you cut his hair and talk to him?"

Mandy smiled at her friend. "Sure, what did you want me to say?"

After he had tapped her neck, she looked down at her chest. "Tell him to back off, in a nice way of course. He's trying to date me and two weeks isn't enough time for me to mourn."

She didn't want to get involved in this. Helping clear someone's name was one thing, being their relationship bodyguard quite another. "I'm not sure I know Ken well enough to talk to him about this."

"It's too much, isn't it?" Her eyes filled with tears. "It's just, every time I think about telling him myself, I get upset and start crying."

Middle school had been a long time ago. Mandy smiled instead of giving in to her urge to frown. "Thanks for volunteering me, and yes, I will talk to Ken about easing up." Patting her on the arm, she added, "Send him in anytime today."

"Great! Thank you so much." She took a tissue from the box Neil offered her. "You don't have to be mean, just firm."

"I'll do my best." She'd dealt with unhappy people before now. Telling Ken to cool his heels shouldn't be too tough.

"Please do. If he finds out I've asked you this, he might get angry. I can't afford that until I learn more about my new business."

The news surprised her, and Mandy wondered where she'd got the idea Debbi would have a hands-on approach. "You're getting into pest control? Not selling Craig's share to Ken?"

She almost nodded. "It's for the new baby's sake. I want them to decide what to do with their father's company." A sob escaped her. "I keep forgetting he's really gone. The funeral and questioning all seem like a horrible dream."

Mandy grabbed a tissue, handing it to her. "Here. I'm sorry, and of course, whatever you need from me."

She blew her nose and Neil paused to let her throw away the waste. Debbi fished around in her purse for a moment before popping a mint into her mouth. It clanked against her teeth as she said, "Good, thank you. I'll text him as soon as Neil is done here."

He gave Debbi the hand mirror. "Get your phone warmed up, sugar. You'll need a bodyguard with this look."

Mandy had to agree, she looked lovely despite the teary eyes. "Good job, Neil. Debbi, I'll call tomorrow and tell you how it went with Ken." She gave her a brief hug once the apron came off. "If you'll excuse me, I have a dozen things to do before leaving tonight."

She hurried to her office and pulled the door to almost shutting. After staring at the wall for a few moments, she thought up the words to use with Ken. Nice, but firm. The standard "It's not you, it's her," excuse. She leaned back in the chair, rubbing her tense neck. Her cell phone's vibrating caught her attention, and she checked her messages.

Seeing a notice about her cell carrier's auto pay feature, Mandy debated for a moment on texting Evan about her talking to Ken. Telling him seemed like giving him routine information, but in crime shows she'd seen, it was always the small stuff that mattered the most, so she typed, *Does it matter that I might see Ken today?*

Not really, why?

Debbi wants me to talk to him about their company. As soon as she hit send, the reason for Ken to kill his business partner seemed obvious. He wanted Bug Off all to himself. She wondered if Evan had thought the same thing. Before she could ask, her phone beeped with a reply.

Good. Ask if he'll swing by here afterward so we can talk about who'd kill Craig.

He might not be able to tell her due to the investigation, but she had to ask. *Don't think it's Ken?*

No. He has no motive.

She flexed her fingers, answering, *Are you sure, not to get all of the company for himself?*

No, he and Debbi had an agreement for the business.

Interesting. Debbie hadn't said anything but Mandy hadn't expected her to, either. *Ok. I'll send him over after we talk*

Now she was dying to grill Evan over why he knew Ken didn't kill Craig. Plus, what did Aaron know? Mandy opened up the finance spreadsheet with a frown. If people would just tell her everything, she wouldn't have to be so nosy.

"Mandy?" Fiona stood at the door. "Angela is running by Sam's Grains for sandwiches. What do you want?"

"I haven't had their hot ham and cheese in a while. And a bag of All Dressed chips?"

"You got it."

She refocused, only pausing with her end of month accounting to thank Angela and pay her back for lunch. Mandy ate while thinking her crew needed better snacks in the back. Maybe deli stuff for sandwiches, too, and soup. They could eat here when the weather was bad out. She made a note to go shopping for her crew on Monday.

"Boss?" Neil poked his head in the door. "Ken's here."

"Already? I didn't get a chance to call him with a time. Damn." She threw

Betrayal

away the sandwich wrapper. She pocketed her cell phone and stepped out into the main area.

She went to Ken, sitting on one of the sofas. "Hello, there!" She let him pull her into a half hug.

"Hey, Mandy. I called Debbi this morning to talk, and she mentioned coming here." He stepped back and held his cap in both hands, mashing the brim. "It reminded me I needed a trim, and I figured why wait."

She smiled, hoping to reassure him. He weaved from side to side just a little as if nervous. "Sure. Have a seat in our extra booth."

Ken followed her and settled in. As she wrapped an apron around his neck, he asked, "I don't suppose this is a good place to ask if the Senators will make it to the playoffs?"

Mandy smiled as everyone looked at each other in the mirrors. "Most of us like the Leafs. Angela over there likes the Canadiens."

He chuckled as Angela. "I might have known. Isn't there always one person in the group skating the other way?"

"Usually. My brother is a Canadiens fan, while the rest of us like the Leafs." She ran the electric razor over his neck. "We think he was switched at birth. Somewhere out there, a Leafs baby is wondering where his family is."

Ken laughed. "I'll bet."

She brushed the tiny hairs from his neck and face. He was a nice looking man, closer to her father's age than hers. "You weren't too shaggy when you came in. I took a little off the top, and a lot more from the sides." She took the apron from around his neck and gave him a hand mirror.

"Looks good." He lifted to one side while handing her back the mirror and retrieved his wallet. "How much do I owe you?"

Mandy made a follow me motion and went to the register. "An even twenty."

He stepped up, giving her his debit card. As she took and ran it through the system, he leaned in and said, "Debbi mentioned you wanted to talk to me about something?"

She gave him the receipt, watching him sign. "Yes, but I have a feeling you won't want it public. Maybe later?"

"Are you open to bribery?" He grinned, taking his copy. "I could probably take you for a coffee or something?"

A twinge of guilt hit when thinking of her salon, but she shrugged it off. Good deeds counted as work, right? "Great idea. Let me get my stuff right quick." He nodded

Betrayal

as Mandy retrieved her purse, closing her office up behind her. "Fiona? I might be back late, so don't wait on me to close."

The woman waved her on. "No worries, we'll be fine."

She turned to Ken. "My car is out back, did you want me to drive?"

"My car is already warmed up, and I don't mind." He opened the door, cold air rushing into the salon

"Sounds good." She followed him out of the front door to his vehicle. The late afternoon sun touched the west horizon, turning everything golden red. "It's almost warm out here."

"Should be in the teens all week." He opened the car for her and held the door until she got in.

"Thank you," she said when he found his own seat. The interior smelled like Ken's cologne times two. Nice, but a bit oppressive. He drummed his fingers on the steering wheel to an invisible beat. Had he always been twitchy, she wondered. She guessed he was nervous about what she had to say on Debbi's behalf. Mandy thought of several questions to ask him before discarding everything as too intrusive.

"What do you want, Mandy?" Ken asked.

"Hmm?" She looked out of the

driver's side window to see a menu and microphone. "Oh! A single single." After he had ordered, she grinned. "Sorry. I was in my own world."

"Not a problem." He drove up, taking the drinks and giving her hers. "In fact, I wanted to give you a penny for your thoughts, but only have loonies."

She laughed. "I'm ok with the price increase." She dug around in her purse. "Here, let me pay for my drink."

"No need. I can treat a lady once in a while." He set the coffee in the cup holder and pulled away from the drive up window. "So, what's this big deal Debbi wanted me to see you about?"

"Ah, well, it's this. She likes you very much as a friend. She's terrified of offending or hurting you in any way. You've been a wonderful business partner to Craig and one-half of a successful team. She's hoping you give her time to grieve as well as time to learn the business. She wants to be a—" She paused, suddenly not sure she had a right word for the relationship Debbi wanted. "…partner to you and the company."

"That's nice," he answered, distracted by the traffic. "Hold up. Did she think I was coming on to her?" He shook his head at Mandy's nod. "She is so full of herself. Don't get me wrong. Debbi's a lovely gal, but me and Craig's wife hooking up? Not gonna happen." He stopped at a red light. "Is this why you had to talk to me?"

"Mostly. Partly." Mandy glanced at him, not happy at how his frown matched the tone in his voice. "I mean, Debbi was afraid of hurting your feelings."

He snorted, and she grinned, glad Ken's mood lightened a little. Maybe now, he could explain a few things before taking her back to work. She added, "Plus, now that you mention it, I'm wondering about the pills you have on their boat."

"What about them?"

The rumble in his voice unnerved her. He'd returned to twitchy. "I don't suppose they matter."

"They do, or you wouldn't have mentioned them." He eased to a stop at the light and turned to her. "So? What about my pills being there? Lots of other peoples' were."

She returned his stare. Mandy didn't want to risk offending him. "We knew Craig had been having headaches and wondered if you'd meant to help him by putting your migraine meds in his baby aspirin bottle for him to take."

"We?" He gunned the engine through the intersection.

Mandy held onto the side door's handle. "Yeah, Evan, Aaron, and me."

"I see." His jaw tensed. "A cop, a doctor, and a hairdresser? Sounds like a joke to me."

Ken's derisive tone irritated her. She tried to keep her voice steady while saying, "I suppose so." Mandy stared out of the window at the barren trees mixed in with the evergreens. "Where are we going, anyway?"

"Just out sightseeing. Talking about medicines, no big deal."

This felt off. His attitude, the wasting time, and nervousness pointed to something bothering him. She'd known Ken for forever. He was a good guy, and she suspected being called up by the police would unnerve anyone. "All right, sounds good."

After a moment, she glanced at him. He seemed a little more relaxed and to reassure him she added, "We all three agree about what must have happened. Craig had a headache, knew you had them too, and took your high powered medicines to find some relief."

"I didn't give them to him. Sharing medicines is illegal. I wouldn't do that."

His lips were pressed so tight together after his denial, a white circle lined them. She took a sip of her coffee. Her hand trembled when she placed the cup back into the holder. "Of course, you wouldn't. I'd never think that."

"Good, because I didn't." He took a deep drink of his coffee. "I can't believe Debbi had you do something as asinine as talk to me about her feelings. Did you know I'm supposed to go in yet again and give the police another statement about Craig's death?"

She bit her lip, chewing on a bit of chapped skin. "Evan texted me this afternoon and mentioned wanting to talk with you about him. If you want, I could go with you to the station for moral support. You know I'm not expected back at the shop for the rest of the day. I don't mind."

He sighed. "It's fine. I can take care of all this myself."

She smiled at him, her grin fading when he didn't look at her. It didn't matter. At least she'd cleared up the Debbi thing. Evan and the officers would talk to him, and Ken would see he had nothing to worry about. Mandy stared out of the window. She liked him well enough, but in this short time cooped up, his whole mercurial nature left her tired of catering to his moods.

Soon, they reached the back of her salon, behind Mandy's car. She grabbed her purse and empty coffee cup. "Thanks for letting me talk with you. I hope everything goes well for you today."

"It will."

She tried the door handle, but it didn't release. Her car didn't have this child safety feature, and she asked, "Can you unlock the door, please?"

"No. I don't think so. You're going to text Evan, telling him how I'm on my way to the station-house, and you'll see him later." He dug in his coat pocket with his left hand, pulling out an old style revolver from his jacket's right pocket.

Her mouth watered as her stomach clenched. She swallowed, unable to move. "Ken, I don't think this is a good idea."

Ken pulled back the hammer. "Do it." He lifted the pistol.

Betrayal

Chapter 11

Mandy took the phone from her purse, her hands shaking. She glanced at the gun. Still pointed toward her. "Does it matter how I say it?"

"No, but let me see before you send."

She typed, *Evan, saw Ken, he's headed to the stationhouse now*. Mandy tilted the little screen toward him. "Here."

He scanned the text. "Good, hit send and put the phone in your purse."

"Why?" she asked. When Ken waved the gun at her, she said, "Right." Mandy turned the ringer to silent and slanted her purse's opening away from him. She mimicked putting the phone in a pocket, like a magician, and let it slide down her leg. Her thigh pinned the device between it and the seat. "Done." She zipped up her purse. "Do you want me to toss this in the back seat?"

"No. Give it to me."

Her heart sank. He'd dig out the phone, or try to. Then he'd see how she hadn't followed his orders. She slid the purse to him, and he set it on his lap, preoccupied with rush hour traffic. "Why don't you drop me off with my belongings, and talk to Evan about the baby aspirin mix up? You can't be in trouble for an accident."

"No. I'm not taking that chance." He rolled down his window and threw out her purse.

She leaned sideways to see her bag hit the ground and bounce once before resting against her car. Everything in her makeup back was probably busted to pieces. Some of that stuff had been splurges, too. "Damn it, Ken! That's not trash!"

Mandy twisted around to watch her business, car, and purse fade as he drove off. She felt the phone slide under her leg a little more and closed her mouth. One of them pissed off was bad enough. Especially since he'd not lowered the gun. She tried a laugh, anemic even to her own ears. "I hope nothing broke. Sure you don't want me to go with you to the station? I don't mind."

He stomped the gas. "Shut up about the police. I'm not going there."

Mandy kept her eyes open and her lips sealed. Ken's hands shook every time they left the steering wheel. She needed to watch for a good opportunity to slide the phone into her coat pocket. Traffic from Dartmouth to Halifax crawled during rush hour. If she'd been able to get a message to Evan, he'd be able to jog by and rescue her.

Ken set the gun on his lap. "Don't get any ideas. I can still get to this quicker

Betrayal

than you can."

Once past the worst of the bottleneck, he turned onto the 306. The trees passed too quickly alongside them, or she'd consider grabbing the wheel. She snuck a peek at the dash to check their speed. She knew the highway. Well enough to give K by K directions so far. She wiped her window with a cuff to see. Her side of the car was foggier than his. She tried to keep her breathing slow and easy.

He drove several kilometers over the speed limit for a good ten minutes. "I didn't plan on this."

"Oh?" Mandy said, hoping to lead him into saying more. She had to keep him talking. Her playing therapist might help him understand returning to town was the best option for both of them.

"None of it. Damn!" He hit the steering wheel. "Damn it all to hell!"

Her therapist idea a bust, she stopped just short of patting his shoulder. "It's okay, Ken."

"No, it's not. Craig wasn't supposed to die. You weren't supposed to die." He kept squeezing the steering wheel his knuckles alternating between white and red. "None of this was supposed to happen."

She shivered when he referred to her death. So the gun wasn't a scare tactic? She swallowed down the coffee-flavored bile. She needed to be calm and hoped her mood was contagious. "Of course, you didn't. No one does. I'm not dead yet, so you're doing good, right?"

"Not yet, and I'm not good," he growled. "I let Craig have my Naratriptan meds. As much as he wanted for his headaches. I'd never even read the warnings until after they found him."

She felt between her leg and the seat for her phone. "Did you personally give him the drug or did he take it from the boat's medicine cabinet?"

His eyes welled up. "I gave it to him. He'd been in pain for a couple of days, and the stuff's a miracle worker for me." He wiped the tears with the back of his hand. "I figured what could it hurt? Worse case scenario is it didn't work. I had no idea."

"Oh, Ken, I'm so sorry. You didn't mean any of this to happen. You poor guy, trying to help a friend. We need to go back and let the authorities know what happened. They need to know the truth."

He grabbed the gun from his lap. "Don't patronize me."

The muzzle of the weapon held her attention. "I'm not! I promise!" Mandy lowered her voice from a panicked screech. She needed to stay calm. "If this had

Betrayal

happened to one of my friends and me, I'd be heartbroken, too."

"Really?"

She stared straight ahead at the road. His sad tone would have tugged at her heart any other time but now. "Of course, I would. It's tragic. Craig was a great guy and a good friend to both of us. If I'd tried to help him and, well, I'd be heartbroken."

"Thank you. I appreciate that."

Any minute now, Mandy thought as they left the town behind them. Her fingers ached from squeezing the handle. Even worse, the coffee hadn't settled. She wanted to throw up, but not in the car and not going a hundred kilometers an hour. "Ken? Right now would be good to turn around and go back to town. Now is very good."

He shook his head. "We can't. You understand why I have to kill you, don't you?"

"I'll admit, I'm not getting that part of all this." Dark blue sky broke through the clouds. They'd been going southeast for long enough to have run into the ocean by now. "You're not a killer. You don't have to do this."

He stayed silent for a few moments before saying, "When I suspected my prescription had killed Craig, I searched online for the drug. I'd read what could happen to the person distributing the stuff, what prison time, what fines they'd have to pay. I'm not going to prison for helping a friend."

She put her hand on his shoulder, and he flinched. Mandy pulled her hand away. "You just need a good lawyer that can argue your case, tell the judge you meant no harm."

"Or, since you're cozy with Constable Rogers, I could kill you and dump your body." He didn't respond to her gasp. "They'd ignore me to focus on finding your killer."

Mandy stared at him. This couldn't be real. "Ken, there are so many reasons this won't work. Do this and you'll actually be convicted of murdering me. That's not what you want. No one wants that." She clasped her hands in front of her. "Please. Turn around, take me back, and this drive will have never happened."

"Name the reasons this won't work. Because right now, I shoot you," he said, patting the gun on his lap. "I dump your body, maybe someone finds it and voila. Another unsolved murder."

Her brain stopped working. How could Evan solve this? Oh God. Would Aaron see her body when they brought it to the hospital? He'd seen Craig's. Why not hers, too? Mandy's eyes filled with tears. She couldn't let it come to that and took a deep breath. She had to pretend this was happening to someone else to get through the panic. "All right. Gun ballistics, first. They'll know it's you if you shoot me."

Ken chuckled. "Nope. This was my great grandfather's gun. It's not registered."

She opened her mouth to protest and then stopped before mentioning his fingerprints on the bullets. Another murderer had been caught this way in one of the crime shows she'd watched on TV. Keeping quiet might help Evan to find Ken if the worst happened. Blab to Ken and he might wipe off the bullets. She'd have a chance to run, but where? Could she run faster than he would reload? She didn't know.

Nothing else came to mind as a good reason for him to stop. Mandy tried to give him a smile. "Maybe there weren't as many reasons as I'd thought." She ran a hand through her hair. The hairs tangled in her fingers like those in a hair brush. She paused. The setting sun illuminated the lipstick smeared on her Tim's cup, and she nodded, taking the providential hint. Distract him with one type of evidence only to leave another kind in his car.

She let the few strands fall from her hand onto the side floorboard. "My coffee is in here, you know. They'll get my DNA from it and find out I was here for a while."

He frowned and went back to squeezing the steering wheel for a moment. "Yes, you had left it after we went out." He grinned, his grip relaxing. "I dropped you off at your car. Your purse proves it. I came out for a drive alone to clear my mind after talking with you. It's going to be a little late before I get back, but not too bad."

With every word he said, Mandy's heart thudded harder. She saw no way out unless he unlocked the doors so she could hop out and roll away. The forests lining the road made hiding behind trees easy. Smacking into the trunks wouldn't be good at their current speed. The ditch might help out with that. She clung onto the useless door handle and realized she had no choice. Even if she went nuts and smashed the window, she'd not be able to get out. "Where are we going?"

"A walk along the beach under a full moon would be romantic, even when it's this cold. We're not a couple, but I don't think that matters in this case."

She gave a weak laugh. "Good, because I'm too freshly divorced to like that idea."

"That's a shame." He shifted in his seat. "I'd thought about snapping your neck.

Betrayal

Quick, clean, and wouldn't hurt you. Then, I'd wanted to roll my car off a cliff to say the accident injured you. None of my ideas work because it'd be too easy for them to figure out."

"I agree. All of them would leave evidence." She chewed on her chapped lip until tasting iron. They stopped at an intersection. As soon as he looked left over his shoulder, she palmed her cell phone into her coat pocket. He turned off onto a side road, and Mandy knew the sign. Ken actually was taking her to the beach.

She'd need to find a reason to be alone between now and when he shot her. A single text to both Evan and Aaron, and they'd find her. Maybe not until too late, but certainly before her body was gone for good. Ken's voice startled her when he began talking.

"None of this was supposed to happen. I'd gone to Craig's boat that night and found Debbi. I thought I lucked out when she didn't notice me swapping out my meds with something harmless from the cabinet. I grabbed the first over the counter bottle I saw and dumped them in. Cops usually didn't pay attention to that sort of stuff."

Before she could censor herself, Mandy said, "Really? You thought anyone would be fooled by baby aspirin and that yummy orange smell?"

"I know. I recognized the smell when opening them. Only thought about scraping off the baby aspirin part at home later that night. I couldn't go back without looking suspicious, or I would have."

He seemed so sad, she almost felt sorry for him. She squinted at him, thinking. The sympathetic angle might work better than appealing to his ethics. "Sorry. I don't mean to give you a hard time."

"No, I should have thought it through. Now they could get me on tampering with evidence. I'm usually more methodical." He waved a hand in her direction. "Like this strategy I had for you. I've not planned any of this very well."

"Who does? I mean, cold-blooded killers do, but you? You're an ordinary nice guy in a tough spot." She shook her head for emphasis. "There's been so many times where an innocent man fled and made things worse for himself."

He laughed. "Nice try, but I'm not going back until you're dead. I want the police on your case, not Craig's." Ken pulled into an empty parking lot. He shut off the engine and headlights. The doors clicked open. He picked up his gun. "Let's get out and start that romantic stroll."

Betrayal

"You're not thinking straight, Ken." Her voice shook, and she cleared her throat. "If we go back to town, nothing will happen to you, I promise."

He lifted the weapon. "Or I can shoot you hear and drag you there. Either way is good."

She stepped out, searching for a place to hide. Her dark coat would protect her for only so long. His doors clicked locked. She startled at the sound and then almost laughed. Who'd be way out here on a February night to steal a car? No street lamps lit up the place, just an enormous full moon hovering on the horizon.

Mandy shivered in the cold. She'd not noticed her sweat until just now and was drenched. She fastened her coat buttons. A porta potty to the right of them caught her eye. As much as the idea didn't appeal, she asked, "Can I go to the washroom first? That coffee has gone right through me."

"Sure. Why not?" He motioned with the gun. "I'd loan you my phone to use as a flashlight, but that'd be a bad idea on my part." He grinned. "Just don't fall in."

She tried to give him a smile. "Ha ha. I'll try not to." She stepped inside, the smell attacking her like a physical thing. Before closing the door, she said, "You might hear some unladylike sounds."

"No kidding. Just go already."

"Okay." She worked the simple lock closed, trying to stay clearheaded. Her stomach threatened to vomit up her coffee. The thought of splash back almost led her to throw up on the floor right then. She put a hand on her belly to calm herself and it helped a little. Good thing, because deep breaths would be distracting and disgusting.

Mandy wanted to turn on her phone and call everyone on her contacts list. Or should she just stay in here? The walls seemed too thin to stop a bullet. He'd run out eventually, but how many times would she be hit before then? Mandy narrowed her eyes. There was a reason fish in a barrel was a cliché.

She peeked out of the broken door handle's hole. Ken was a distance away, looking out over the ocean and moonrise. He might be far enough away to not hear the texting taps of her phone, but the porta potty echoed like an amphitheater. She turned her back to the door and retrieved her phone. Mandy touched it awake, and the screen shone like a floodlight. She swiftly dimmed it. The gravel outside crunched and warned her of his approach. She held her breath.

"Are you about done in there?"

His voice sounded just outside the door. She exhaled and hollered back, "Just about. I'm having a tough time finding the toilet paper in the dark."

He paused a little while before saying, "Get a move on. I still need to establish an alibi."

"Gee, how inconsiderate I've been, dawdling around, not wanting to die," she mumbled. Louder, she said, "Found the tp! Almost done." Huddled over her phone, she texted Evan and Aaron both, *Help! At Crystal Beach with Ken! Kidnapped with a gun!*

As soon as she hit send, Mandy put the phone in an inner coat pocket that zipped and staggered out. "Whew! Don't get near me for a while. That place is nasty." She went to his car and tried the handle. "Do you have any hand sanitizer? I keep some in my purse, but you know where that went."

"I don't have any." He waved the gun toward a path. "Come on, let's go."

Mandy did as he ordered, but took her time. A stiff breeze blew into her face. Little ice crystals pelted her skin, giving her an instant Botox treatment. She knew this trail. The path led to a rocky shore stretching south for miles. Each step brought her closer to dying. No matter if he shot her outright or just left her here to walk back to town, she'd freeze. Slow, she decided, walk slowly, keeping him preoccupied until the guys arrived. It was all she had left. She turned back to him. "How far?"

He stepped up to her, too close, and pressing the gun against her back. "I'll tell you when. Get moving."

She obeyed, the slender trail stretching out in front. Dark vegetation provided contrast to the pale gravel path. The landscape changed from low scrubby trees to shrubs with an occasional taller tree. The glacier-smoothed boulders gleamed in the rising moonlight. Ken was right. With anyone else and under almost any other circumstance, this would be romantic. The brightest stars shimmered in the night air. The rocky ground crunched under their feet. Just when she was about to ask if he'd reconsider this whole idea, the path stopped at a flat granite outcrop.

The rock sloped toward the sea, broken up by larger boulders and deeper crevasses. When she stopped at the edge, Ken stepped up to her, the muzzle of the gun again at her back. "This looks like a good stopping place."

She froze, unable to think at first. Mandy had never touched a gun and now? One was touching *her*, ready to fire. She struggled to be calm. "I don't mind going further. It's a beautiful night, after all."

"It's shit out here. Stop stalling. I

Betrayal

need to get back." He took a step away. "The easy thing would be to shoot first and kick you down to the ocean. But, shell casings. It's dark, and I can't count on finding them all. I'd rather not leave the evidence."

He'd given her an idea. Sending him to the car while, she found a hiding place might work. "You could use a flashlight to—" Mandy began. A hard shove from Ken had her falling through the air. Her her hip, shoulder, and finally head, smacked hard against the rock. She slid a foot down the slope before friction did its job and stopped her.

Shock and pain kept her still. A moan escaped her. Everything hurt. She rolled to her stomach, the side of her head throbbing in time with her heart. Mandy tried to see if her hip was as swollen as it felt. She struggled when her arm wouldn't lift up without a burst of pain.

"I can see you moving. Damn it! I didn't want to do this."

A zing sound and spark hit the ground between her and the water. She screamed and tried curling into a smaller target. The next hit her arm with a nudge and searing pain. Ken was too close to avoid her. She had to run.

She got to her knees, survival

instinct overriding everything. More shots zipped by her as she scrambled to a low rock to hide behind. More bullets zipped by her, and she cried, "Damn it, Ken! You don't have to do this. I'll keep my mouth shut."

The final bullet smacked into her upper thigh before she could reach safety. The fire in her quadriceps overpowered the one in her arm. She staggered, falling down as if he'd hit her in the chest. Mandy tried to relax into the rock. The pain tasted like tin foil lining the back of her throat.

She trembled. How many times had he shot at her? Two hit, four didn't. Six times and his pistol wasn't one of those magazine ones reloaded with a cartridge. She took a deep breath, letting it out slowly. In case Ken had brought more bullets, she needed to lie still enough so he wouldn't see her move.

"Mandy?" he said, edging closer.

She didn't take the bait and stayed quiet. On her belly, her face was turned toward the ocean. The breeze blew icy little drops onto her exposed skin.

He eased down closer, one of his shoes skidding out from under him on the smooth stone. "Whoa!" He nudged her arm with his foot. "Hey, come on Mandy. I'm sorry. Let me take you to the hospital."

Sure, he would after she died. If he'd

Betrayal

kicked her a little higher up, catching her shoulder, she'd have cried out from the pain. A cell phone's tunes floated out, high and thin in the cold air. She stopped her shallow breathing. Her phone was turned down, wasn't it? Mandy couldn't remember all of a sudden.

"Hello? Yeah. Just out for a drive, needed some time to think. Yeah, sure, I'll come on in. She told me you'd called, and I'd meant to get there earlier." Ken put a foot under her side and wiggled it. "Time got away from me. Ok, yeah, it'll take me an hour. Bye."

His phone rang again. "Yes? Um-hm. No, not in a while. I dropped her off at the salon an hour ago."

She thought about shouting loud enough for the other person to hear. No, she decided. If he believed he'd killed her already, he'd leave. She could find help if she didn't freeze or bleed to death first. She kept her eyes shut. Mandy didn't make a sound and worked to be dead weight.

"Why? Uh huh. No, I have no idea where she'd be right now. Sorry, I couldn't help. Okay, bye."

Ken gave Mandy a slow kick, not hard and sharp. The force sent her rolling down the smooth slope. She tried to be limp yet protect her face. Mandy held her breath to keep from crying out each time she landed on her injured arm or leg. She fell face first onto the black wet rocks.

A wave crashed into Mandy, rolling her back further onto the shore. She peeked out from her wet eyelashes to see Ken turning and hurrying away. Cell phone. Her inside pocket kept electronics safe, but could it withstand the sea? She needed to call someone, anyone who'd answer. If Brad had done something like this to Aaron, no wonder he still ached.

Everything hurt on her, even the whole right side of her body. She needed to wait until sure Ken was gone. As waves washed over her with a flash of cold pain before numbness set in. Sleep sounded so good right now. A car started in the distance, and she lifted her head, straining to listen. It had to be him leaving.

Mandy needed to get out of there. She tried to crawl up the incline to reach at least as far as the dry rocks. Once clear of the waves, she rolled over to lie flat on her back. The smaller moon comforted her as she retrieved her cell phone.

Aaron reread the text. *Help! At Crystal Beach with Ken! Kidnapped with a gun!* His phone rang and his heart sunk when seeing the caller id. "Hey, Evan. Tell

Betrayal

me that was a prank and you two are laughing at me."

"No, I can't and hoped you'd be kidding me, too."

"Shit." He ran a hand through his hair. "What do we do now?"

"I'm calling 911, getting an ambulance out there in case he's shot her."

He went for his coat, shaking it to hear if the car keys were in the pocket. "I'm going, too."

"Think that's a good idea?"

Aaron paused in locking up his house. It'd take a lot more than Evan's disapproval to keep him away. "You're going, right?"

"Yeah. So meet you there?"

"As soon as possible." He clicked off the phone, turning up the sound to the max before putting it in his pocket. Aaron didn't want the road noise to drown out the sound if Mandy called or texted him again. Thanks to shaking hands, he had to enter Crystal Beach into his GPS twice. The route plotted, he took a deep breath and headed her way.

Trees growing up to the side of the road left him feeling claustrophobic. Now would be a rotten time for a moose or deer to jump out of the brush. Aaron kept his gaze sweeping from one side to the other, looking for eyes glowing back at him. The

GPS voice sounded almost comforting as he left the 306 for a narrower road.

Minutes seemed like hours until he turned into the beach parking lot. The moon gave an eerie glow to the water and sand. No one else was there, no other vehicle. Only a porta potty stood at the back of the lot. He turned the car to where his headlights illuminated the small structure and got out. What if he found her in there, dead?

He stopped for a moment at the mental image. If she'd been shot, but not killed, he needed to help her. His heart thudded hard. But if she'd been killed already? He shook off the fear. Mandy couldn't be in there and couldn't be dead. He'd not allow it. Aaron opened the door to find the place empty. Foul smelling, but empty.

Aaron leaned against the doorframe. One location was done, leaving him the rest of the province to search for her. He let the door shut and went back to his car. After turning off the lights, he grabbed a flashlight from under the seat. Two paths led out of the area. One went to the beach and the other somewhere else. He couldn't see where, exactly.

Brushy trees, not much taller than him lined the trail. Aaron tried to remember if he'd ever noticed Ken's dominant hand. A

Betrayal

righty would choose the right side if the beach didn't matter. He glanced at the ocean before sending a text telling Evan where he was and began a fast jog toward the trees instead of the coast.

He started wheezing, the cold air hurting his lungs and he coughed. He slowed the pace a little, letting his system catch up before running again. The asphalt and gravel path ended abruptly. A side footpath, like one deer or cattle might cut, meandered onward along the rocky cliff. He glanced to his left at the beach one more time, searching for something human shaped on the white sand. Nothing, so he turned to continue on.

He reached the top of a hill. The land fell away below him in a gradual decline. Wind and water erosion rounded the rocks. The smooth surfaces didn't trigger his fear of heights and falling, so he continued past the path's end.

Nothing seemed out of the ordinary at first glance. He turned on his phone's flashlight function and swept the rocks. He took a few steps toward the water, still searching for any signs of her. "Mandy! Can you hear me?" he hollered.

"Help," a wavering voice croaked out in the thin air.

Laura Stapleton

Chapter 12

Aaron's head whipped round at the sigh-like word. "Mandy?" He saw her up ahead and to the left, lying in the shadow of a boulder. He shivered and had done the same when Brad hurt him. He slid down the rock slope to her, careful to not injure his knee. She'd need every ounce of his strength and more to survive. "Mandy, sweetheart. How ya doing?"

He checked her pulse, strong, but her skin cold to his fingertips. Aaron smoothed the hair from her forehead, the damp curls clinging to his fingers. She'd freeze to death before too much longer. "I need to get you warmer."

She moaned and reached for his hand. "I'm all wet."

He held her fingers, giving them a squeeze. "I know, sugar. Can you feel your toes, wiggle them for me?"

"They're numb now, so cold." She turned to him, her teeth chattering and put a hand on his leg. "Is this good?"

When her feet moved, he let out a pent up breath. No immediate spinal injuries. "Perfect, sweetheart." He bent down, lowering his ear closer to her mouth. "All right. Take a deep breath and let me hear you exhale." When she did, he detected nothing rattling in her lungs. "I'm going to help you get this coat off. It's soaked. If you don't mind, I'll need to take your shirt off, too."

She crossed her arms and winced. "No, too cold."

"You'll wear my coat, and it's warm from me." He loosened her hands where they gripped her forearms. His heart stopped when seeing the bullet hole in her upper right arm. "Shit, Mandy. You've been shot." He lifted her upright. "Come on, sweetheart, help me out."

"My leg was hit, too." She gasped when he pulled her right arm out of the sleeve. "I'm not wearing your pants. You'll freeze."

He bit his lip, wanting to laugh and afraid of sounding hysterical. She'd already lost this argument. He'd make her wear his pants as a tourniquet if it saved her life. "Good to know. Where did the bullet go?"

"The meaty part up here." She turned toward him, lifting her hip.

He leaned over to examine the wound. Very little blood, considering. If the shot had hit her femoral artery, she'd have bled out by now. He swallowed the lump in his throat. His phone blared out a signal. He ignored it to help Mandy remove her other

Betrayal

arm from the coat. Aaron placed it over her legs to help keep her warm.

When he began to pull off her shirt from over her head, she lifted her arms and said, "I'll regret this in the morning."

He smiled at her. "How so?"

"Letting a guy undress me without dinner first."

Aaron chuckled, happy to keep her talking. He took off his coat and wrapped it around her. "Let's get you to a hospital so I can take you anywhere you want to go. How about that, sweetheart?" She slumped over onto him, unconscious. "No! Mandy? Shit. Mandy? Wake up, honey, stay with me."

His phone chimed a message reminder. He retrieved it, praying for good news. Evan had texted they were on the way. He sent a quick reply to take the right path, not left. Aaron stood, struggling not to panic at getting her to his car. "Damn it all hell! Can no one think of a better way to kill people than tossing them down a hill into the ocean? Really?"

He wiped his eyes and knelt back down to her. He searched for her pulse, not feeling it at first, nearly crying when the vein fluttered. "Okay, sweetheart, I'm going to take you to my car and warm you up. Stay with me."

Aaron glanced up, hearing the sirens

first. "Mandy, honey, wake up. The ambulance is here for you, nice and warm." He put his hands under her, lifting her while ignoring his protesting knee. Some hero he turned out to be. He carried her to the parking lot with a slow walk. Even then, his breathing protested the cold air and her weight in his arms. He steadied his heart rate and counted while he inhaled then exhaled. The sirens, growing louder, stopped up ahead. Their absence was a relief to his ears. He didn't have far to go. Flashlights and people ran up to him, Evan first.

"You found her!" Evan shown the light up and down Mandy. "Damn, Aaron, did you see her leg? She's been shot."

"I did, and it didn't hit an artery. She'll be okay," he said in between panting for air.

"You all right?"

Aaron nodded despite his body's protests. "Yeah, let's get her somewhere warm."

"Here, let me take her." Evan took her limp body from him. "This isn't her coat."

"No, hers is still where I'd found her." He leaned forward, hands on his knees. "It fell off of her legs when I picked her up."

"Murphy, Davis, we'll need someone to secure the crime scene. Find the shell casings, photograph the area, you know the drill." He started toward the parking lot. "I'd ask you to tell me what you did back there, but think you need a rest yourself, doctor."

Condescending little punk wasn't that much younger than him, and Aaron ground out, "I'm all right."

"Out of shape?" he hollered over his shoulder.

"No, healing from a punctured lung."

"Damn." Evan slowed and glanced down at Mandy. "Hey, there's my girl. Trying to wake up, huh? Don't worry, we'll thaw you out right quick."

They reached the lot. Police cars and an ambulance filled the place or seemed to. The lights comforted Aaron with their presence while the flashing gave him a headache. He followed Evan to the back of an ambulance. The paramedics took Mandy in, covering her with a blanket and removing her shoes and pants. Aaron asked the closest person, "Where are you taking her?"

"Dartmouth Regional."

He nodded as the doors closed. His hospital and he knew Dr. Shaw would take care of Mandy. As the vehicle left, he turned to Evan. "What about Ken?"

"We caught him coming back on the 349. Stupid bastard. I'll have his hide for this."

Aaron began shivering, clenching his jaw to keep his teeth from rattling. "Has he said why he took Mandy?"

"Not yet, but he will by the time I'm done with him." Evan looked Aaron up and down. "Go on with her. She'll want one of us there to tell her what happened. Also, do you have her folk's number?"

"No."

" I'll call and tell them where to meet you. As soon as we're done at the house, I'll be there, too." He held out his hand. "Text if anything happens, okay?"

"You got it." He would have said more, but Evan turned and went back down the path to the crime scene. Aaron started his car, the blast of air painfully cold. He reduced the fan and entered his hospital into the GPS. He'd not been this far out of town since he drove in and sped up, wanting to be at the hospital already. A moonlit drive through beautiful country meant nothing if the woman he loved died tonight.

He coughed. "Damn," Aaron whispered. Loving her wasn't a surprise so much. He loved steak and a good action movie, but his can't live without her love did surprise the hell out of him. Nothing in the world mattered to him more than seeing Mandy recover.

Aaron wiped his eyes. This happened

Betrayal

to be the worst year in his life to fall in love with someone. No matter how beautiful, kind, funny, charming, or just perfect she was, now was not the best time. He wanted to be completely free of British Columbia and obligations toward Brad. She deserved no less than everything from him.

The GPS spoke, saying to turn right at the next intersection. He both appreciated Evan and loathed him. If he'd not been there to help, Aaron might not have made it back to his car. But then, he knew Mandy's parents well enough to call out of the blue. Aaron wanted that familiarity with them, too. He shook his head and refocused on the two lane road. All of this would be great to mull over later when Mandy was healing up and knew he loved her.

He drove to the hospital, finding Emergency and pulled into patient parking. The cocoon of warmth he'd been in helped him breathe. He had hurried into the hospital before the cold air affected him. A small crowd stood around the information desk. He wanted to part them like the Red Sea until realizing they were Mandy's family.

The receptionist, Jenny, gave them all a baleful stare as if used to the protests. "She's still in the back."

Karen asked, "Can we see her?"

"No, they're warming her up and

prepping for surgery." She looked around. "I probably shouldn't have told you this much, but you are her family. Ms. Hays wasn't conscious enough to sign any consent forms."

Marty spotted him first. "Aaron, I suppose you know what happened?"

Everyone turned to him and stared. He glanced down to see if any of Mandy's blood was on him. He was clean. "I do, most of it."

"Will she be all right," Shawn asked. Karen took her husband's hand, and he put his arm around her.

"She should be. Let's go over here and have a seat." He asked Jenny, "You'll tell us when she's in recovery?"

"I may not be on shift, then, Dr. Nicholson."

Her eyes widened at his expression, and Aaron knew the woman sensed danger. He was too scared and angry to be patient. He cleared his throat. "I'd suggest you write a note, then, that as soon as Mandy Hays is in recovery, you or the next person sitting there is to inform the family."

She started scribbling with a pout. "The surgeon usually talks with the family anyway."

"I know that. Now he's sure to." Aaron turned on his heel before losing his

Betrayal

temper completely. The family sat with each other in a secluded corner of the room. He went to them, finding his own chair. "Mandy should be okay. They're working on her now."

"What happened?"

With three sets of eyes focused on him, Aaron began, "She was brought in with hyperthermia and two gunshot wounds."

"Two? Oh, Shawn!" Karen held on to his arm.

Mr. Hays cleared his throat. "Where was she shot?"

"Once on her leg and once on her arm."

Mrs. Hays gave out a little sob. Both Hays men leaned toward her, putting their arms around her. Aaron gave Karen a smile. "She'll be all right." His phone buzzed, the tone overly loud in the waiting area. Everyone stared at him until he lowered the volume. He read the text to the family. "Evan says they have the suspect in custody, which I knew. They'd caught Ken on his way back to town."

"Ken?" Shawn asked.

Aaron offered, "Ken Cole."

"That can't be right," Karen said.

Shawn nodded. "He's one of my clients and the nicest guy. A bit crass, but decent."

He didn't care if Ken invented a cure for cancer. Aaron would never consider him anything but heinous. "He's who kidnapped Mandy."

"Why?" Marty asked. "Why would he do such a thing to her?"

His phone chimed again. He'd received an email from Evan. "Let's see what the cops say." Aaron opened the app and scanned the message. "Evan says Ken confessed to everything. He'd given his medicine to Craig for his headaches, tried to hide it, and when asked to come back in yet again, wanted to—" His heart stopped, and he couldn't say the words at first. He blinked a few times to halt the stinging in his eyes.

"Are you all right?" Karen went to him, placing a hand on his forehead. "You're running a little fever."

"I'll be all right, thank you." He looked back down at the message. "It says Ken wanted to kill Mandy to distract the police from Craig's death. He wanted it to seem like murder, instead of an accident like Craig's." Aaron drew in a shuddering breath. Seeing Ken's plans in black and white hurt his chest. "Ken felt bad, thinking he'd left her for dead, and confessed to everything."

"I hope they nail him to the wall,"

Betrayal

Karen exclaimed.

Aaron tried to not smile at how much like Mandy was like her mother. The thought of what she and Shawn were going through as parents sobered him. He continued, "When I found her, the suspect had already left her there. I'd almost turned around because the parking lot was empty. Mandy's text had said Crystal Crescent, and so did the sign. When I found her and saw how seriously she'd been injured, I started to carry her back to my car. That's when Evan and the others got there."

Marty stuck out his hand. "Thanks, doc, for finding her and saving her life."

"Evan was there, too," offered Karen. "He's such a nice young man. I'm glad he could help you get Mandy to the ambulance."

He shoved aside the twinge of jealousy and smiled at Mandy's mom. It wasn't tough for him to say, "So am I." Aaron patted his bum knee. "My body isn't at a hundred percent, and it's frustrating. I forget I have limits."

Shawn chuckled. "Happens to everyone." He looked at his hands for a moment before staring at Aaron. "Tell us your honest and professional opinion. No bullshit. Is she going to come out of this all right?"

Without being in surgery with her, Aaron could be a hundred percent sure. With all of her family staring at him, he wanted to stay positive. "Yes, sir. Her injuries didn't seem that serious at first glance. And besides, we can't let it go any other way."

The constant jostling had stopped, and Mandy tried to look around her. Even with the warm air, her bones felt icy. How did someone thaw frozen bone marrow, she wondered. They must have given her something good because she felt the blankets covering her, but not the heart pounding pain from earlier. After a metallic click, the room brightened enough to show through her eyelids, and she tried to lift a hand.

"Doctor, I think she's awake."

Mandy said, "I am, I think, but can't open my eyes." She moved her head from side to side a couple of times. "Is something wrong with them?"

"I don't think so. Let me check." He pulled one eyelid up, letting it down after her ow of protest. "Did you see anything?"

"Yes, and it was too bright. They must be tired, then." The people around her resumed their noises. The last thing she remembered was pain and cold, and then Aaron's warmth as he checked her pulse.

Betrayal

"Do you know Dr. Nicholson? I love him. He rescued me."

"Dr. Nicholson is usually in our Emergency Department, and he rescued you, huh?"

She recognized the doctor's voice and nodded. "He's my hero."

"Sounds like it. Now, just try to relax."

Mandy sighed, ready to take a nap. "Where am I?"

"At Dartmouth Regional's operating room," a nurse replied. "You'll be asleep in a minute or so, and we'll remove a bullet or two from you."

"Will I be okay?"

"Yes, you'll be fine. Dr. St. Clair is one of our best, and he's who'll be operating on you this evening." The nurse put a mask over her face and said, "Count backward from ten, please."

"Ten, nine...."

Laura Stapleton

About the Author

With an overactive imagination and a love for writing, Laura Stapleton decided to type out her daydreams and what-ifs to share her lovable characters and their worlds with readers. She currently lives in Kansas City with her husband, daughter, dog, and a few cats. When not at the computer, you'll find her in the park for a jog or at the yarn store's clearance section.

If you enjoyed this story, please consider leaving a review.

Find Laura online:
https://twitter.com/LauraLStapleton,
https://www.facebook.com/LLStapleton
http://lauralstapleton.com.

Subscribe to Laura's newsletter and keep up on the latest updates and new releases.

Made in the USA
Charleston, SC
03 September 2016